OLIVIA AND THE SOCIETY

Anusa Nimalan

Olivia

And

The

By Anusa Nimalan

"When I'm old and dying, I plan to look back on my life and say, 'Wow, that was an adventure,' not, 'Wow, I sure felt safe.'"

– TOM PRESTON-WERNER

CHAPTER 1

"Professor, Professor", the voice nervously called from the shadows of the doorway to the enormous library.

"What is it!" Came the gravelly response impatiently.

"We have found her!"

A smile curved the Professors's cruel lips. "At last," he breathed. "Now we can complete our mission". He continued to smile into the fire, "At last."

"No, no, no.... " I have must have missed it, it has to be saved. "Shit, shit, shit."

"Whats up sweetie?," a teasing voice said from the next cubicle.

I looked over at my best friend Daisy, blowing my hair out of my eyes and pushing my glasses up. "I have lost the marketing spreadsheet! Why does this always happen to me?" I moaned, as I banged my forehead down on the table in front of me.

"Because you actually care," Daisy smiled widely, at the back of my head. I could not see it but I could hear the smile in her voice, "I do not take my work seriously and things always work out, well for me. It's the way that I like it."

I lifted my head, pulling off the post it note that had attached itself to my forehead. "Karl is gonna be so pissed." I thought through again, I had uploaded the original and spent hours making the changes. I had been checking and double checking. I saved regularly, so where was it. I pushed my glasses back and with a feeling of stomach churning desperation I searched the files on my computer again.

Daisy continued looking over my shoulder and giving me advice, which was so not useful in my mind fog of panic. I could feel the sweat start building under my arm pits.

Karl popped his head into my cubicle and hissed "Where is the report Olivia? Send now, so that we can present it." Without waiting for a reply he moved on, calling out to someone else.

I put my head back down on my folded arms and just closed my eyes.

Olivia pushed my head aside and took my laptop, humming her favourite pop song. "If you don't stop being so bloody cheerful, I will show everyone that picture when you were drunk last Christmas"

"Oh that's not nice and here is me helping. What would you give me, if I find it?"

"My kingdom for my file," my voice muffled.

"Well then, your kingdom it is and I won't forget that you owe me one. Here it is!"

My head popped up like a startled prairie dog, I pulled back my lap top and started disbelievingly at my missing spreadsheet. Smiling widely, I put it down and jumped up, hugging Daisy tightly. I sat down, "You are amazing, this is why I love you." With speed I quickly attached the spreadsheet and emailed it onto Karl, with afterthought I also sent it to his assistant. I would not put it past him to say that he had not received it.

"Well now that that drama is done, the adrenaline crash that will follow demands coffee, so let's get some. You amazing friend of mine."

Daisy clapped happily and then high fives me, "You know that I never say no to coffee, it's the elixir of the gods."

I grabbed my shoulder bag and my never far from me old beaten up leather jacket. As I swung it on, Daisy asked for the thousandth time, "When are you ever going to get a new jacket?" Daisy shook her head with a defeated smile, as she grabbed her puffy jacket and shiny purse.

"When will you stop asking that, you know that answer as well as I do?" As we skirted past Karl's office, "It was my Fathers' and....."

"..It reminds you of your Father and feels like her is still with you." She ended in a sing song voice but took the sting out with a smile and a one arm hug.

I hugged her arm back, "You just want to take me shopping".

Daisy laughed and punched my shoulder, opening the door, "You got me, I always want to go shopping and you don't. I wonder if that should be my favour? This takes more thought."

"And now I have a bad feeling about this, you realise that it was a figure of speech, right?"

Daisy put her hands over her ears, "I am not listening, Olivia owes me a favour." I shook my head as I followed her.

It was cold outside, the wind coming straight into my open and I would admit, only to myself and not out loud, old jacket. I tugged the jacket closer, seeing my breath in the air. We turned to the coffee shop down one of the many warren like side roads. As our feet headed towards Louise's. We loved it, it wasn't a franchise and the owner Louise was like family. The bell over the door tinkled a greeting as we went in, almost blown in by the cold air. The warm air inside seemed to hug us, Louise looked up from behind the counter with a welcoming smile. "Hi girls, sit down and I will bring your coffees over."

We grabbed our favourite table, in the corner by the book shelves. As we divested ourselves of our coats and bags, Daisy remarked, "I love that we don't have to spend ages deciding on what to order". Though added wistfully "Sometimes it would be nice to puzzle over our coffees and most importantly there are no guys in here. Just old James in the corner, with his head in a book". She looked towards a white headed old man in the other corner, who was here everytime that I came in. As if realising that we were talking about him, he raised his eyes and nodded at us.

As I took a deep breath of the familiar place, "I disagree, I love it here. It's cozy and safe."

"You realise that isn't how people normally describe places right. Safe."

I sat back as I thought about it, safe was the way that I felt while being here, an encompassing feeling that surrounded me every time I stepped through the door. Maybe it was because it reminded me so much of the home that I had with Father.

As if for the first time, I looked around. Everywhere were familiar reminders. Old books, old pictures, the sofas. How had I never noticed before that there were things that had been in my old house. A strange feeling came over me, like a shining of the sand beneath my feet. Before I could think further on it, Louise arrived with our coffees.

"Here you go, my dears, just like you like them?" She placed them in front of both of us and then tucked the tray under her arm. "It's nippy today and I am sure that these will warm you right up."

Daisy grabbed hers, "Thanks, I do not know what else is in this but this is the only coffee that makes me feel awake and warm inside, no other coffee tastes as good."

Louise smiled, "Thank you, I always aim to give my customers what they need."

She held my gaze, "You usually jump on yours just like Daisy here?"

I started, I had been wondering what else I hadn't been noticing before. "I was just wondering how do you know exactly what we like? Is is magic?"

If I hadn't been looking so closely, I would have missed it, a strange look passed over her face but like a thought it was gone as quickly.

I wasn't sure what it was but the feeling of unease increased,I took the coffee realising that Louise was waiting for me to do so.

Another customer arrived and Louise turned away from us reluctantly. She looked back over her shoulder and I lifted the coffee to my mouth. Her shoulders relaxed as I did so. As she turned away and Daisy was checking her phone, I poured my coffee into a nearby plant pot.

I sat back, wondering if something was wrong with me. I had just wasted a coffee, that I usually loved, I even came here on my days off. Why was I questioning it?

Daisy was talking now, complaining about the text that someone had sent her. I was pleased that she had not noticed my preoccupation, she would want me to explain something that I couldn't explain.

Louise was back at the counter, casting glances over to us and looking slightly concerned. I looked away quickly and happened to look towards the door as the front bell tingled.

The door opened, sending a blast of cold air ahead of it. Quickly a guy ducked in, shutting the door firmly behind him before Turing around. He stood for a moment looking around. He didn't look over to our table, everywhere else but not at our table. He was our age, handsome and yet he didn't look at the only two young women in the place. He was either gay or ignored us on purpose. He walked towards the counter, pulling his gloves off.

"Olivia!", turned my attention back to Daisy, who had her head tilted to the side, smiling at me.

"Sorry."

"I can see why you are distracted", Daisy said looking over at the guy who was talking to Louise. Louise glanced at us. "He is really cute, I take it back, now this place is perfect."

I could not help but agree as I looked over at him again. He was leaning into the counter, looking very comfortable. He a long wool overcoat, over a black jumper, jeans and boots. He had a military looking short buzz cut, emphasising his lean face and bright cobalt blue eyes. I had never seen eyes like that outside of the movies.

He happened to turn and caught my appraising gaze. I flushed, always very obvious with me and looked away. Daisy looked at me with sly eyes, I could already see the teasing look in her eyes, that never boded well for me. "A new potential friend?"

"No, stop it, let's go?", I pushed my apparently drunk coffee away and stood. I really hated that I blushed so easily and that it was so noticeable. I wanted out of there now, there was something about that guy that pulled at me and I didn't need that.

I pushed the door open and was out, without waiting for Daisy. I stopped a little way away, while I waited for Daisy. I took the opportunity to pull my gloves on and tighten my jacket around me. Without the coffee, I was feeling the cold more, I wondered where I could get some.

"What the hell was that?" Daisy wheezed out, "You just ran out of there and left me. If you do that with every cute guy, then there is no hope for you."

I shrugged, not knowing how to explain that so many things had felt wrong. "Come on we are going to be late for work and seriously you have to do some exercise. You should not be that short of breath."

Daisy complained as we walked back to the office, I tuned her out and kept looking over my shoulder and I didn't know why.

At least when we arrived back at work, Daisy had moved on with her topic of conversation. One of her favourites, Daisy telling me about her date last night. I remained zoned out with the occasional nods and noises, which was all she needed to keep going.

The afternoon seemed to pass slowly, with some more mind numbing spreadsheet work. Interspersed with more information than I needed about her dates private anatomy. Really details that no one should know.

I finished off my last job of the afternoon and looked out of my window. I loved that my desk was in a corner next to a window, it made work more bearable. I could see the trees across in the small residential park over the road. The trees were looking winter bare but still beautiful, like silhouettes. I leant back in my desk chair and sighed. As I focused on the trees, the sounds of the office faded away and almost believed that I could hear the sounds of the park, the wind blowing through the remaining leaves on the trees, moving the branches. I took a deep breath in and I could smell the leaves and the cold. It was so intense that I closed my eyes and just let all it all wash over me, it was like the most realistic meditation or sleep white noise tape. I could actually feel the cold and put my left hand out. As I thought the I felt tree bark under my hand.

"Olivia!" I sat bolt upright, startled. I opened my eyes, to see an angry Sarah by my desk scowling at me. Her shrieking continued, "What are you doing? Sleeping at work?"

"Hello Sarah," I shook off a feeling of disorientation as quickly as I could. I had learnt that when Karl's second in command was around it was better to just be pleasant. It gave her no ammunition to go to Karl about but had the added benefit of also really annoyed her. She was in it for the power and the ability to stomp on any defiance. I wasn't sure why Karl had her, as he could do all of that himself. Sarah obviously sensed that I was not going to give her what she wanted, turning on her 4 inch heels, swishing her hair. As she had to leave with a parting shot, "Watch it Olivia, I have my eye on you."

I watched her go, choosing to admire the shoes. I wished that I could wear something them, not something that I could wear but I could wish I could. Though obviously without the awful personality. "Daisy, do you think that I could pull them off?"

Daisy laughed fondly at me, "The last time you tried, you twisted your ankle before the News Year Eve party and spent it with your leg up covered in ice".

I grimaced remembering the complete embarrassing episode. Ah well I could always dream about wearing shoes like that.

I got up, time for the loo. As I got up crushed leaves fell from my cold hand. What the fuck! How had those got there? I looked over at the park again, realising that my clothes and hands felt tingly as when you came in from the cold and rewarmed.

That was beyond odd, I thought about it and then decided that I would go wit the let Olivia pretend that nothing happened.

I pushed away from the desk with a determined air and made my way to the staff kitchen. A tiny hole in the corner that HR had insisted on, it had space for a kettle and small fridge only, maybe a single person, if they didn't turn. I greeted a couple of colleagues but didn't stay to chat, still a little freaked by the thing that did not happen. I poured some of the ready made coffee and took a deep sip. Ahh, that was what I needed despite the scared tongue. It had none of the depth of flavours of Louise's coffee but I was grateful for the caffeine hit. Catching sight of Sarah, I quickly took my coffee back to my desk. Where I sighed deeply.

I usually loved all the little jobs and things that made up my day but I just felt dissatisfied, uneasy and restless in myself. I had a couple of tasks that I could be busying myself with but I just didn't seem to have the push.

As if called, my gaze wandered to the window again. As I focused on the outside I realised that someone was staring at me from within the park, I probably wouldn't have been able to see them if it had been summer but with the missing leaves I could see an outline of a form.

No, they couldn't be looking at me, just at the buildings in general. Our building had the deep tinted glass, that meant that we could see out but that people outside couldn't see in. But the tingling feeling at the back of my neck and unease along my spine felt like I was being watched. Something felt really wrong. As I started to duck down, a bus went by and when I looked again, the figure was gone. I scanned the park cautiously but I couldn't catch sight of he, she or it. I laughed at myself, no one could move out of sight that fast, I must have imagined it.

I took a breath feeling my heart rate and breathing slowing down. I centred myself, as my father had taught me. Feeling my breath enter through my mouth, enter my lungs and hold. I did a minute and opened my eyes, feeling calmer and more in control. As I quickly glanced around, I breathed a sigh of relief that no one had noticed my day dreaming.

Quickly I finished off some tasks, sent some emails and with relief realised that the work day had ended. I stood, moving over to Daisy, "Almost done yet?"

"No, I haven't finished yet, I got distracted by my texts. How do you manage to get everything done?"

"Is it ok if I go? I have had it with today." I fidgeted on the spot as Daisy usually liked to leave together but I felt a strong compulsion to leave. Daisy knew this, she pouted and whined at me, "If you help me, I will be done sooner."

I shook my head, "You sure this is how you want to spend the favour I owe you. You know my rule, I don't do your work anymore. It's a slippery slope that I have been down before." I gave her a hug, as I spoke.

She sighed but with a smile, "Fair enough, text you later."

I shut everything down and made sure my desk was tidy for tomorrow. I liked a tidy neat desk, it settled me, for my own mental health I avoided looking at Daisy's. It was overflowing with this and that. She assured me that it was organised chaos but I didn't believe it.

Swinging my jacket on, I headed to the atrium and the large glass doors. I paused as I tied my bright yellow scarf, a bit of sunshine in the cold.

Pushing out through the doors, I walked with my head down. Looking at my feet, letting their rhythm be my focus. It was a 30 minute walk home, which I liked. I got to walk by the Thames for part of it. At my favourite spot, I stopped looking out over the rolling water. I took a deep breath, smelling the water. The day's irritations fell away and I took another. I put my hand out to feel the wind, while I focused on the water, I could almost feel how cold it was. I leant over the wall more, suddenly I pulled back as I actually felt wetness on my hand. I stumbled back abruptly, bumping into someone walking past. I apologised without looking at him, trying to process how my hand had got wet. As more people pushed past, giving me vexed looks I realised that I had to move. I wiped my wet hand on my jeans and walked briskly off. I felt a strange foreboding, something was happening and I just didn't know what it was.

I jogged the rest of the way home, which sounded like it

should be part of a healthy routine. I had tried jogging before and I managed to blow my right knee within 10 minutes, so I had never done that since. So that fact that I had managed it without thinking now, actually scared me. I wasn't red, sweaty and wheezing by the side of the road. I moved into a run, running easily, my technique good. No Tom Cruise running style buttery good. People scattered out of my way, cars using their horns as I ran across roads.

I pulled my keys out of my inner jacket pocket, fumbling with the front door lock, I continued running up the three flights of stairs to my top floor flat. I fumbled with the key again, slamming the door behind me. Then double locking, after a pause, I put the chain on too. Then with my back to the door, I slid down it to the floor.

I raised my right hand to my face, realising with surprise that I was shaking. There was my hand, though it was dry I could clearly remember how it felt. I couldn't get away from the fact that there had been no way that I could have touched the water. Not possible.

Right what this called for was alcohol, with that focused thought I got up and had a shot of tequila. I have often thought that there isn't much that a shot of tequila couldn't sort. It took quite a few more before I started feeling less like a deer in the headlights.

CHAPTER 2

Okay that might not have been a good idea, was the thought that went through my head as I slowly opened my eyes.

My head was pounding, made worse by the light streaming through my windows. I had obviously forgotten to close the curtains. Moaning softly, I buried my head in my pillow. With relief I realised that it was Saturday and therefore no work. I felt like something a cat might have dragged in.

It was a brutal reminder of why I didn't usually drink. My thoughts tried to remind me of why I had started drinking yesterday but forcefully I refused to let them dwell there. Better to focus on making myself feel better.

Knowing that a little effort now would make me feel better sooner. I slowly opened one eye and reached for my water glass. Taking a gulp, I felt it immediately sooth my throat but sitting up made my head pound more. Slumping back, I gathered my strength, sat up and with determination made it to the bathroom and some paracetamol and ibuprofen. I decided against brushing my teeth, too much effort and crawled back into bed.

Job done, I thought and lay back down. My phone made a noise and with one eye I grabbed it and beadily tried to focus on the screen. It took a minute, to see that there were a couple of missed calls and texts from Daisy, plus an unknown number.

Resting the phone my chest, I calculated how irritated Daisy would be if I didn't get back to her now versus later.

Signing, I decided to get it over with and called her. She picked up on the second ring and shouted, "What the fuck happened to you?"

Feeling my headache worsen, "For the love of God, please stop yelling".

There was a pause, where I could sense her deciding whether to go with pissed off or curious. Curiosity won, "Are you hungover? You don't drink, well not without me. Whats happened?"

"I just got a little carried away, don't ask, I don't even know why. Now if you have any sort of mercy in your heart, let me just sleep and recover."

"Okay but remember we have plans tonight, you promised before and I am cashing in the favour you owe me. So are you going to come out."

"Yes, yes. What ever, please just let me sleep."

"Happily sweetie, now just set the alarm for 4pm, so you have plenty of time to get ready. To make sure that you don't back out, I will come to yours."

We exchanged good byes and thankfully I lay back down. Then I set my alarm, maybe two just in case. Rolling back, I snuggled under the blankets, not having the energy to close the curtains. I immediately fell into a deep sleep.

Next thing I knew was my phone's alarm going off, I slapped it down and then the next one went off. I awoke with the feeling of getting too little sleep, slightly nauseous. I wondered if I could just ignore Daisy but knew that nothing would stop her and she was my best friend.

I felt like I had dreamt but I couldn't hold onto what they had been, just fear. I took a couple of deep breaths, to centre myself and the feeling thankfully receded.

With that when I opened my eyes, I realised with relief that I did feel better. Great, but lets hope that the feeling sticks. I had a quick shower, some water and then a greasy breakfast, feeling like it couldn't hurt.

With some reluctance I started getting ready. It was worth making a proper effort, as otherwise Daisy would decide to redo it herself.

I dried my hair and put some leave in conditioner, letting the curls bounce. My shoulder length brown hair was easy to manage, in that I left it alone. Some BB cream, powder, blusher, eyeshadow, eyeliner and mascara and I was ready to go. I did love my eyeliner, possibly a little heavy on that.

I wondered if I should go the extra length and put my contacts in but thought that was a step too far. Though I didn't know where we were going, I went with a black cocktail dress, tights and some heeled boots. I knew that Daisy would roll her eyes but I put on my chains. These were a collection of chains, with various charms including my Fathers signet rings that wound around my neck to various lengths. My Father had gifted them to me and told me that they would provide protection, I was not sure what he meant but I had to admit that I always felt better with them. I usually wore them every day but had left them in a cleaning solution yesterday.

Once I had the chains on, I felt confident enough to let my thoughts touch on the strangeness of yesterday. I wondered if things might not have been different if I had drunk the coffee or been wearing my chains. Obviously there was no way I could know.

I glanced at the clock, noting that I had not done too badly on time. While I was waiting for Daisy, I decided to have some quiet time, as I doubted that there would be much of that later. Pulling my legs up on my favourite window seat that looked out over the road, I decided to loose myself in a book.

I was pulled out of the book by my doorbell. I leant to look out and saw Daisy. I buzzed her in, pulling my trusty leather jacket on. As I opened my door, Daisy swept in and did a twirl. As always she looked amazing in an extremely short dress with a lot of bling and her hair up. I whistled. At the wave of my hand, I also did a twirl. With her hands on her hips, she pursed her lips and then said, "Fine."

She sounded a little disgruntled, I grinned, "You wanted to dress me up, didn't you?"

Sheepishly she looked away, "You got me, You never let me

play."

Daisy insisted that we have some wine, after a couple of glasses I managed to get Daisy on the road. The Uber stopped outside a gentleman's club. It looked grand, there was even a doorman. I turned to Daisy, hissing under my breath, "You should have told me. I would have made more of an effort."

She looked at my face disbelieving "No you would not have." I had to be honest, that was probably true.

I followed her, as she swept up the steps, her heels clicking. With confidence she announced, "We should be on the list, Daisy Smith plus 1."

The doorman looked like professional security, all muscled, with an unfriendly forbidding face. If I was on my own, I would have turned back by now. He looked us up and down, spending more time on my jacket, which I self consciously tugged on. He then with distain looked at his iPad, nodded to himself and opened the door. Daisy, obviously not put off by his demeanour, smiled, turning to wink at me. She went through the doors with no hesitation, I lingered, not having a good feeling. I had suddenly developed a feeling of dread in my stomach. The doorman blow out an annoyed sound, I looked up and he narrowed his eyes, partially closing the door as if challenging me. I quickly scurried up and through the door, knowing that I couldn't leave Daisy.

It was darker than the bright lights at the entrance but as my eyes adjusted I saw a small cloakroom, manned by a very smart teenager. Daisy had already handed in her wrap, she was literally bouncing on her feet. "Come on, leave your jacket here, you are not wearing that inside".

With some reluctance, I shrugged it off and handed it over, receiving a ticket stub. With some curiosity, I asked "How are you on a guest list for something like this?"

"I feel that is a little rude. I was out with this guy, the one that we are meeting today, he mentioned this society. Apparently it is amazing and empowering, lots of celebrities are part of it, though he couldn't tell me their names. It recruits once a year, at parties like this." Seeing my eyebrows raise in question, she hurried into speech. "I know that you will think that this is odd but it really isn't not. I wanted to see this for yourself." She whined and I sighed, as we approached the curtain at the end of the corridor. "Okay, okay."

The curtains lifted up by themselves and a gasp of awe escaped me. The room beyond was amazing, beautifully framed by the curtains. A huge ballroom, lit by multiple fantastic beautiful crystal chandeliers. Large ornate mirrors covered the walls reflecting all the light. There were tall cocktail tables scattered around, there was an actual small orchestra played music on the raised stage at one end. There were about hundred or so people milling around, with smart teenage servers carrying trays of little bites. "Wow."Daisy was giggling with delight.

The people were all around our age, with various levels of smartness. The girls varied between being in cocktail dresses through to ball gowns. Daisy squeezed my arm and squeaked, "How amazing is this? I am so excited, I have never been to something like this." Snagging two glasses of champagne, she handed one to me. We clinked glasses. I couldn't help but smile. I have to say what ever my odd feelings were, I had to admit that it was all impressive. Since I was here, I might as well enjoy it.

I sipped the delicious champagne, loving the sensation of the bubbles. Daisy and I moved towards the centre of the room, where I admired the room.

As I surveyed the room, I noted that there were many doors leading from the room. They appeared closed with security stationed in front of them, very serious security. It seemed a little odd. As I had been pondering this, Daisy had joined some guests and started a conversation. Shaking off my questions, I joined in.

The other guests were very excited and happy to be here. They were all very excited about potentially joining something that they actually knew nothing about. I signed, may be I was too cynical but they really did seem too trusting to me.

As I was standing and smiling at the right times, I thought that I saw the same figure that I had seen outside my office window. I stiffened and moved forward, adjusting my glasses but there was nothing there. I finished my drink and grabbed another flute.

A loud gong sounded, I actually felt myself vibrate. I turned, along with everyone else, silence fell over the room. On the stage there was a stunning women. She had alabaster skin, short blonde asymmetrically cut hair. She wore 6 inch heels, a form hugging black silk evening gown with a low cut back.

She raised her hands, "Thank you for all coming, I am afraid that Professor May could not make it but he welcomes you. We are all very happy to have you join us on this special occasion, or should I say opportunity. I have friends here who will be coming round to welcome you. Please feel free to ask questions, we are hoping that some of you will be able to join us in our quest for truth." She smiled thinly around at the room, as she gestured with her hands, some people fanned out into the room.

Well that wasn't suspicious at all. I joined one of the groups that had one of the welcoming committee. As I listened, I realised that it was all very vague. The one thing that they did was to touch each person, be it a stroke down the arm or a handshake.

Not feeling comfortable with that, every time someone moved towards me, I would strike off towards another group. The selling point seemed to be that they would be a family, who would understand them.

I made my way back to Daisy, who was having her hand held by a very cute guy. She was giggling and stroking his arm. I internally eye rolled, and said "Hi."

"Hi, Olivia this is Marcus, isn't he cute. He is so clever. He said that I am a perfect fit for the Society."

I silently groaned, that was a guarantee for the start for one of Daisy's overblown infatuations. She was a sucker for someone to look after her.

He smiled with too many teeth, "She is perfect and I am

looking forward to helping her on her journey." Okay, now I thought that he also had an annoying smarmy voice. He didn't look at me, just kept his eyes fully focused on Daisy.

I had to ask, "What is that you actually do?"

He looked annoyed and reluctantly slid his gaze over to me, giving me an unfriendly look. "We improve the lives of the members of our family and the world."

"It looks more like a speed dating thing," I said off hand.

He sighed deeply and leaned in closer to Daisy. "Some people just don't have the vision that you do. I would love to take you somewhere more private to talk?" He stroked her cheek with a finger and she looked smitten.

Daisy looked over at me, "Give it a rest Olivia, I know what I am doing. Why don't you talk to someone, you might learn something new. Just keep an open mind for once." With that parting shoot, she stalked off with her man.

I was left with my mouth open and fuming. I have had enough of this crap. Daisy was an adult and I was going to leave, I would check in later.

Suddenly I felt the hairs rise on the back of my neck, like I was being watched but as I turned I saw no one specific. With that final push I went to the cloakroom. I presented my ticket to a different bored teenager, grabbed my coat and pushed out of the main door.

The air though cold felt amazingly fresh and I felt so much better for it. I turned up my collar, sunk my head down and walked towards Trafalger square. There would be the winter market there and I always enjoyed that.

CHAPTER 3

As I walked I continued to take deep breaths of the cold refreshing air. I entered a kind of meditation as I concentrated on my steps.

Feeling more calm, I was able to feel more generous towards my friend. I smiled at some of the kids running in and out of the crowd, their parents trying to keep pace.

Picking up my pace, I walked past Leicester Square which was busy as always. Moving around the tourists taking pictures I headed down towards the National Portrait Gallery.

I saw the little Christmas market, there were a mixture of different stalls. The most popular seemed to be around the one serving hot beer. My focus was on the ones with the handcrafted stuff. I always loved things like this, though I knew that I was paying extra for the location.

I spent time looking through the stalls, half listening to all the different conversation, in varied languages around me. One of the things that I loved about London. Finally I decided on a beautiful glass figure, which had enchanted me. There was an inner glow from the tea light embedded within the female figure, which stretched upwards. I nodded at the lady behind the counter and asked how much it was.

"100 pounds love, it's one of a kind."

I pursed my lips, not really sure, I was awful at haggling. I did really want it but didn't want to waste money.

A voice next to me said, "It is nice but that seems like day light robbery!"

I turned my head and took in the man next to me. He wasn't looking at me but the stall owner, "You could try to give her a better deal."

I felt a little embarrassed about a stranger getting involved. I wanted to get out of there. I spoke to the stall holder, ignoring the man, "I am sorry but that is more than I can afford at the moment." With an apologetic and wistful look at the figurine, I turned away.

"I think that we could have gotten that for you, why did you bail."

I took a breath and turned to face the voice. I took him in, a handsome guy, who looked vaguely familiar was standing with his arms folded looking at me. He had a smug grin on his face. I bristled, more at myself, as I had thought that he was attractive and that he had obviously seen that I did too.

"Excuse me, I did not need your help. If I really wanted it I would have been able to get it myself, without an audience. I am not the damsel in distress that you thought, so thanks but no thanks."

His smile got wider and he tilted his head to the side, lifting his left hand and rubbing at the stubble on his chin. "Well that told me. As you have hurt my feelings, how about you buy me a drink?"

Seriously, I was impressed by the shear cheek. Looking again, he looked okay, well more than okay. He was wearing a smart fitted suit on a trim muscular body that looked expensive. I felt myself flush and looked up, catching another fleeting smirk. Jerk.

"I am so flattered, really," I drawled sarcastically, "but I am not that desperate."

"I have obviously messed this up, how about we try this again?"

Despite myself I smiled, damm. He was very charming and I just didn't have the resistance. "Well as a favour to you, how about we join the queue up outside the beer stand and talk in the queue?"

"I like the compromise. It is a skill that I don't have and it is one that I admire."

That's honest, I thought and very typically male. As I turned away, I glanced over his shoulder, seeing a man duck his head down.

I shivered slightly, the feelings that I had at the Society coming back, things felt off and I wanted nothing more than to be home. I realised that the guy was waiting for me to move but that his eyes were scanning around me. Though he appeared relaxed, on closer observation he was tense.

I decided that I should heed the warnings that my feelings were giving me, "I am sorry but I forgot that I have to meet someone. Maybe another time." With a ghost of a smile but no eye contact, as I didn't trust myself not to give in. I brushed past him, he didn't follow but gave a mocking wave goodbye. On retrospect I did stop at the stall, buying the figurine. I did look over my shoulder the whole time, not wanting to be seen by him. Though I did get a discount.

I kept my eyes up, scanning the crowd feeling the hair rising on the back of my neck. I could not help but continue to glance around, feeling as if I was being watched. I couldn't see anyone.

I did manage to shake the feeling off, as I walked further away. Once I saw the Thames, I slowed down, the being watched feeling had dissipated and I felt myself relax. I took some deep breaths but I refused to reach out. To distract myself, I pulled out my phone, no messages. That was odd, normally I would have received loads of one liners, with lots of emoji's and exclamation marks, Daisy classic. Pursing my lips, I looked out at the water, feeling unease return. I pushed out a breath and tried to push it aside. She was her own woman. Putting the phone away, I headed for home and my PJs.

CHAPTER 4

I woke up the next day with the winter sun shining brightly through my curtains, the light catching on my new glass figurine. I watched the light play through the glass, shifting and throwing rainbows on the wall.

I felt happy, warm in my bed knowing there was no work and no expectations (and no hangover). Really sometimes it was the little things.

I lazed around for another hour, watching some morning TV and then got up to make some breakfast. As I was making it, I looked out of my kitchen window. The window was quite small and overlooked a bit of greenery, the sun was streaming in, making a little difficult to clearly see. But it looked as though there was someone standing there, looking towards my window. I immediately shifted back, though there was little likelihood that they could see inside. After a moment, I moved forward and peeked through but there was no one there.

Well, there goes my carefree mood, suddenly feeling uneasy and uncomfortable I moved back from the window. I sat at the small snug table and realised that I couldn't ignore what was happening. Too many strange things were happening, but first coffee, nothing can be done until I have my double shot of Nespresso. With it in my hand, I grabbed a notepad as well, which helped make things clearer. Strange people following me, the cult like Society, Daisy not sending messages, the way that I could touch things far away, Louise and her coffees, strange guys. Wow, now I could feel the start of a headache.

I had always aimed for normal, I wanted to be one of the crowd. This had probably been because my childhood hadn't been that normal.

I looked over at a picture of my father, Marcus Jones. He had been a teacher, though I had never seen him teach. As long as I could remember he had been home with me, it was just us two against the world. We had always had money, I had a trust fund, though I didn't need to work I did because that was what people did. He had never really spoken of my mother, just said that she had died giving birth to me. There were no photographs, they had all been lost somehow. He did tell me that she had been an amazing person, with my smile. He had always been there, for every school events, homework, always pushing me to think about the why's.

It had been him that started the tradition of going to Louise's, when was that. I remember something happened but I could not remember what, something that had scared him, I remembered that. I also then remembered that I hadn't gone to school for a month, maybe when I was 10? We had met Louise then and I had started getting my daily drinks on the way to school, I had thought it a nice new tradition.

I had enjoyed any time with my Father, he had loved me but he had not been demonstrative. It was as if he, in retrospect, had always been on guard. He had never lied but could avoid giving me answers and I learnt to drop some things. I could always tell when he or anyone was lying, the lie triggering a sour taste in my mouth. I had thought that everyone could do this, therefore I had never lied. Gradually through school, I had realised that other people didn't but I knew, withodght being told that it was not something to talk about.

My Father had died when I was 18. He had for the first time, said that he had to go away for some business and he had never come back.

It was something that I had not realised and I realised that I did not know how exactly he had died. My Father's lawyer had done everything, discouraging questions and I had been so shellshocked that I had asked many.

Everything had already been set up, including the sale of our old house, this new flat and the details of my trust fund. The funeral small, simply the lawyer, Louise and myself. I had never seen Louise outside of her cafe, she had made me promise to continue coming to her cafe everyday, in memory of my Father.

She knew more than I did, for sure. I felt better having reached that decision and also that I had faced some things. But first I rang Daisy, it went straight to voicemail, odd but I uneasily left a message asking her to ring me when she could.

I got ready with my chains and my ever-present leather jacket. It felt good to have a plan. As I walked to Louise's, I kept, what I hoped was a subtle eye around me, as I walked. Nothing seemed odd and I didn't have that feeling of being watched.

As I approached Louise's place, I realised that it was closed though the lights were on in the back spilling light onto the street. I cautiously approached the window from the side and peered in. I saw Louise at the counter, her back to me while talking on the phone. It must have been some phone call as she was gesturing wildly.

I took the opportunity of her description to really see her, she was tall about 5'8, short white blonde buzz cut hair. She had strong features, reflecting a strong woman.

I knocked on the glass door gently, she swung around violently, almost dropping the phone. Her face looked shocked to see me but that expression disappeared quickly replaced by a smile, that didn't extend to her eyes. The weariness in her eyes led me to believe that I shouldn't trust all she would say. Why did people always have to mix half truths, everyone was hiding something even if it was from themselves. She cut her phone call off and came to the door, looking behind me, as if to check that I was alone. She undid the locks and opened the door partially. I slid through the gap and Louise locked the door behind me. Now that I was there, I was not sure where to start and nervously pushed my glasses up.

Somehow my nervousness seemed to relax her more, and she smiled more genuinely. "Do you know how long I have seen you do that when you are nervous?"

"I know that we have known each other a long time. I am asking you to help me now. There are some things that have been bothering me."

Her smile dimmed a little and with a sigh, she gestured to one of the seats. "Let us sit down, there are some things that you should know." As I sat down, "Would you like a hot drink?"

"Not coffee."

"Why?" Louise asked innocently, tilting her head to the side.

I folded my arms across my chest and indicated that she should sit opposite to me. "How about we start with why does this place remind so much of my old home?"

She sat down facing me, with her hands flat on the desk. "Your father was my friend and set things in place in the event of his death. He wanted me to be there for you and at some point help you with questions that might occur." As she say my expression, she hastened to add, "It was my pleasure to be there for you both." She tried to hold my hand but I pulled them back.

"What about the coffee? There is something strange in your coffee. Why do I need it? Because I do, don't I? Well you and Father thought so." I rubbed my arms, worried about the answers that I might get.

"Before we go any further, what happened? Why are you suddenly asking these questions? It would help me know the context."

I pursed my lips, buying time by looking around at the familiar things. I realised that I had to be honest, in return for a honesty. What ever I feared it would be better to be more knowledgable.

"This is going to sound unbelievable, I am not sure if I heard this myself, I would believe it. Let me get it all out, whether it is real or fantasy, let me finish." Looking down at the table, rather than at Louise, I tole her everything that had happened. Once I finished I let silence envelop us, then I lifted my head to see her expression.

She had a thoughtful expression, there was no pity or horror.

She stated simply, "Hmm. I had thought that this would take longer, if at all." She stood and paced a little, "First, you are not crazy, it is good that you told me everything. Second, your Father loved you and always wanted what was best for you, to protect you. Third, you are special, more special than you could possibly know. You have some extra, gifts, than other people. The coffee was to chemically suppress them, so that you would not attract unwanted attention, the best chance at a normal life. It's that what you always wanted?"

My mouth dropped open, Louise smilingly reached over and closed it for me. I gasped, talking deep breaths, I needed air. As she sat, I stood. "You know what, I think that I could do with a strong drink now."

"Me too, I agree," Louise bustled off and grabbed a bottle from behind the counter.

I smiled weakly and joked, "Not coffee!"

I sat myself back down and put my forehead down on the table, closed my eyes as I took some deep breaths. Slowly my heart rate slowed, my anxiety reduce its hold on me. I smelled the peppermint and some whiskey from my mug that appeared in front of me. Louise smiled sympathetically, nursing her own mug.

"Absolutely nothing but tea with a shot of whiskey, I find it soothing."

As I allowed the burning heat to wrap itself around me, "So all those coffees over the years, what was in them?"

"A mixture of unusual and rare herbs, with special chants said over them. It was something that had never been down before, so it was a bit hit and miss. Do you remember what you could do?"

I shook my head in denial as I dropped my eyes.

"I think that you do Olivia, try to remember, I know that you have buried them far in your memories."

I closed my eyes, focusing on the little details, in the sounds and smells around me. I told myself that I could do this, that I needed to. This was the way to know about myself and my

Father. As I entered a mediative state, I could see images float through my mind, I let them pass. They did to be going back in time. A small child crying about a lost toy. Her disbelieving face, sniffing as I returned a stuffed bear. "How did you find that, mum said that she had lost it last week." Another memory, I was telling a teacher that they were lying, the teacher all red and fuming. Me, crying being comforted by my Father, assuring me that everything would be fine. I don't know what had happened but there were many such scenes.

Father becoming increasingly worried, talking to teachers, other parents, Louise, on the phone. Then I was in another new school, new children, new home.

I opened my eyes, gasping as I clutched at my chains instinctively, "Why had I forgotten, there are more coming, its like a dam bursting."

Louise lent over to me and held my hands, saying nothing but sympathetic.

I leant back, my head hitting the wall. "I am not normal, I never was. Is this why I am always trying to fit in and not stand out?"

"No one is truly normal? Its an urban myth," Louise quipped.

"I have to admit that you are taking this much better than your Father predicted."

"I am trying to be pragmatic and the freak out, which is going to happen later, now this feels like something that I need to know."

Louise sat up straighter, letting go of my hand, despite myself I missed the warmth and I felt alone. She wrung her hands. I bit my tongue, to stop from pushing her again. I realised that sometimes people had to do things in their own way and in their own time. I would not be leaving without answers. It seemed like an age, while I watched Louise fight with herself, enough time that I had started to get uncomfortable and start fidgeting. I took off my jacket and scarf, carefully unwinding it without messing with my chains.

Their jingling caught Louise's ear and she turned towards me.

Her eyes a-lightened on them with a sort of recognition.

"You still wear those?"

"Of course, they are nearly always on me."

She moved back to sit opposite, "Can I ask, why do you wear them?" I shrugged, not exactly sure, why I wore them so much, it just felt right, necessary. She leant over touching the chains separately. "These are truly special, they shield you, and will help you focus. It is the way that the stones are linked together which help your energy. When you have it on, what do you feel?"

"I..I feel stable, is that strange but without I feel like I can be blown around and with it I am held steady. I always wear them either around my wrist or neck. There was one time I did not.. I can't remember exactly but something really bad happened. Something awful.." I paused, feeling a block. "Why can't I remember? The other memories are coming back but not that." I stood up while speaking, hugging my arms, feeling suddenly sad and scared.

Louise signed deeply, "I myself, don't know what happened, just that it scared your father a lot. That is when he found me. He kept secrets, so many secrets, he said that it was safer that way. He didn't need to tell me about the chain, I could feel how your energy was dampened after you wore it. You are right, I am letting my own discomfort put you in danger. I need and want to help you not put you at a disadvantage. What I am going to tell you, is from the bits that he told me. You had better sit down."

I did, feeling scared and excited that I was going to be finally learning answers to questions that I had not even known that I wanted to ask."

"Your father was a hard working man, very driven. He came from a middle class background, but as many young men, felt that he should be so much more. He saw education as the way out, so he studied hard, went to Oxford. Where he did feel people that thought like him, felt like him. There was one, a William May, they were friends. They established a club, the Society, perhaps it was one that they resurrected. I don't know. Its purpose, their desire was to establish a new order, a way to make the world the way that they wanted it.

So to be in it, you had to be special, useful because otherwise what would be the point. To make real change you need money, influence and the followers. So they looked for ways to have all of that and their research lead them to the occult. Unfortunately they got lucky and found an entity to help them. It must have been so seductive and therefore addictive, to them and others. They continued to build the Society after they left university. Remarkable fortune followed them, in ten years they had became so powerful in 10 years. All through the right people, in the right place at the right time.

I did wonder, if they had wanted to do good, what a world we could be living in right now. But people aren't always attracted to the good, people are people.

At the core, there was a select group. They had decided that people needed to evolve, that they would combine the entity in some way. Making new better beings, that would give them more power. So they developed new rituals to combine their entity with those that they recruited, well the women that they had recruited. Breeders, to make the next all powerful generation. These offspring were to be brought up within the society, indoctrinated really."

Louise paused, taking a shot with shaky hands. I followed her example. I have to admit that I found it difficult to listen, it sounded so fantastic, the plot of a movie. I realised that I would have felt better if she had been lying but she wasn't. I would have tasted any lies. I had a feeling, well I knew that this would not have a happy ending.

"Your father become disillusioned with the Society, in the way that they were using the recruits and I would imagine in controlling them. He never said but by then he had you, and he didn't want you to be a part of it. He wrestled with himself for a long time before he broke away. He disappeared with you, I don't know how he managed that. They have a long reach and so I think that he made then leave you both alone. He had prayed that you were without gifts, normal, then they would continue to stay away. So when you started displaying gifts, he did what he could to keep you safe."

She paused, for breath, her throat must have been dry by now, I topped her up.

I gave a snort of laughter, trying to process what was happening. Was I okay? No I didn't think that I was okay, there was nothing that was okay here. But I had asked for some answers, I had them, I knew that things would never ever be the same again.

I glanced over at Louise, I could see that she was trying unsuccessfully to hide her worry.

I grimaced, feeling almost overwhelmed by all the thoughts going through my head. It is what it is, I thought, there was little to be gained by fighting against things that had already happened. Even less point hoping that they were otherwise. Time for the next step. "Am I in danger?"

"Yes but remember to them you are valuable, but once they have you, you will lose all freedom.

"That relieves me a little, but if I don't join them, what then?"

"I don't know, but actually hurting you would probably be a last resort." She shrugged her shoulders.

"What can help me?" I asked anxiously.

"Learning what you can do, becoming as skilled as you can and avoiding them while you do this." Louise answered promptly.

I sat back again, thinking over my life so far, what I could remember had been pretty boring. School, uni and then working at a boring job. More pathetically, I didn't even need to work but I thought that it made me normal. A childhood of trying to fit in had disabled me, where was my drive, my ambition. I realised that I had just been trending water in the only life that I had. What an absolute waste. Had I made the world better for having been in it? Hand on heart, No. This did not make me feel better.

Maybe this could be the something that made my life worthwhile, with a direction. My father had sacrificed to keep me safe but now it was my time.

"Do you know anyone who could help me learn?"

Louise nodded, "I think so, I will call around."

I leaned forward and held Louise's hands, looking her deep in the eyes. "Thank you for being there for me and my Father. You are my family but I have not been there for you. This must have been hard, again I am grateful."

Her eyes teared up, she sniffed but smiling, "You are your Fathers daughter, it has and continues to be my pleasure. Do you want to have some more drinks?"

I laughed, "Why the hell not."

CHAPTER 5

I groaned, my arm was lying across my face. Oh my, another hang over. This could become a habit. My Alexa alarm was ringing, painfully. The weekend was over, I should be getting ready for work. I lay there, thinking.

I had something bigger, greater to do. I didn't need to work, no one would die if I never went back. The routine hum-drum was no longer needed.

Decision made, my hang over receded and I leapt out of bed. As I grabbed my lap top, I really felt energised and that this was the right decision. I fired off emails to HR, citing personal issues with my notice, to include my leave for my notice period. I emailed my few outstanding projects on.

Daisy leapt to mind, I checked my phone, no missed calls. That buried feeling of worry that had been at the back of my mind turned into dread. Settling in my stomach. I rang, the phone didn't even ring through. Biting my lip, I checked her social media and they had all been closed. This was so not Daisy, she lived on these sites, it was her way of being seen and liked.

Desperate, I called her mum, who answered but was obviously distracted. It felt like I had to remind her of Daisy, she had never been what anyone would class as a good mother but seriously. With frustration, I told her how worried I was and finally she admitted that she had not spoken to Daisy for over a year. "Don't worry love, she will turn up. Ask her not to ring me, I have a new guy and he doesn't know I have a kid." I wish I had rung from a landline, so that I could have slammed it down.

With my heart racing, I reviewed what I knew. Daisy had not contacted me for 3 days, her phone was off, all her social media accounts had been closed. Officially worried, I thought about what I should do. Slowly I got dressed, my chains, leather jacket paired with conservative black trousers and a white shirt.

I made my way to Daisy's flat share in Brixton, her flat mates hadn't seen her for 3 days. She had only what she had on when I left her. Daisy had never worn the same thing for more than 24 hours. Okay, now I was well beyond worry and accelerating towards fear.

Determined I left, turning right towards Brixton police station. I waited in a queue, distracting myself from my worry, observing the people around me. There were certainly some strange people about, I listened to a couple of their conversations. An elderly lady who felt that she had been jilted by a younger man, after she had given him a lot of money.

Finally it was my turn, after I stated that I wanted to report a missing person, I was asked to wait.

A lovely young officer came down 20 mins later, taking me to an open plan office. I gave all Daisy's details, along with pictures and the contacts I knew. He was nice, but obviously dealt with a lot of this, he kept reassuring me that she was okay and had probably taken off with a guy. Insistently I gave the details of when I had last seen her and the weird feeling that I had gotten from the place. Once I had said Society, he suddenly sat up and paid full attention. He asked me to repeat the details and then with no explanation got up and left.

I was left with my mouth open, what just happened. I leaned over and could see him heading up to another floor. That was more than a little odd I thought but stayed put. Another 20 mins went by, my right leg was really bouncing with my impatience. I could feel my anxiety and now annoyance mixed with fear building up. I stood up and started pacing, Daisy. Some of this was my anger at myself, I realised that I was angry at myself because I had left her. My best friend. I closed my eyes to recall the man that she had been with, why couldn't I recall his features. I had a good memory for faces but all I was drawing was a blank. Trying to force my memory, I screwed my eyes up tighter, nothing.

I was so caught up, that I didn't notice someones approach. The first indication was a polite cough. Startled I looked up. An officer stood behind me, smiling. He was cute, slightly rumpled, brown hair and beautiful brown soulful eyes.

"Hello, I am Detective Jason Seymour", he held out a hand. I stared at it but finally pulled myself together and shook his hand. He smiled, charmingly and I felt myself flush. How embarrassing.

He moved into a seat and gestured for me to sit. I sat, folding my hands onto my lap. He looked through the forms that the other police officer had filled in. "I understand that you are very worried about your friend."

Pulling myself together, I leant forward to make sure that he understood how concerned I was. "I am, something is very wrong. She would never go for this long, without a change of clothes or shut down her social media. Trust me when I say this, she is in trouble."

He frowned down at the paper, "I am inclined to believe you, you don't seem the type to panic unnecessarily. Let's go through the details again and make sure we have everything."

He took me through the forms and extra details, I was impressed by his professionalism and reassured. After an hour, he felt that he had enough details to be going on with.

While he was making some notations, it suddenly all seemed to overwhelm me. "Are you okay?"

Startled, I smiled apologetically, "I am really worried about my friend and guilty that I shouldn't have let her stay."

"Would she really have listened to you?" He leaned forward with a very sympathetic look.

"No but I can not help but feel I should have tried harder, whether she listened or not." I defiantly lifted my chin, meeting his eyes.

He leant further forward and placed his hand on mine, "I admire your loyalty. Trust me, I will do my very best for you ... and your friend."

I smiled sadly, "Thank you, I so feel better knowing that you take this all seriously."

Moving his hand reluctantly, he pulled a card from his wallet. "I have got your number, I will be ringing to let you know our progress. Here is my card, let me know if you hear from her or if you just need to talk."

I stood, "Of course and thank you again." I held my hand out, as he stood, seeming to tower over me. I felt protected, my anxiety had lessened, it was reassuring to share the responsibility.

As if he wanted to continue our meeting, he said "Let me walk you out." I blushed, fussing with my glasses, I smiled shyly. It wasn't the best time but he really seemed like a nice guy and cute.

He made small talk, which kept me at ease, as we walked out. I found him charming and despite my worry, I found myself chuckling. "You are very good at making me forget why I came here?"

He smiled leaning lazily against the outside wall, "Then I have done my duty and more." He paused and moved a little closer, looking down, "I am going to check on you later, so expect my call. Okay?"

I looked down too, fussing with my chains, shyly smiled "Yes, I would like that. Thank you again." As I was aware that I hadn't made an idiot of myself yet, I walked away. I forced myself not to look back, walking to the station.

As I had started not to feel safe conscious, safe in the knowledge that the detective couldn't see me anymore, I glanced in the window of a shop. In its reflection, I saw the guy from the Christmas market, Mr Charmer. He was staring at me from the other side of the road. He didn't seem to have any shame, he confidently, as if he had every right, continued to stare at me. Then as I was deciding what to do, he started across the road, with a challenge in his eyes.

I looked around nervously, surely I was safe on a crowded road. Feeling a little more confident, I held my ground. I needed answers. He stopped in front of me, seeming totally at ease. He was tall, I looked up at him, pushing my glasses up, a question in my eyes.

He looked down the road, where I had come from, "Trouble?" His voice was deep and gravelly, his eyes watched me intently.

"As I don't know you, explain to me why should I tell you anything?"

"I thought that we might be able to help each other?" He stepped forward, into my personal space. Though my face heated, I refused to step back and stared him down.

"Thank you but I have some official help already." I snapped back, thinking of Detective Seymour. Despite myself, my face heated.

He frowned, moving forward again, bending to look into my eyes.

Now I stepped back, "Hey, heard of personal space?"

"I was wondering who you were thinking of." He straightened and held his arm out. "How about we try having that drink now?"

At first, I couldn't believe that his gall. But as I stepped back to get some distance, I saw a coffee shop. I had a feeling that he would continue to follow me, he seemed persistent and determined. So I might as well get this over with. "Since you insist."

He smiled widely, a little crookedly, which was annoyingly cute. He gently took hold of my elbow to steer me, which made me pull away. I walked briskly forward, entered the coffee shop first, leaving him to follow. As I looked around, I spotted a free two seated table. I took the chair against the wall, leaving him the chair with its back to the room. With some satisfaction, I noted that he looked at it with dislike and raised his eyebrows. With ease he lifted the chair and placed it beside me, so that we were both facing the room.

After we had both sat, he nudged me with his shoulder, "Well this is nice."

With a huff, I pushed my chair a little way from his, "You need to learn and respect personal space."

"I have never really had a problem with it."

A young waitress came over and asked for our order, in our bored way. He ordered a latte and he ordered a flat white.

As she walked away and his attention had turned back o me, I asked flatly "So why are you following me?"

He shrugged, answering flippantly, "Should there be a sinister reason, don't you know that you are very pretty?"

Despite my annoyingly easy blush that had stained my cheeks, I rolled my eyes, pushed my glasses back up. I think that my silence expressed my opinion on that.

He moved his chair, so that he was angled towards me, leaning forward, he stared at me. It was as if he was measuring me up, it caused me to shift uncomfortably in my seat.

"Okay, so you don't believe in compliments. So moving on, why were you at the police station?"

I thought that some truths might be helpful and I might get some information back. "My best friend has gone missing."

There was a thoughtful look in his eye but no surprised, "Where did you see her last?"

So he does know something, I thought, he had a coiled energy about him. Like a dog that has caught a scent. "At an odd party three days ago. She wouldn't leave, she stayed. Now tell me what you know."

He looked uncomfortable and did his own shifting. He took a breath, "Because the same thing happened to my sister, last month." He spat out the words as if they were causing him pain, he looked away, trying to avoid them.

"I am so sorry," without thought I placed a hand on his arm. The muscles tensed under my hand, he was still for a moment and then he pulled away.

To lighten the mood, he said "Now who is ignoring personal space".

I could tell that he was being defensive, not comfortable with the weakness that he might have shown. "Where did she go missing?"

"London, same place I saw you. I had been trying to get in and

I did manage but then I was asked to leave. They obviously knew that I had been looking around."

"I thought that I had caught a glimpse of you, how did you get invited?"

"I have my ways. How did you get invited?"

"My best friend was invited and she insisted that I go with her. It felt off, something was wrong there. So I left."

"You were the only one who left, that's why I followed you. I thought that perhaps you might know something."

"I thought you would have stayed to pick up some more clues?" I realised that we had leaned closer into each other, engrossed in our conversation.

"No one was talking. It was a dead end. So I thought that they would want you, that someone would come and pick you up, you seemed the kind of person that they would want in their group." I wasn't sure what to make if that, it gave me a creepy feeling. A frown appeared on my face, there was a lie in the story but mainly truth.

A distraction arrived in the form of our coffees. I took my mug, appreciating the heat. It felt like something important was happening here, that he would be important to me. I had never really had or to be honest been open to these instincts before. This was a new world for me and I already knew that I needed to start trusting my feelings.

I held out my hand, "We missed out a step, in case you didn't know, my name is Olivia Jones."

He looked at my hand strangely, looked up, as if to assess this about turn. Smiled broadly, as if he had won something and took hold of my hand in a firm handshake. "I am Grayson Moon."

I continued to hold his hand. "I know that we don't know each other, but we have something in common. We have lost loved ones. I need any help that you can give me, but I also need to know what is going on, the stuff that you aren't telling me. I have to be honest, I am having a really weird week and I have decided that facing things head on is the only way to go." I tilted my head to the side, nervously pushing up my glasses, that had slipped while waiting for his response.

He chuckled, clearly amused as his fingers stroked my palm. As tingles shot up my arm, I tried to pull my hand back but he held on, gently but firmly.

"Olivia, it is a pleasure to meet you, I am impressed by your honesty. I was not expecting it and I usually expect everything. To be frank, I am not sure whether I can be completely honest. I usually work alone." He seemed to suddenly realise that he was still holding my hand and stroking it, he pulled back gently letting his fingers trail.

I was silent, caught by the sensations. I shook my head clear and frowned at him. Smiling mischievous, amused and satisfied by my response, he took a sip of his coffee. I followed suit and took a gulp of coffee, though typically started choking, as it went down the wrong way. Desperate to look more grown up, I asked hoarsely, "Do you have a picture of your sister, just in case I see her?"

He pulled out his phone, the smiles having disappeared. He showed me a shot of a beautiful young asian girl about 19. She looked back at me, caught having been laughing. No, I had never seen her before. As I was passing the phone back, it flipped to the next picture. I pulled the phone back and smiled. The photo was Grayson and his sister, they were smiling at each other. He looked very carefree and open. So unlike the man that was sitting across from me.

He saw my expression change as I saw the second photo and leaned closer, his hair brushing my face. When he saw the photo he took the phone back, smiling down at the picture. "Before you ask, she is younger and obviously I am adopted, in case you were embarrassed to ask. Our Dad was a great man, and since he isn't here I am responsible for her." Sighing, he breathed out and said under his breath, "God I hope that she is ok?" He allowed his body sank back in the chair, his eyes closing.

His distress was palpable, though I loved Daisy, losing a sister must be different. I had always wished for a brother or sister, it had been a lonely childhood.

I placed my hand on his arm again, he opened his eyes and looked at me. His eyes were a brilliant blue and it seemed that time stopped. I caught my breath, feeling something happening. Some sort of connection forming, which intensified as he placed his hand over mine.

My phone loudly rang, breaking the moment, Grayson pulled back. Distractedly I looked at the unknown number but answered and the smooth voice of Detective Seymour spoke. "Hello Olivia, I hope that I haven't caught you at an awkward time?"

I turned slightly, angling my body away from Grayson. "No, its fine Detective, do you have news?" Hope mixed with caution rose in my chest.

"No I am sorry but I was just following up, checking on you. I wonder whether we could meet tomorrow, I can give you any updates." I could taste the ghost of a lie but about what, perhaps he just wanted to see me? Odd and a little unprofessional but it would mean that he put more effort into the search. Though I couldn't see him, I could feel Graysons disapproval and from the corner of my eye, I saw that he had crossed his arms.

"That would be fine Detective, could you let me know when and where."

"I have to go but I will text you. Take care Olivia."

After he had hung up, I turned towards Grayson, "What?" I said defensively.

With disapproval and something else, clear in his voice, "Nothing, obviously I thought you had more important things to worry about rather than getting a date."

His words stung, I responded impulsively, "Actually that was the Police who is helping me. He wants to meet tomorrow. Is that not important?"

He flushed at my tone but evenly said, "And professional?"

"It's none of your business, who I meet. Back to the basics, what did the police said about your sister, it might be worth letting him know."

Grayson looked pissed, but stiffly said, "Nothing. They said that they had followed all leads but there was nothing to point to her whereabouts or that it was anything but a runaway. Like your friend, her phone is off, all her social media shut down. I did flyers, hired a private investigator and nothing. There were a couple of leads but they all seem to fizzle out or were shut down." He leaned forward to whisper, "I can't help thinking that there is a conspiracy behind this. I think that these people are protected."

I nodded my head, my mind buzzing. With the background that Louise had told me, then yes they were being protected. I felt bad that I did not feel ready to share this with him yet, to be honest he would probably think that I was crazy. Settling for, "I have a feeling that you are right." Pushing my glasses up again, I anxiously ran my fingers over my chains. Feeling settled and just processing, I didn't notice Grayson reach over and touch one of the strands.

"These are unusual," he mused looking down at them.

Startled, as no one had touched my chains before, I placed a hand over his to stop him.

With almost a shove, I was somewhere else. It was hot, a solid feeling of heat, like a desert. I looked around, it was like a film. From afar, I could see Grayson wearing an army uniform and holding a gun. No-one seemed aware of me, he stood with a group of similar dressed men, suddenly there was an explosion, everything and everyone flew to the ground. I gasped and suddenly I was back in the coffee shop. Grayson was standing over me, holding my arms, looking scared. "Are you okay? What happened?" He almost shouted the words, worry underlying the harshness of the words.

I blankly liked at him, felt that I opened and shut my mouth a couple of times, with nothing coming out. Shocked beyond belief by what I had just experienced. I thought to say, I was okay but I had to repeat it in my head before I could say it out loud. "I am .....", I opened my clenched fist and red sand fell from my hands. I shot up from the chair, "What the...."

Grayson also stood, "What is going on Olivia. You need to tell me, what just happened."

I mumbled, almost incoherently, "I have to go, sorry. Call me if you hear anything, here's my number." I quickly scribbled my number on a napkin and thrust it at him, then ran out of the shop.

I heard Grayson call out behind me, but luckily a large chattering group of teenage girls entered and he was held up by them. Moving fast, I ran to the station, making it onto a train just pulling out. As I got on the train, I panted from the panic still running though me. The other passengers glanced and then ignored me, thank you London.

I sat down, knowing that I needed to start this training. I could see why someone would want me and this gift.

CHAPTER 6

By the time I had left the undergound, I had managed to calm down, slightly. I certainly went up the stairs with less drama, than I had arrived on the train. The cold was welcome, cooling my still flushed cheeks. I pulled my jacket closer. As I stood at the entrance waiting for the light to cross, I pulled out my phone. There were several missed calls from an unknown number. I suspected that they would be from Grayson and I was right. I sighed, added his contact details, so that I would get some warning next time. I texted him that I was fine and that I would get back to him later. That would not be well received, almost immediately a text popped up from him. 'I will call you tomorrow and you had better pick up'. Not controlling at all, though he probably didn't see it that way. I shoved the phone back into my pocket. Pushing on, I passed a quiet gardened allotment, one that I often came to in the summer. As I looked around, it struck me how quiet and isolated it was. I had an overwhelming urge to try something out. Glancing around, I went through to the back.

I rubbed my arms, trying to get some heat into me. I was also a little freaked by what had happened with Grayson. That was beyond normal, it seemed that things were moving fast, as those suppressing chemicals wore off. I could feel the urgency in my need to try out some more of these gifts. I stepped up behind a tree, using it to hide me in case someone came in. Furtively I looked around and took my gloves off. I blew on my hands, feeling like a boxer getting ready. Biting my lip, I looked about 20 yards away, where there were some abandoned gardening tools. Closing my eyes, I focused on finding my calm, my space within me. Slowly my breathing deepened, my heart rate slowing.

Through a lot of background noise and thoughts. I continued to focus, as I did so I felt something gathering in my centre. That had never happened before and it distracted me. I had to restart and find my focus again. Opening my eyes against the now bright light, I focused on a small gardening shovel. With pure focus, I opened my hands and reached out for it. Frowning, I focused harder, nothing. Absently I planned with my chains and I felt something stronger within my focus. More confidently I tried again, letting go of my disbelief, my lingering doubts about the reality that this could work. I started to feel strange, my hand tingling. Closing my eyes, I pictured the spade clearly, the way that it was resting against a tray, the drops of water that were running over its surface, the rust at the handle. I focused on how it would feel in my hand, the cold metal, the wetness, the smell of the earth. My hairs at the back of my neck lifted, my breath stilled.

I opened my eyes and looked down at my hand. There, sitting in my hand was the spade. I stood still and then took a step back, dropping the spade. Oh my god, I slowly sank to the cold ground, the hard anchoring bark of the tree against my back. Though I had told myself, that this was possible, I obviously had not.

Way to lie to myself, I banged the back of my head against the tree, looking up through the bare branches. I am going to end up in a lab getting dissected. Paranoid and now more than a little scared, I scanned the allotment again.

With a little shrug, I shook myself, stood up and did it again, and again. Twenty minutes later, I looked down at my mixed collection of garden tools and rocks. Realising that I needed to work with something heavier, ignoring the image of my brain coming out of my ears. I gauged the weight of a wheelbarrow, well I did need to practice distance and weight. Maybe a private hall or gym would be better to start, than alone, in case I did something wrong and got injured.

Proudly brushing off my hands and putting my gloves on, I glowed with sweat but also the feeling of accomplishment. Louise would be impressed, which made me think longingly of hot food and drinks. I stamped my feet, to warm them a little, only now realising how cold they felt. I held back a little before the entrance, using the fence to check the road. No-one seemed to be paying me any attention. Though I couldn't shake off a feeling of being watched. Pulling my cooler up and my head down, I stepped quickly onto the road. Moving briskly, feeling the cold, I made my way to Louise's.

It was open and appeared quite busy, the light spilling out onto the road. Pulling open the door, I quickly went in, pulling the door shut behind me. Louise and her assistant were busy serving behind the counter. I joined the queue, happy to feel my hands and feet warming up. By the time I got to the counter, I had warmed up enough to remove my gloves and scarf. Louise smiled at me, "It's busy right now, but I will bring your drink over and we can catch up."

"Coffee and a scone please." She nodded and shooed me away to an open single table in the corner. I quickly ran to it and collapsed into the single padded chair. I took off my jacket, hanging it carefully behind my chair. Casually glancing around the cafe, I felt comfortable and had lost the feeling of being watched. Relaxing, I pulled my phone out. First I checked my work emails, reassured that all was well and that I wasn't leaving anyone in the lurch. Though it didn't feel good that apparently I wasn't indispensable. Thank you Father for the trust fund, which enabled me to be independent.

Moving forward with my training, I started to look up gym spaces that would let me hire. I looked through for the privately owned ones, as they were more likely to let me hire for myself. There was one, a little outside London, I sent an email request with my phone number. It would be good to practice with weights. A more accurate assessment of my limits was definitely needed. There could be so many variables, could I move something between places or was it only to me.

I also had that not a date with the Detective Seymour and I didn't imagine that Grayson would be leaving me alone.

Sharon, Louise's employee approached with my coffee and

scone. Thanking her, I promptly demolished the coffee and scone. A quick look showed me that Louise wouldn't be popping by yet, she still had a crowd.

Looking again at my phone, I thought of what Louise had told me yesterday. So much had happened, that it seemed longer.

So time for a little internet research. Not expecting much I searched for anything on my Father, nothing but his obituary. I looked sadly at the photo, so many secrets. Then Professor May, there were so many hits. His professorship, lectures, philanthropy. A lot of photos, it was strange to see pictures of this, my nemesis. There were pictures with famous actors, politicians, philanthropists. I have a nemesis, not odd at all. He was striking, blonde white hair, short cut, high cheekbones, a very direct stare. I hated to say, attractive for an older guy. Clicking on one video after another, after digging my AirPods out of my pocket, I played it. He was charismatic, forceful and obviously out of my league.

Chewing my lip, I could imagine that this man would get what ever he wanted. I could imagine that little would stop him, not scary at all that he apparently wanted me. He certainly would have the resources to find me.

I leaned back, with all his resources, he had to know where I was. Why hadn't they come already? I sat back tugging at my chains, trying to think it all through. I couldn't even pretend that I could imagine what he was thinking, he thought globally and I did not. The amount of time, investment to ...create, make me wouldn't be written off. What ever deal that Father had done, might and probably wouldn't be honoured now that I was obviously not normal. I couldn't be naive enough to imagine that I wasn't being watched.

Also bouncing around my thoughts, were what if there were others like me. Images of x-men flew through my head. I had always been open to possibilities but really, wow. Maybe having that coffee hadn't been a good idea.

A sudden presence appeared at my table, with an aura of worry. I looked up into Louise's worried face, she looked at me and sighed heavily. Pulling over a chair, she put some cake in front of me. "You looked like you needed this. Tell me what has happened?"

Smiling, "You are a mindreader.." Pausing I looked at her, "You aren't are you?" I was only half joking, as my fork hoovered over the cake.

"Go on, tuck in. Of course I can't, can you?"

"That's not funny," I took a piece and felt it melt in my mouth. Exactly what I had needed, the familiar, amongst all the chaos. Louise looked at me fondly, tucking some hair behind her ear, as she scanned around us. There was no one nearby but she leaned close to me, talking softly. "I felt something, I thought that perhaps you had used your gifts? Are you okay?"

"When did you feel it?" I asked, leaning forward as well, wondering if she had actually felt me.

"About 2 hours before you came in?", she saw the confirmation in my face. Excitedly she asked, "You were practising weren't you?"

I put my fork down, having demolished the cake, I eagerly nodded, happy that I could share this. "It was amazing." I told her what I had done but finished, worried, "Can other people feel what I did?"

She looked worried, "Yes, so I think that it would be better if you practised further away from where you live. Though I would like to see it," she said wistfully.

Smiling, I assured her "Of course you will but when I am sure that I won't hurt you by accident. Any chance that you know anyone to help me because I am just winging it here."

She looked worried, "I thought that I knew someone but when I approached him, he was almost too interested. I got a bad feeling from him, I refused to answer his questions but he became really pushy. I was surprised because he knew your father, I hope that I haven't made things worse."

"It's not your fault, I guess that there are only a few people that I can trust. Let me have his name, I can tell if he is lying, there maybe something that I can learn from him."

Louise leant back, toasting me with her own coffee, "You are becoming the strong and resourceful young woman. You have dealt with all this better than I could have hoped for."

"I never gave you a reason for thinking otherwise, I have been wasting my life but not any more." Sometimes we need adversity to see who we really are, I hope that I was up for whatever was coming.

Nodding, Louise pulled out her phone and air dropped the number. I had a quick check to confirm I had received it, I would call him later.

"Louise, I am aware that you have been doing so much for me, but that I don't know about you. Would you mind if you filled me in?"

I was rewarded by a shy smile, which became broad. "Settle in then Olivia, it is one hell of a ride." I listened intently but there was no lies. Louise had been brought up in a family that were comfortable with the supernatural. They were known for their sensitivity to the other unseen world and easily walked it. Unfortunately she had fallen out with her family, over a man. He had some abilities, and had been very charming but then had left her with nothing and joined the society. She had not gone back or approached her family, just built up her own knowledge base and made her own way. She had met my father during this time and he had helped her find this place , focus and financial security.

I smiled as I left a couple of hours later, stepping out . I could see my breath. It had been nice, I felt a lot closer to Louise and I understood her, a bit more. I seemed to have gained some homework, Louise had given me some of her books.

As I shifted my bag, I heard my phone bing and pulled it out. A text from Grayson, 'Wrap up warm and travel safe.' I thought about responding back but then thought better, hanging around in the cold and dark was not a good idea. I looked down at my scarf, its bright yellow almost glowing in the lights that were on around me. Looking around, I didn't dwell on the fact that he had known when I had left Louise's. Perhaps a better wardrobe might be best, if I wanted to attract less attention.

CHAPTER 7

Despite my fears and I had fallen straight to sleep, with surprise I awoke feeling energised. Blinking at the sunlight that streamed through my window, I really have to remember to shut them. Swinging my legs out of bed, I did my morning yoga. Stretching after, I could feel my newly found focus.

While having breakfast, I allowed myself to check my phone. Disappointingly there was nothing from Daisy. There was one from Grayson, he was planning to canvas around the Society building and wanted to know if I wanted to meet him. I had planned on doing that and he probably had more of an idea about how to go about it. I sent a yes and asked him to confirm location and time. Detective Seymour had sent one with a time and place for meeting up. I hoped that they didn't overlap. Checking my emails there was good news from the gym that I contacted, they were happy to let me use it in the morning.

It seemed like I was going to have a busy day, I felt excitement about what might happen. Since I had a busy day ahead, I had better get started. I rang the gym, arranging to meet the owner at 10am, I could be alone for a couple of hours. I could ring the trainer after. I used my little used car share app to rent a car for the ride to the gym, it would probably be better that it was not obvious where I had gone. Confirmation came through that it would be available in thirty minutes.

Singing, I showered and changed into some yoga clothes, grabbed some water and protein bars. After some thought, I also grabbed a note book, perhaps I should record my progress. I made it to the car in good time, set the address in my phone and set off.

I took a circuitous route to get to the gym address,

inadvertently by the fact that I got lost. Pulling into the almost empty car park, it looked like an old fashioned boxing club. The gym owner turned out to be lovely, though initially he frightened to me. He was an older muscled man, I am sure that he must have been very impressive when he was younger. He died ask any questions, just looked me over and accepted my cash. I opened it up, it was dominated by the central boxing ring, with gym equipment scattered around. It was old and worn, with absolutely no security cameras. Perfect.

As I had seen in films, I started some stretches and a run. Realising that it was dangerous to wear my chains around my neck, I transferred them my wrists. Taking some sips of water, I realised that I had procrastinated and stood 5m away from the weights. Centering myself, I held out my hands for a 1kg weight. I concentrated, concentrated and then concentrated some more. Slowly there was a tingle that built in my hands and without warning a sudden heaviness. Breathing out slowly, I opened one eye to look down at the weight in my hand. Feeling a smile tugging at my lips, I pressed them together and concentrated on moving it back. With a step back, I wiped sweat from my forehead. There was the start of a headache at the back of my head. I guessed that I was using my mind like a muscle and I would need to build some power and stamina.

Jogging on the spot, I decided that getting something into my hands was all well and good but impractical. So instead of holding my hands out to receive I held them palm down, over the floor. This time I concentrated on the weight and once I had a feel of it I focused on where I wanted it. This took a little more effort, concentrating strongly.

I sat back on my legs, panting. It was astounding, strange, alien but through I didn't want to fully admit it, it felt natural. Something that seemed to complete me, I felt as if this was something that I was meant to be doing, using. So I kept going.

A couple of hours later, my phone alarm rang and I realised that I was drenched in sweat, surrounded by weights, stacked haphazardly.

I collapsed by their side, pulled out a protein bar and demolished it. That and some water eased my headache, I massaged my neck with my free hand. Eying all the weights, I was impressed by the fact that I had managed to move them all.

Needing some more rest time, I pulled out my phone ringing the number that Louise had given me. It rang, I hung up after a couple of rings, not really sure if I should leave a message. As I was standing up, it rang. "Hello?"

"Is this Olivia?", the quiet voice sounded old and harsh, I couldn't even tell if it was a man or woman.

"Yes," I answered confidently, hiding my nervousness, I hoped.

"Ah good, good. I am Marcus, I think that we have a mutual friend in Louise and your Father? She has told me a little about your situation and I think I can help." The words sounded reassuring but there was a lie in there. He continued eagerly, perhaps a little desperately, "I thought that we could meet today."

I decided that this was not someone I wanted to meet but rehabs there was something I could learn. "I am sorry Marcus but today is not good, can we meet tomorrow?"

"That is disappointing, I have actually already travelled down to meet you. You know that I knew your Father, I can tell you so much." A low blow I thought.

"I am afraid that I can not, Louises' tomorrow at two? I am sure that she will also want to meet you." I firmly said.

He had gone quiet and I wondered if he would agree, with some injected warmth, "Well if you can wait that long, then so can I. If I can pass on a warning, trust no-one. You are more special than you know."

"Thank you, I will see you tomorrow." I disconnected, staring at my phone. There was someone with a back story." I would worry more about it tomorrow, I texted Louise to let her know. Then feeling cool, I got up to do some more.

Much later, I lay on my back on the dirty floor, breathing harshly, my head pounding. Covering my eyes, I dragged in more breathes. Rolling over, I stumbled over my bag, pulling out paracetamol and ibuprofen. After a had taken them, plus a full bottle of water and another protein bar, I collapsed onto one of the mats. I was too tired to care about all the possible things that were on the floor and this mat.

I closed my eyes, waiting for everything to kick in. I was going to need to be on the go soon. Letting my head flop to the side, I was almost alarmed by the fact that I had moved everything in here. Thank goodness I had been returning everything back. As I stared up at the ceiling, I was taken back bay the things that I could do with only one session. A little scary really and I now I knew why people might want me. I was going to have to think everything that I thought I knew.

I rolled over before my thoughts became too overwhelming. As I stood shakily, my legs feeling like jelly. I was going to have build stamina. Trying not to think what this could actually be doing to my brain. At least I couldn't hurt anyone by accident, as I still had to focus. I grabbed my sweatshirt, realising that my headache was wearing off. With relief, I grabbed my stuff, turned off all the lights and locked up. As I drove, I was struck by how vivid everything seemed to be, like ultra HD. I returned the car and dragged my tired boys home. I was so out of it, that it took a moment to realise that there was a beautiful flower bouquet waiting for me. They were beautiful, I had never gotten flowers before. Scooping them up, I juggled everything to open my doors.

Dropping my stuff, I placed the flowers on the breakfast table. Excitedly I pulled out the card, 'We will meet soon, keep safe'. Leaning back against the table, I tapped the card on the table. Who were they from, the message sent a little fission of foreboding through me. As I heard the card and it touched my chains, I feel into a daze. Though it I saw a face, shit, Professor May.

Dropping the card, I collapsed back onto a chair, putting my head in my hands. I had thought that it would be unlikely that being in the one city and with all my feelings of being watched, they didn't know that I was here. This was a reminder that they knew and were going to pick their time. I might have been in denial but this had hammered it home.

My home wasn't safe and neither was I.

So what should I do about it. Rubbing my arms, I stared blankly at the wall. Thoughts tumbling around my head.

I needed to train, hone my skills. I had a feeling that any weakness was like blood in the water to a shark. But ...I think that it was going to need to be somewhere else, I needed to be off the grid. But leaving Louise and Daisy, that didn't feel right all all. I was going to have to talk to Louise, find somewhere else. As I looked around my little kitchen I realised the time, I was going to be late.

Rushing into and out of the shower, I quickly dried off, towel drying my hair and dressing as quickly. My outfit was simple, comfortable black leggings, a black rolled neck cashmere jumper, my chains and some comfortable black boots. I left the room, only to return and apply some mascara, eye shadow and powder, with a tinted lip balm. As I looked at my reflection, I shrugged my shoulders, well I was a woman. Locking the doors, I paused, something telling me that I might not be back. A strange thought.

Brushing my unease aside, I hurried into London, not without keeping an eye out around me, Wondering who was watching. Then I became distracted wondering what news Detective Seymour might have. Panting, I was a little early to arrive. As I approached, I saw that he was already there, facing away from me and angrily shouting at someone on the phone. Despite sliding up behind him, I couldn't catch any of the conversation. He turned suddenly and hung up. It was smooth but there was definitely a moment of suspicion and then he smiled charmingly. It was a good smile, despite myself I blushed and smiled back.

I might have overdone it, as he blinked in surprise but then widened his smile. It was definitely a less than professional smile, my heart rate picked up.

Clearing my throat, I tried to rein it back a little. "Is everything alright, did you hear anything?" My concern returned full force, I was left feeling a little guilty about the smile.

He shook his head, "I have not heard anything yet but trust me, we are doing all that we can." That was a big fat lie, he did it so well, even faking sympathy in his eyes. If I didn't have my gift I would have believed him. I looked at his phone, "Oh that was a colleague trying to take my annual leave. Can you believe it, not all police men can be trusted." He laughed and I pretended to do the same, anger coiling inside me.

"That's terrible, you really must have a tough job. Thank you for wanting to check on me." I tried to look coy, I had never tried before, so wasn't sure that I was getting it right. Looking up through my eyelashes, I saw with some relief that he looked delighted. I must be okay at this then.

Taking my arm, he directed me, "I hope you don't mind but I actually booked us a table to eat, I am starving?" He walked me to a restaurant, I would have protested but I was also starving. I call it a fact finding mission. He created the server and we were led to a table. As I took my jacket off, I was woman enough to be glad that I had made a little extra effort.

"You look great Olivia," I smiled, as if I had received many such compliments. He didn't need to know that it wasn't true, though I couldn't help but push my glasses up and fiddle with my chain links. "Let me give you a summary of what we have done so far." He talked very seriously and I could see the professional that he was. He spent ten minutes telling me all that he had done, I was almost nauseas with the lies. He appeared so earnest, looking me straight in the eye, reaching over to hold my hand and offer me comfort.

I thought of Daisy, her innocence, wanting to belong so desperately. I prayed that she was okay. I looked away, not sure that I could hide my hostility right now. I knew now that Grayson had been right , the police were not going to help me. Sighing deeply, he tightened his grip, "Olivia look at me, I know that you are right and that Daisy is in trouble but so are you. Tell me what is going on with you, I can help, you are not alone."

"Thank you Detective, I am okay, It is just alot, Daisy is the only family I have and I find it hard to think of her being hurt. I need your help to find her, then perhaps we could be more. I think that I should not let you split your focus." I pulled my hand away as if I was reluctant, slowly rather than the quick way that I wanted to. He let me but his other hand spasmed, as if he wanted to stop me. I left my hand on the table, though I wanted to rub his touch off.

We ordered and ate together in a quite comfortable silence. We made small talk, trying to draw Information from each other. I didn't let the circumstances stop me from eating, I hadn't eaten much all day. He asked me to call him Jason, he told me funny stories from his job, I could sense his love for his job and the good things that he had done. It made me wonder about the lies, about what the Society had on him. The time passed, I declined dessert, aware that I had to meet Grayson.

I excused myself to the bathroom, as I made my way back I saw that he was having a heated discussion with some man. I held back, hidden behind some well placed ferns. He left as Jason stood, looking him down. A waitress came back with the bill and I intercepted her, "I need to pay because you are helping me."

He tried to argue with me but I won and paid. "I won't argue anymore as I know that I will pay next time." We walked together to the door, "I need to go back to work, what about you?"

"I have to meet someone," at this he tensed up, so I added "Just a girl friend, who might be able to help." He relaxed, as we both stood awkwardly outside the restaurant.

He nodded again, his hands in his pocket. "Be safe and I will text you later, if that's okay?"

I nodded a goodbye and started to walk away, turning slightly as I did. Catching him nodding to someone in the shadows. Realising that I was most likely going to be followed, I sped up as if cold. It would be better if I lost this tail, can't believe I was saying that. My life was a novel, maybe a movie.

CHAPTER 8

I had been moving fast for the last 10 mins, ducking and diving in and out of crowds. It was making me dizzy, the only plus point was certainly working off my food. The less than positive note was that I hadn't managed to lose him. Obviously I had paid no attention to every movie that I had watched. It was like he had a sixth sense, by now he must know that I was trying to lose him or was just crazy.

Pausing behind a handy pillar, I caught my breath. Peering around it I watched him approach, he stopped, closed , then headed towards me. I moved around to another, a nasty thought had come to mind, he almost looked like he was concentrating as I did when I was using my gift. Hmm. Quickly tagging onto a passing tourist group, I smiled and answered their friendly questions. Waving bye, I lost myself in the crowd. I had an idea but needed some distance and quiet to concentrate. An alley appeared to my right and I ducked in. Moving into the shadows, I closed my eyes and felt for my core, my stillness. As the outside noise muted, I tried to sense around me. There was something, a sense of someone, I opened one eye and saw him approaching from the same direction that I had sensed him. With a sense of desperation licking at my insides, I held onto my chains tightly and just concentrated on fading into the background. Coating myself in a sense of being invisible, after a while something seemed to settle on my shoulders. It itched a little but I stayed with it. I immersed myself in the feeling, unaware of my surroundings, any noise. After a while, with a no sense of how much time had passed. Leaning my head back, I felt sweaty and drained, a headache starting to make itself felt. Looking around, I couldn't see my shadow.

Bringing my shine unto my face, I realised that I was really late and that there were several missed calls and texts from Grayson. I didn't bother to listen to the messages, the texts were agitated enough. Reluctantly I concentrated again looking for that feeling I had felt from him. It was harder, as I was more tired but I persevered and then felt the faintest sense moving away from me. Sagging back, I felt relatively reassured that he had moved on. Reluctantly I called Grayson.

Who immediately exploded on the phone, "Where the fuck are you?"

"I'm okay in case you were wondering. I had someone following me and it took me a while to lose them."

I could actually hear him grinding his teeth, in a more moderated tone, "Where are you? I will come and get you!"

Wearily, though I would have liked have been able to go for angry. "I am not a bag, I will come to you." Rather than become more annoyed with his attitude, I hung up. While imaging his face, I also realised that I was going to have to get a new phone, there were more digital ways to track me.

Moving off I kept an eye around me, running my fingers over my chains. Moving confidently, I walked along side other people, moving from group to group. As I approached the meeting point, I stood by the side of the pavement and sent my senses out. I didn't feel anything else, gladly I walked on, my headache now full blown. Less focused now, suddenly from behind, I felt breath at my neck, and a low growl whispered in my ear. "I was getting worried." My heart sped up again, though I had recognised Grayson's voice. I moved away, rubbing my neck. I was annoyed by his attitude but his voice had felt nice, too nice. I didn't need rescuing or any more complications. Obviously he hadn't got the memo, as he approached me again, crowding me against a wall. I certainly didn't feel cold anymore, as his body heat warmed mine. As he brushed some of my hair out of my eye, I couldn't help but shiver. He leant down, with one arm braced on the wall behind me and whispered. "I am very very glad that you are okay but don't do that again."

"Have you heard of personal space," with reluctance I pushed him back a step. Feeling overheated and annoyed that I did, "You are not the boss of me, Grayson. Don't push it." With reluctance I stepped further away, though from the look in his eyes, he knew why. Git.

He had turned so the he was now nonchalantly leaning against the wall, with his hands in his pockets and his ankles crossed. He looked at ease, though his eyes were intently looking at me. He scanned me up and down, then with a shake of his head he pushed off. "You are going to be trouble."

I couldn't help it, I snorted in annoyance. "Any chance that we can grab something to eat, I have a really bad headache."

He came closer but didn't crowd me, "You don't look too good, fine. While you eat, you can fill me in."

I was really fighting the headache now, not knowing how much I was actually going to be telling him. I was a freak and I couldn't trust any one. I had to remember that, however cute anyone was.

He held his hand out directing me towards the row of restaurants nearby. He walked by the side of me, but with a definite gap between us. I tried not to acknowledge that I was disappointed by the distance. We entered an Italian and Grayson ordered for us quickly, he then left telling me to drink water. As the food arrived, he came back with some painkillers. I thanked him and took them quickly. I essentially inhaled my order, it was enough for two people. I leaned back, patting my stomach, feeling much more alert. I liked up into Grayson's shocked open mouth. What could I say, I had eaten way more than I had ever done before. I expected that he was used to a more lady like person.

He smiled, "Wow, you really were hungry, I am glad that you liked it. Shall we say that you were a little hangry before."

"You should never say that to a woman," I huffed, still a little embarrassed.

"Don't worry, I don't mind, it's good to see a woman eat,"he smirked. Then ignoring my angry gaze calmly finished his food.

I strewed and sipped on my drink. With a sigh, I realised that I owed him some appreciation. Reluctantly, "Thank you, I do feel better now. Though I don't agree that I was hangry. I am sorry that we are now behind schedule."

He shrugged, "It is probably better this way. Come on, let me educate you on detective work."

I gritted my teeth as I followed him out, I was sure that he was saying these things to wind me up. As I caught another smirk.

Pulling my jacket closer, as we stepped out into the chill, I looked around. No shadow. Grayson led me around a lot of backroads. Then we were outside the club. It loomed darkly in front of us, it appeared sinister and ominous. There was a warning there in the building itself. Perhaps I was more sensitive now because I could feel the darkness. I couldn't believe that I hadn't felt it before, it was so strong. I shivered standing outside, as Grayson looked around.

Surprisingly there was still a far amount of foot traffic despite the cold. Passing couples snuggling close to each other, drunken groups weaving their way down the street. All were engrossed in their own lives and none paid us any attention.

The private buildings nearby, all had security cameras but their alignment showed that they wouldn't cover the building. Someone must have paid for that. Surprisingly there were no cameras on the Society building, I wondered why.

Grayson was staring balefully at the building, as if he could interrogate it by sheer force of will. He glanced over at me, feeling my gaze perhaps, "Shall we see if they forgot to lock up?"

I nodded slowly, realising that was why we had come. There was little that we would find out without doing so, I found my fingers itching to get inside. I let myself be open and decided that I should go with instinct. Moving forward, I swung around to the left of the building. Grayson surprisingly joined me without a word. Hugging the dark shadows, we passed several doors. None felt right, I continued around the back of the buliding. There were some loading bay doors, one of which was partially opened. Grayson held me back and took the lead, peering through the partially opened door. There were some voices in the distance, Grayson peered up above the door and sharply pulled back. "Camera", he whispered pointing up.

I didn't look up, not wanting to take the chance that it would catch a good view of my face. Grayson timed the camera and signalled me to stay put. He slung forward, disappearing into the gloom.

It was hard to wait patiently, the shadows freaking me out. The voices started to sound louder, hesitating for a moment and then I slipped in as well. I guessed at the direction that I though Grayson had gone. I tried to avoid the cameras movements, keeping myself behind several large crates, I pushed further into the loading bay. Taking my phone out, I put it on silent.

Taking my surroundings in, there were several well lit doors. Knowing that Grayson would come back soon, I decided not to take more risk and just see what these crates were about.

They all had overseas addresses, I took pictures of all the labels. Then I took my gloves off and touched the crates, hoping that I would feel or sense something. Almost as soon as I touched them, I was paralysed by fear. It caused me to fall back on my back, stunned. Then there was a hand over my mouth, muffling my involuntary scream.

Belatedly, with relief, I recognised Grayson. He looked worried, silently helping me to my feet and back to hide behind the crates. Refusing to touch the crates again, I eyed them warily. Grayson looked between me and the crates, I shrugged and mouthed 'later'. He nodded and returned his eyes to the doors. He pulled a short stick out of his jeans and flicked it, on which it immediately extended into a long baton of sorts. Pulling up his scarf to cover his mouth, he indicated that I should do the same. I also took my chains off and wrapped them around me hand, let Grayson think that it was for self defence. He wasn't wrong, just not the traditional style. The voices were closer now, though with the echoes I and Grayson couldn't locate where they were coming from. With alarm I then heard a vehicle approach the door we had come through.

Grayson indicated the doors but which one. I closed my eyes, trusting that I would pick the right one. Moving forward, I went to the second one. I was being pulled this way. Grayson hung back but I pulled him insistently forward. He looked back and then tilted my chin up, so that I could look into my eyes. What ever he needed to see he did and followed me through without hesitation.

He moved ahead of me, quickly and stealthily, checking doorways or corridors before letting me move forward. He appeared very professional. The voices had faded behind us, I felt that we should continue on. We came up on some stairs and moved on up. The lights were off here, but the corridors were wider. Then I felt a pull to the right and I tugged Grayson back, pointing silently.

We came upon some offices, there must be something here. I went into one, and stood overwhelmed by the amount of paper, computers, files. Grayson paused beside me, he grasped my hand and whispered "You start here, I will look around." He rested his forehead on mine, "Stay quiet."

It took a moment for me to pull myself together, standing, I bite my lip and thought. It had worked so far, let me trust myself again. Putting my hands out in front of me, I pictured Daisy, my memories of her. A tug to the left, I followed it without thought. Around to another door to a file room, flicking on the lights. Letting myself be least to a drawer, they opened soundlessly. I pulled one and then others out, once I felt released, I had twenty files. They were thin, I sat on the floor and started opening them. I took pictures of the pages. They were like personal files, I was sweating now but I was too scared to take off my jacket. I paused when I came across Daisy's but I couldn't wait. I just kept taking photos. I felt the need to hurry, there was a noise in the corridor. Faster and then I clutched them altogether and stuffed them in a drawer. I spun and flicked off the light, as the outer door opened. I hid behind one of the tables, crouched underneath. And held my breathe. The office light flicked on and then off and the door closed with a locking noise. I didn't move, my breathing loud.

Moments passed and I slowly moved into the other room, then to the door. Very slowly I turned tiger handle, locked. Now I felt the perspiration under my back and arm pits. Forcing myself not to panic, I touched the door lock. No, I was unable to focus. I took deep breaths, saying that I have got this. Again, I touched the lock, thinking of what I wanted, for it to unlock. Heat flared from my fingertips, I jumped back. It felt like static but there was a click.

I punched the air, I was badass, pulling myself together I eased the handle down and opened the door. Again I was pulled to the right, I moved slowly, sliding my feet forward to make no noise. The guard had lowered all the lights and the gothic architecture was starting to look scary. The shadows appeared to be reaching for me. More stairs and again I felt a pull up. Pausing, I reflected that this was probably not a good idea at all.

Undecided, I heard a noise from the left and my feet decided that I was going up. The stairs curved around, the bannisters smooth against my sweaty palms. Moving up, quicker through moonlit windows. At the top, it opened into a large atrium with a curved dome like glass ceiling. There were oil paintings on the walls, I was glad that the darkness hid most of them. Moving towards one off the walls, I placed my palm against it and had sudden image of Daisy. I gasped, lying both hands on the wall. Cecilia laughing. Without thought moved along the wall, trailing my finger tips against it. Again, images of a party, dancing. Circling the room I felt nothing more.

Pausing, I felt my phone vibrate, a text from Grayson, a question mark. Hoping that it was Grayson and not some one using his phone. I texted back my location, to which he responded with a curt instruction to stay put. Bossy much, I slipped my phone back in my pocket. I spun in a circle, there was something more here. Again I felt around the walls. As I passed by a section, I paused and went back. Bending forward, I slowly ran my fingers over it and felt an edge. Pulling my little pocket knife out, I wedged the blade into the crack. There was a slight movement, there must be a catch for the mechanism somewhere. Pressing my hands flat against the wall, I willed it open. There was a click and the hidden door swung inwards.

Peering into the extremely dark opening, I paused. Touching the walls hesitantly, I felt fear, making me snatch my hands back. Something very bad had happened here, oh god Daisy.

Standing there lost in my thought and fears, I felt hands on my arms. I shrieked and leapt into the air, as I was turned around. Grayson made urgent shushing motions, while trying not to laugh. I punched him in the arm, which he pretended to hid a smile. I hit him, feeling my heart with the other hand. He pretended to rub his arm. I hissed at him, "What the fuck. Don't do that."

He tugged on my hair and bent down to whisper, "Worth it." He looked past me into the darkness, pursing his lips. Trying to avoid looking at him, I saw that he had a bag with in.

"Shopping?"

"I found some discs and thought that I should take them. There are more guards, I think they are doing their rounds, they will be up here soon. I guess that this is the way that we should go." Pulling out a small touch, he shone it around the walls. Though powerful, it didn't illuminate much. I moved closer to him, needing the reassurance. As he looked around to me, his touch lit some of the paintings. The things were clear now, demons, tortured humans. I pushed his touch away from them, I was having a very visceral feeling about them. I felt sick to my stomach. He must have seen something, as he held out his hand to me.

Swinging the touch forward, we could see narrow windows and doorways down the sides. He gave my hand a squeeze and moved forward. As soon as my reluctant feet followed, the door swung closed behind me. Tentacles of fear deadening and slowed my limbs. Grayson tugged me forward with him. We both looked through the first opening, a monk like cubicle. As we moved forward, they were all the same.

The foreboding was getting stronger, I refused to sense

anything, fearful of what I might find. I was clutching Grayson's hand with both of mine. I was immensely glad that I was not sensing anything from him. It made me avoid touching the walls, that seemed to be closing in on us. Though that was probably my imagination. Though Grayson also seemed to be moving pretty fast now.

It seemed like ages until we came to the end of the corridor, which ended in a metal spiral staircase. I looked up, it seemed to extend another 2 floors and then down into the darkness. We hesitated, Grayson checked his watch, looked at me and then started down. I agreed with the direction, I really wanted to be nearer the exit. The stairs creaked under us and we slowed down. Grayson held up his hand and I paused, he went down to the next floor and disappeared. I looked up and down, feeling the darkness closing in. I didn't want to hold onto the side but I did after I had pulled my gloves on. The feelings of fear were slightly less and I could hear crying. Without a doubt, Daisy and Cecilia had been brought through here.

I felt anger towards the people that had done this, this gave me the strength to reach out with my senses. Down, I followed it, knowing that if I hesitated I might never move. Without the touch, it was like being in an immersion tank, cocooned. Nothing but the pounding of my heart.

I felt the stairs with my feet, time seemed to loose all meaning. I lost count of the stairs and the levels. I imagined that I was below street level now. The air smelled damp and cold. Tugged deeper, I followed.

CHAPTER 9

It felt like I had been walking for ages in the darkness, I had opened my phone light but it didn't seem to penetrate the darkness. There were noises, almost like whispers that licked at my awareness. I was trying very hard to ignore them. Though the hair on the back of my neck was standing up, I didn't even want to feel the sweat that was gathering under my arms pits.

I was well aware that if this was a movie, I would be shouting at the TV, not to go there. Yet I knew that there were answers down there, I also had a sense of urgency that licked at my heels. Despite myself I started to move faster, despite the risk of falling.

Suddenly looming in front of me, appearing as if from no where was a set of heavy gothically ornate doors. I almost ran into them, they appeared so suddenly. I paused, catching my breath, after a moment I carefully placed a hand on the door. Yes behind this one, I pulled on the heavy handles and they opened smoothly, which I felt was a bit of a let down.

Again, no lights. It felt like a large room, though I couldn't see the walls. I pulled off my jacket, scarf and hat and carelessly dropped them on the floor. Flashing my phone light around, I identified a light switch and flicked it on with relief. It came on suddenly, temporarily blinding me.

The room was rows and rows of large crates, some stacked on top of others. Not let myself get overwhelmed, I held my hands out, strangely there were two different directions. Focusing on a thought of Cecilia, I moved to the one that became stronger. I halted about twenty yards in on the right, About 20 yards into the room, I came upon a particular crate. I searched around for something to help pry it open, finding one I walked back. Knowing that I could easily get lost in here, I carefully traced my path back. After a pause. After a pause I also texted Grayson, realising that he probably didn't even know where I was. He was probably really pissed and I would be too. Realising that I never used a crowbar before, I guess that I should try to loosen the nails first, hopefully by the time I had done that Grayson would be here. As I gave it my all, all I managed was to hang in the air over the crowbar, even with my full weight. Well that was embarrassing, as I let go falling back on my heels.

As I was wondering what I was going to do, I saw a torch light coming towards me and a whispered call of my name.

I had to admit that I was very happy to see him, the darkness had really got to me. I spontaneously hugged me, he stiffened and then hugged me back hard. "You are in time, do you know what to do with this," holding out the crowbar.

"Ah, you just want me for my muscles," though he took his jacket off and went to the crate that I indicated. "I guess that I am not going to bother to ask whether this is a good idea or not."

"Look, at that we are really starting to know each other", I hissed back, with a smile. Despite the situation, I did take a moment to admire his muscles. He grunted with the effort and his muscles coiled.

He stepped back, panting, "This thing is on tight."

Well now I didn't feel that bad, "Lets do it together." At his raised eyebrow, "Well it hasn't moved yet." Without another word or facial expression, he inserted the crowbar back in a corner. We both grasped the crowbar but I in addition used my power. It slowly gave way and then with a pop it lifted.

"Well done," Grayson grinned like a little boy. "Lets get the rest." We worked our way around, I helped behind the scenes as it was. Good for my secret but not for the muscles, which of me were burning at the end. Grayson unfairly looked good with the sheen of sweat.

We lifted the lid off, I noticed that we both paused and looked at each other before we peered inside. Inside was a large silver coloured metal box, strangely there was a small circular viewing window. We couldn't see from where we were, so Grayson gave me a boost up and inside. Reluctantly I put my feet on the box, which didn't give. Slowly and carefully I made my way to the viewing window and looked inside.

I involuntarily gasped, looking into Cecilia face. I helplessness looked at Grayson, my mouth open in shock.

"What, what is it." I beckoned him in, with some difficulty he vaulted up and scrambled in by my side. Placing his hand against the glass, he bowed his head. I placed my hand on his back, knowing that he must feel awful. He looked over to me and placed a hand on mine, "Thank you, I don't know how but you helped me find her."

I solemnly nodded and looked away from the exposed emotion in his eyes. I wondered how we were going to get her out. She looked like she was asleep, and from my sci-fi watching the closest thing it resembled, was a stasis tube. It was beyond my understanding, meaning I was not sure how to get her out safely. Grayson was no use at the moment, just staring down at his sister. Knowing that I needed two brains, I kneeled in front of him. Taking his face in my hands, "Grayson." Nothing, he looked shut down. I gently held his face in my hands, "Grayson," I pushed some energy through my hands. He looked sharply up at me, "We found her, know we need to get her out. I need you, she needs you." Still nothing. Instinctively I leant forward and softly kissed him, he didn't respond. With a little more desperation, I slanted my lips, moving them softly but firmly against his cold lips. He shuddered, then his arms came around me, one moving up to cup the back of my head. He took control and deepened the kiss. I pulled back, knowing that he was back with me and aware of the inappropriateness of the location of this. As I opened my eyes, I found that he was staring intently back at me, still holding me.

He touched his forehead to mine, "Thank you again." He let me go and looked down around the sides, to where there might be some panels. We couldn't reach them, "This is going to be a problem." He pursed his lips, which I unfortunately couldn't help but focus on. "Come on, let's get out." He jumped out first, landing easily like a cat. I clambered out with much less finesse and he had to help me down. "Can you see if the door we came through locks, or if you can barricade it, at least so that we get some warning if anyone comes in. I am going to call a friend."

I ran off to the doors, there was a lock but it required a key. I tapped my lips as I considered the nearby furniture. There wasn't any, nothing but the crates and now that I knew there could be a person in each one I was reluctant to use them. I looked behind me, to check that Grayson couldn't see me. Putting my hand over the lock, I thought about how I wanted it to lock. I heard a click and made my way back to Grayson and Cecilia.

"Lance, I am going to need help. I am sending some photos. I need to know how to turn this thing off, safely, its got my fucking sister in it. Also let Michael know that I need him to come now and bring it all." He turned back and started to try to take the sides of the crate down. He looked utterly focused.

I hesitated, thought of Daisy and followed the pull. Passing so many crates, I didn't stop until I felt the pull to one in particular. Damm, it was underneath two others. Looking around, I realised that there wasn't much time for messing about and I was really pissed by these monsters who put people in boxes. Holding my hands out in front of me, I considering pushing the crate off but realised that it would make too much noise and might hurt the person inside. So I moved it, like a game of Jenga. Grunting, as my mind took the strain, I was thankful that I had started training. I didn't even try to find a crowbar but I lifted the lid off the crate. Clambering in, I saw Daisy. I had found her, as I focused more. I realised that she did not look peaceful, like Grayson's sister. She looked and I could feel the pain, the fear. I could also see that there was a head wound. Except for the pain and fear, there was so little energy there. She was slipping away.

Desperately I felt the heavy lid fly past my head, I felt the wind as it wizzed past. It hit another crate, the bang was loud, too late. Straddling Daisy's chest, my breath coming short and fast. I slammed my palms on the centre of her chest, my chains intertwined between my fingers. I closed my eyes and thought how I wanted her to live, to be full of life. I let memories engulf me, the surrounded me like I was in the eye of the storm. Something shifted inside me, an acceptance of the power that I had.

Without warning I heard Daisy start screaming, it reverberated in my head. I desperately cliched my head as the scream echoed through my head. I pried my eyes open, with difficulty I focused on Daisy's face. I fell to the side, with my head bursting. It was like she was in a nightmare, her eyes blankly open and that awful scream.

I knew that she had to be quiet but I couldn't move, my head was bursting. It felt like something was going to blow. Then I felt darkness around the edges of my sight and I welcomed it, then nothing.

CHAPTER 10

I was home, in my old home. I touched the furniture as I walked through the house, knowing that this wasn't right. I was somewhere else, something had happened but I couldn't recall the details. It was as if there was a fog surrounding them.

So I focused on where I was, it even smelled like I remembered. As I stood turning in a circle, I hear a familiar voice, I stalled. It wasn't, it couldn't but then he spoke again. As if from a starting block, I darted towards it. "Father?"

I came to an abrupt stop, "Olivia, what ever is the matter?" He looked up from his papers, sitting at his old familiar desk. His smile the same, his glasses slipping down as he looked at me over them. Slowly I moved towards him, my hand out. Disbelievingly I moved slowly forward, not really wanting to know if it wasn't true but also that I desperately wished that it was.

My shaking finger tips touched fabric, I sank to be knees in front of him and hugged him desperately. Tears running down my eyes, "Father, father, farther.. I have missed you so much." He made comforting noises, as he lifted me, hugging me to him.

"My dearest daughter, I have missed you too. I can see by how grown up you are that I have been gone a long time. I am sorry that I left but I am so proud of you." He lifted my chin, so that he could see my eyes. "This isn't real, you being here means that you have awakened your gifts, my curse. I need you to listen and focus, we have a lot to talk about."

I pulled back, knowing that I did need to listen but all I could focus on were the details of his face. I had not thought that the last time would be the last time, if I had known I would have memorised his face. My eyes trailed along all the little details that I had forgotten. I started to trace the details with my fingertips. "I want to stay here with you?"

He smiled sadly, stroking my hair, hugging it lightly as he had always done. "Always running, never still. This is a kind of interactive memory that I left for you, we are in your head."

Sitting back, I held his hands firmly so that he couldn't leave, I hoped. "How much time have we got?"

"Not a lot. I was a young man who wanted the world to listen. I knew that it could be better, I could do that and have a real place in it. I have to admit that I wanted an important part and place in that. I met someone who thought like me, agreed with my way of thinking. It was very easy to get carried away, searching for knowledge beyond the accepted limits." He looked away, "It was addictive, so addictive." Taking a breath, he straightened up, taking a deep breath he turned back. I continued to look at his face, knowing that I loved him but that I was going to learn things that changed how I would remember him. Pain blossomed in my chest. "He looked towards the occult, the supernatural and the unexplained. These changed us but more him, I didn't see it. I was so caught up in the power and the potential. Slowly I realised that there was a cost, he didn't care to who. I think that the best explanation is that he became possessed. My friend, my brother became someone else." He held a finger to me, "I am not excusing myself, I did these things too. I was changed but I pulled back. He didn't realise at first, I think all he could see was himself but then he noticed. I wonder why he didn't try to control me as he had done others but perhaps there was still some loyalty. Maybe he needed me as a link to his past, from a time before." He gently touched his forehead to mine, "It was you, you brought me back. I could not bring you up there, with them, with him."

Standing, he walked to the window. I was aware of the cliché that was, a window in my mind. However hard it was, I needed to listen, that he had wanted me to know him. I stood and came to the window too, looking out onto nothing but swirling mists of white. Turning my back to it, leaning against the window frame, "What about my mother?"

He sighed, "I only met her the once, it was in a ceremony of power and fertility. It was a powerful ritual, inviting something in, a way of creating something more than a normal human. She was beautiful, she believed." I closed my eyes, knowing that there had been no relationship, it had been a kind of one night stand. "I knew that it had worked straightaway. Everyone felt it, I was allowed to spend time with your mother while you were growing and we came to care for each other. She was very special, it was this that really showed me the wrongness of what we had become." His face relaxed, as if he was remembering a better time but then his eyes tightened.

"I did not hide my feelings, which I was not meant to be feeling. It was meant to be clinical, part of a bigger picture. May knew or suspected, I was sent away, limiting my Time with your mother. When I would return, your mother was sadder, withdrawn, she lost so much weight. She would never tell me but I came to suspect that May had been doing more to her, to you. Finally when I came back for your birth, she was not strong and she didn't survive your birth. I blame myself and him for that." His voice broke, he turned away from me.

I didn't know what to think, I had just become numb. All this time, I had hoped that I had had something with my mother. I had not had the chance to spend any time with her. I could feel anger at my father coiling inside me, I walked away from him to the doorway.

"Wait Olivia, I know that this is hard to hear but you need to hear it all. I know that I have let you down and you must be so angry at me. He swallowed, "She died in my arms, asking only me to save you. I was in shock but I couldn't not help to see the avarice in May's eyes. I could not let him have you both. So I played nice, while I started to plan. I gathered information, he had done so much that I had been blind too. Each thing that I found, made me more and more desperate to get you away. You made it all worth the risk. We left when you were one, unlike the other children created, no power was felt from you because I had started to dampen your powers. May let us go, with a little blackmail."

I got up, restless and started to pace. It seemed impossible to process everything. All the what ifs. Swinging around to stand in front of him, with my head up , I looked at him defiantly. "What am I? Am I human?" My heart thumping, as I voiced my greatest fear out loud.

My father stepped towards me with tears in his eyes. "You are human, just special, augmented."

My eyes must have rolled, he sighed again. "You have some, something from another dimension."

"That is no answer. You don't know do you, you messed with my genetics but you aren't sure. It's like a child playing with the building blocks of DNA. How many children were born from this, how many survived?" My voice raised, I was so angry at decisions I had no control over. My fists clenched by my side and I could feel power rising inside of me. Stepping back, I tried to calm myself. How could my clever, loving, kind father have done this. "You don't know what I have in me, do you? I could hurt people, be a danger to people." I spat out the last words, my thoughts now chasing themselves in my head. I held my hand for silence, as I tried to calm down. Minutes later, I opened my eyes and nodded to my father. "Does May know more?"

"You must stay away from him Olivia and anyone with him. It's too dangerous, you are too special, you are my little girl." He hugged me to him, despite me instinctual stiffening he persisted. I relaxed into this greatly missed physical contact.

"I have had people following me, they took my friend. I had just found her, almost dead. I had to push energy into her, so much. I passed out and then I was here."

He collapsed into his chair, his hand covering his eyes. "Oh Olivia, you must have sent up a flare of power, they will definitely come for you now. You have to try not to do that, until you have learnt to shield." Muttering under his breath, "I left you so unprepared."

"How should I learn? Do you know anyone? Louise found

someone but I don't think that I should trust him, he lied and was so desperate to meet me." I rubbed my arms, remembering the feeling.

"I don't want to say it but you can't trust anyone. I trust Louise but you must never underestimate what people will do for power." He looked up, "You are going to leave soon and I am grateful that we have had his time together. I am sorry that I am not the man that I have wanted you to think that I am." He hugged me tight, "Remember this information, my bank. I have left you things that will help. You will need to learn to protect yourself and others."

My head had started to pound, my vision was starting to fail. I clutched him tightly back, I needed to memorise everything about him. I repeated the information that he was desperate to give me, as he was insisting. As well as telling me that he loved me so much.

He grasped me stronger and stronger until suddenly he was gone. No..

CHAPTER 11

Groaning I turned over onto my side. My senses returning sluggishly. With my hand, I felt what I was lying on, not a bed. Hard old worn leather, a car seat? Not knowing how I got here or who was with me, I cautiously cracked one of my eyes open. I was lying on the back seat of an SUV, its windows blacked out. Voices were arguing from the front seat, relaxing as I recognised Grayson's. "I don't care what you think, she is coming with us, I am not leaving her behind."

"She is an unknown risk, with all that we have done, how did she just walk straight to your sister and the other one. You don't think that was suspicious, stop thinking with your trousers."

I grimaced, happy that Grayson was protecting me but that was disgusting.

"I am going to ignore what you just said, it is my call. Just drive, we need to get them, all back."

"You always have to be a boy scout, don't you?" came the wry response.

Reassured that I was okay for the time being, I closed my eyes. My headache had reduced a little. I had used so much energy and needed to recharge with food and fluids. Thinking back I was impressed and a little scared by how badass I had been.

I also realised that I no longer felt a hole in my heart from the loss of my father. I felt healed, I had my closure. People had told me that he was always going to be with me and they were right. Though not in a normal way.

Slowly, I checked my pockets, nothing there except I felt my chains. Thank god. My head started to pound again and I closed my eyes and let myself drift off. I would worry about everything else later.

I awoke when the SUV hit some bumps. Opening my eyes, I slowly sat up. Grayson head whipped back towards me, I gave a small smile, he smiled in apparent relief. "You're awake, thank goodness." His eyes were warm, not hostile or suspicious. I breathed a silent sigh of relief, realising that I would have felt hurt if he had looked at me differently. My father's warning sounding. I turned back to the front window, we were entering a large yard and there was, what could be only called a mansion, in front of us. Impressively huge and gothic. Dawn was rising behind the building, framing it nicely. It was all rather impressive.

I heard a grunt and turned towards the driver, white in his thirties, shooting me very hostile and irritated looks. Brightly I said, "Thank you so much for your help." The result was that his expression turned even more sour.

Laughing quietly, I decided to take some pity on him and slipped back into my seat. Grayson smirked and turned to the front, as he received a glare too.

We stopped, our tires crunching loudly on the gravel. It was then that I saw the other vehicles stopping beside us. Anxiety started to hit, as I realised that I only knew Grayson here, wherever the hell I was. Remain calm. I watched as Grayson and sour pants got out, calling greetings. Slowly I opened my car door, relieved that I wasn't locked in. As I stood nervously by the SUV, Grayson came to my side. "Come on, I got you." I certainly hoped so.

What got me moving was when I saw that Grayson's sister was being offloaded, still in her container. I gripped Grayson's jacket tightly, "Where is Daisy?"

"Relax, she is already here. She had to be heavily sedated." Grayson swung me around, "Come on."

"Really." He nodded and I hugged him, feeling such relief. The relief after all that had happened and that I was feeling. Surprised, he held himself stiff and then tightly hugged me back, his head at my neck. Flushing it suddenly hit me, I had never hugged a man before, especially one that I kinda liked. His body was hard and full of muscles. Hearing cat calls and whistles, I sheepishly pulled back, "Sorry."

He didn't let go but held me at arms length, "Not a problem, any time." Clearing his throat, he sent rude hand gestures to the cat callers. Tugging me along, "Lets get inside."

I allowed myself to be pulled forward, as any burst of energy that I had on arrival was flagging fast. Stumbling, I almost went down but Grayson pulled me sharply up and into his side. We entered the building.

It was bright inside and my headache rebounded with a vengeance. The pounded made me feel as if I was going to pass out. Grayson must have felt my increased weakness and swung me into his arms. Feebly and embarrassed I whispered, "You don't need to do that."

He ignored me and kept walking, he didn't seem to struggle to carry me. Though I was grateful, I couldn't help but feel embarrassed as to how being this close made me feel. It was quite intense to be this close to someone, I could see the small things that only a loved one might notice. There was a small scar below his chin, I couldn't help but trace it with my finger. His jaw immediately clenched, through gritted teeth he growled, "Stop that or we will be taking a detour."

Not sure what he meant but aware that there was a line that I wasn't in the fit state to cross, I dropped my hand as if on fire. I looked around me instead, though it actually felt better when I closed my eyes. Despite the jostling I dozed off. I jerked my eyes open, when I heard Grayson call out, "Maggie, where are you?"

As a Scottish voice called back, "Back here love, just bring her through." As I was placed onto a hospital trolley, I could make out a very hospital looking lay out. With some relief I saw that Daisy was sleeping in the next trolley to me. With relief, I lay back and covered my eyes.

"Hello dear, now just bear with me, I need to have a look at you and then I can start making you feel better." I opened my eyes, feeling reassured by the middle aged smiling doctor.

"That would be amazing, my head is killing me."

She nodded briskly, turning she shooed at Grayson as if he was a child. "Now Grayson get out, so that I can do my job."

"I would rather stay.." Grayson started but was propelled firmly out of the infirmary. His expression was funny, despite my headache I smiled. If I had been feeling better I would have laughed at the sight and his expression. As I lay back and heard Maggie come back. She took me gently but firmly through a neurological exam and then gave me some huge tablets. Disbelieving I looked at them, wondering how I would swallow them. Maggie stood there, tapping her foot. So I choked them down, almost immediately I started to feel sleepy. So I gratefully did just that.

Later I opened my eyes, blinking the strange drugged sleep away. Strangely I wasn't in the infirmary, I was in a bedroom. I felt down myself and was relieved that I was still dressed, though not with my boots. I heard a quiet snore from my right and turned, in the arm chair next to me was Grayson, asleep. His head was tilted to the side and he had even drooled a little. I smiled, at him and the vulnerable that he made. I had a feeling that it was a side of him that he rarely showed. I was touched that he had stayed with me.

My thoughts were interrupted by nature and that I really need the loo. Luckily there was a door to the ensuite open. After my immediate needs were met, I saw the shower, that looked nice. I shut he door, paused and then locked it. I took a long, hot and well deserved shower. After the water had lost its heat and the room was steamy. I got out and dried myself. As I stared in the foggy mirror, I realised that I was looking at a completely different me. I looked thinner, on closer inspection I realised that I had a violet ring around my brown eyes. Knowing that there was nothing that I could do about it, I opened some of the cupboards, I found a set of slightly large but clean sweatpants.

Pulling the sleeves up and rolling the trousers up, I laughed thinking how this could be marketed as a new diet. As if in protest I my stomach growled loudly. I drank a couple of glasses of water from the tap, left my hair to air dry and walked out.

Hoping that Grayson might still be asleep, I wasn't surprised to see him lazily leaning against the wall with his long legs crossed. His hair was mussed, his hooded eyes ran over my outfit. Despite myself, I shuffled on the spot, I managed to swallow, "Thank you for staying with me."

He looked me in the eye and nodded, pushing off the wall he stalked towards me. As he got close, he bent his head and said into my ear, "I am going to have a shower too, stay here. Its probably better that we will go down together."

I said nothing as he entered the bathroom, with some of his own clothes and the door did not lock. Ignoring the images that had flooded my mind, despite my best intentions, I looked around the room.

It was like a guest room, old fashioned in the decor but there were a few scattered personal items, all men's. Was this Grayson's room? Looking out of the window onto beautiful manicured grounds, I tried to sift through everything that had happened. I realised that I had slept half the day away, I had missed quite a few calls including from Detective Seymour. Goodness knows what he was thinking.

The question now, was I safe? I held onto my chains and tried to sense something. Immediately I felt a general anxiety, fear and secrets. There were a lot of secrets here, it looked like this was not a place where I could fully relax. I sighed, lost in my thoughts until a few scent of shower gel entered my nose. I suddenly became aware of warmth behind me.

He spoke quietly, "I know that we have a lot to discuss. I can not say that I fully understand what happened back there but I am grateful for your help. Know that I am on your side but you are going to meet people that might mean well but will always act in their own best interests. Be careful of what you say." Stepping away, he throw his towel to the side and opened the door. Waiting with a tight but reassuring smile. I nodded that I understood as I walked past.

We came out into a corridor and Grayson led me downstairs. There were quite a few twists and turns, as it was an old house with many newer additions. I very gratefully entered a kitchen area, we were welcomed by a high level of noise. Grayson seemed comfortable with everyone, he smiled and greeted a few people but kept going until we reached the coffee. Wow, I really needed this, I wrapped both my hands around my mug, taking a moment to just smell it. As I sipped the hot coffee and thankfully strong cofee, Grayson grabbed us two already made think sandwiches from a big industrial fridge. Seeing the hunger on my face, he laughed quietly and added a lot of fruit. Placing it all on a tray, he walked through the kitchen to a seated area, with long tables. It didn't appear too busy, with scattered groups of people but Grayson led us to an empty one. I sat down too, after grabbing some napkins from the side.

I literally inhaled the sandwich that he placed in front of me, I couldn't explain it. It was there and then there were crumbs. I decided that I was not being lady like and slowed myself down with my coffee. As he ate more slowly, I tried to get a feel for the other people sitting around us.

There seemed to be a lot of people checking us out, then I realised that it was Grayson that the women were looking at. Annoyingly I realised that I didn't like that at all, though he wasn't mine to be jealous of. Irritated none the less, I turned back to Grayson. He had finished his sandwich and was leaning back drinking his coffee. He caught my eye, "Don't worry, this is a snack. Dinner will be coming up after we meet with the head of the operation. You don't look recovered still." There was a tread of worry in his voice. Not knowing what to say, I smiled vaguely and started to eat some of the fruit.

Apparently realising that he wasn't going to get much more, he sighed and looked around. As he did, he smiled and gestured someone to join us. A couple of people slid in next to us. A red haired guy with a friendly smile sat next to Grayson, they greeted each other in time honoured fashion by slapping each others back. I rolled my eyes at the display and turned to the small blonde woman who sat next to me. She appeared like a doll, all fine boned and fine features. I felt large and clumsy next to her but any insecurity was disarmed by her genuine and shy smile. I couldn't help but smile back, feeling very comfortable with her. Somehow I knew that this was someone important to me and who I could trust. I didn't know why but I knew it to be true. I did glance at Grayson and fleetingly wondered why he had not engineered this feeling in me.

Before I could think further on that thought, Sunny spoke in a musical voice. "Hi, I am Sunny, it's really nice to have a new girl here. Especially as you look like you can have a laugh, everyone is really serious on the cause here," she waved her hand towards some of the others. Who I realised were giving me the evil eye.

I turned away from them, not giving them a response. Out of the corner of my mouth, I asked Sunny, "Seriously what's their problem?"

She smiled, as if amused that I didn't know and tilted her head towards Grayson. "They are very territorial, they want what they were never able to have but it seems that you might have beat them. They don't like to lose, I don't think that they ever have."

Not wanting to touch on that potential minefield. I turned fully towards her, "I have to say that I am very confused. I don't even know what I am doing here? Let alone where here is." I caught the confused but guarded expression the flitted over her face. I didn't want to make her uncomfortable, so that I quickly added, "Don't worry, I don't want to make you uncomfortable, I think that I am going to be talking to someone soon who might be able to clear up my confusion." Her face cleared straight away, she was not one for lying, I think that I will keep that in mind. With very little urging, she gave me lots of gossip about herself and people that I didn't know. I let it flow over me, it was soothing a way.

A bell sounded somewhere and as one everyone got up. I grabbed our rubbish and put it on the side as we followed. Before we actually left the room, Grayson grabbed my hand and tucked me into his side. Sunny had stuck near us and smiled knowingly. I stuck my tongue out at her.

We ended up in a hall, with rows of chairs. Grayson didn't let me go, tightened his grip. I was loath to admit it but I squeezed, feeling reassured by it. As I sat down, tucking my feet under, catching more unfriendly looks from some of the women. I let go of Grayson's hand, he glanced at me and around and then with a smirk placed his arm over the back of my chair. I huffed and turned towards Sunny, who had managed to slip in next to me. She silently laughed, her eyes crinkling at the corners as glanced at the arm behind me. I decided to ignore her too and sat forward, not letting my back touch the back of my chair and Grayson's arm.

There were about forty to fifty people in the room, faces expectedly turned to the raised stage. I realised that everyone in the audience was wearing sweats like me or combats style clothing. I couldn't help but start to feel a little anxious about what was going to happen. Without realising it my foot started to tap, I caught myself but shuffled on my seat.

Without warning, the doors at the back opened up and a group of people entered in a line. All in more official looking fatigues, in their thirties, forties and one guy in his fifties. He was obviously in charge, I shivered when his eyes caught me out and fixed me with a stare. I sagged back when he released me to address the room.

There was knowledge in that glance, I knew that he knew something about me and he wanted it. It would be a bad idea to trust him further than I could throw him. While willing myself not to just run, I felt Grayson place his hand reassuringly on my shoulder. Silent support. When. I looked at his from the corner of my eye, I could see tightening around his eyes.

I realised that I had missed some of his speech, it sounded like it had been delivered many a time. It was a rousing, rallying speech, though vague and referencing the enemy and how we all had to work harder. The rest of the room seemed to be lapping it up, I wondered if I was hearing the same speech. At the end, they all rose, clapping wildly. I stood as well, not wanting to stand out, though my clapping was half hearted at best. I realised that

Grayson's matched mine and his mouth had a pinched look.

The guy on stage was raising his hands, nodding and accepting the loyalty but asking for quiet. "We have also made a huge leap forward, we have discovered one of their bases, seized valuable information and rescued two victims." The clapping and calls started again, hmm, I didn't remember him being there. But I understood good PR was good PR. He gestured to the side and Daisy was wheeled in, I stood on my toes to see her more clearly. She appeared alert enough, a strained smile on her face, she appeared dazed by all the attention.

As the crowd dispersed, we waited to the side, Grayson placed a hand on my arm to hold me in place. I understood that I did have to trust him and he knew these people. I wanted to go to Daisy but as the crowd cleared I realised that she has been moved. Frustrated, I blew out a breath. Grayson must have guessed and urgenty told me quietly, "We have to meet Marcus in his office, just keep it together. I will get you to see Daisy soon." Reluctantly I nodded. I waved at Sunny as she left.

As the crowd cleared, we moved towards one of the older rooms. Marcus was sitting behind an imposing ornate desk. He was reading something on a tablet, as a younger man stood by his side. While we stood waiting at the edge of the room, they discussed what ever it was on the tablet. As he passed it back, he glanced up at us and waved us to some of the chairs in front of him.

We sat in the strangely low chairs, another power play I thought. It did leave me feeling at a disadvantage, Grayson had not sat but remained standing behind my chair. I attempted to look as nonchalant as he did. I was not sure that I was as successful.

The younger man moved away, casting an assessing, appraising look at me. He didn't leave the room, just closed the door behind us and moved to the side where he wasn't in my line of sight. He was still looking at me, I could tell by the hairs standing up on the back of my neck. Great something else that I had to ignore.

After another ten minutes, we were still waiting while Marcus read something. It was successful, by now I was really pissed. As if knowing that I was about to explode, he sat back and put his fingers together. He looked me over and then his eyes moved to Grayson. He smiled, "Grayson, thank you for bringing her here. There is no need for you to stay." At the clear dismissal, Grayson's facade slipped and he looked ready to argue. With an obvious effort he brought himself under control and without a glance at me, walked out.

"Olivia, you remind me so much of your father."

"Thank you but it seems that you might have known him better than I did." I made my tone and voice even with no hint of emotion. I had placed my arms on the armrests, looking as at ease that I could.

He raised an eyebrow at my tone, perhaps he had expected hysterics. I was surprised at myself.

As the silence lengthened, I allowed myself to ask, "How is Daisy? Can I see her?" Instantly, I saw that he relaxed, I realised that I had shown my weakness. One that he was not going to hold back on, as I grimaced inside, I maintained my relaxed facade.

With a careless air, he said, "I am sure, that I can allow a meeting but as you realise she is still recovering. Let me check with the doctor." He glanced over at his man, "Harry could you go check on that for me?"

His eyes didn't leave me, "While we wait, I would hear your side of the story." He folded his arms and sat back as if about to hear a story.

What should I say, to buy some time for thought. "I am afraid that I haven't sorted through my thoughts yet. Also my head still hurts from where I hit it." I rubbed the back of my head for emphasis, I tried to make my expression meek and mild.

Marcus looked amused, at my bad acting, rather than call me out. "I am sorry to hear that, the doctor has asked for permission to run some imaging. I will make sure that happens, I have great hopes for how you can assist me and mine." He leant forward, lowering his head as if to tell me a secret, "Your Father helped to set this whole organisation up, I owe him."

That was an opening, "Can you explain what all of this is?" Suspecting that he would be into a bit of flattery, I continued with interest in my voice. "It all looks so impressive. I don't understand how you got Daisy and myself out of that terrible place." I didn't have to fake the shudder that went through me at the memory.

He nodded briskly in agreement, "Evil. Evil is what lives there, made by evil people. I am hunting them all, I will cause them to suffer as we have all suffered here. I will ensure that they are chased to the end of the world." His voice rose with fanatical fever. He stood at the window, he held his arms out, "We are many, there are many other sites like this. With the information that you have given us, we have a real opportunity." He turned and looked me in the eye, "They consort with demons, to gain power and wealth. They care for nothing and no-one. They have evil ceremonies where they conceive the half breeds of demons. My daughter was taken, she managed to escape but she was broken," his voice broke and I could see the genuine pain that he felt. The pain that had led him to this crusade. "..she came back with one of these things growing inside of her." His disgust made him spit out the words.

I shivered knowing that he would view me in the same way. "I tried to drive the demon out but she just got sicker and sicker. She died giving birth to it. They both died. That demon spawn killed her and I will do all that I can to stop them."

"I started to investigate, I spread the word about their evil. I met people who helped me, like your father. Though he told me much, he couldn't bring himself to do more, he could have done more." There was real anger running through his voice. I felt fear flicker through me, this was a man who would burn the world around him to get his revenge. This was the kinda man who would burn me at the stake.

There was silence, he had turned away lost in his memories. The door opened and his man returned but stood by the closed door. At the continued silence, he made a discreet noise to get Marcus's attention. Marcus straightened up but did not speak again. "People were following me, is that why they took my friend?"

Marcus moved around his table, placed his hand on my shoulder. "I will protect you, it is my duty and honour. You have more than made up for the lack of your father. I have a feeling that you will be the key." There was true sincerity in his voice. Briskly he pushed away and moved back to his seat.

"Thank you Marcus, I feel safer already." He nodded at Harry, who moved forward. "I have things to do, as you remember things let Harry know. I need that information, though Grayson has given us the gist of it. You have an instinct for this." He exchanged a glance with Harry, "I am sure that after your tour, you will be able to see Daisy for a short time." He obviously had dismissed me.

"Harry, show Olivia around. Let Grayson go to report in, you show her around and then come back to me." There was something there, in that way that he wanted only Harry to show me around but there wasn't anything I could do about it. As we approached the door, he called "Harry make sure that Olivia has her own room."

I turned and tried with equal sincerity, "Thank you Marcus and I am ready to help." Marcus looked at me and nodded, accepting my words. "By the way, is there any chance that I could call someone at home, they are probably frantic with worry."

Marcus had looked down, going through his papers again. "We will see about some replacements."

Grayson stood outside, he relaxed once he saw me. As he moved towards me, Harry intercepted and whispered something to him. He must be telling Grayson about my tour, looking at the sour look on his face.

Marcus voice drifted out of the room, "For your safety Olivia, it would be best to remain on the grounds."

I nodded, I heard an order when I heard it.

CHAPTER 12

I didn't look back at Grayson, as I walked with Harry though I could tell that he was looking daggers at the back of my head. Harry was walking stiffly by my side, as if he didn't want to be near me at all but was duty bound to do so.

"Harry, is it okay if we see Daisy first, since she needs to rest up?" I tilted my head to the side, trying to look friendly. He didn't even look at me, that was a wasted effort. He just stopped, paused, looking up at the ceiling as if calling for strength. As none appeared to be forthcoming, sighing deeply he nodded.

Turning us, he walked towards the infirmary. As there appeared to be no small talk, I used the time to try to work the layout of things. I couldn't help but cast little glances out of the corner of my eye, he was taller than me but shorter than Grayson. He was cute in an uptight sort of way.

I could soon smell the infirmary, before we reached it. As Harry pushed open the swinging doors, he called out. A different doctor appeared than the one that I had met. A guy and he was thin to the extreme, he was pale and looked sickly. Unconsciously I moved closed to Harry, this guy was giving me seriously creepy vibes. I was glad that I hadn't been in his care.

He peered at me, lowering his mask, "Ah this must be the visitor." He cast an appraising look at me, running his eyes up and down. It felt like something slithering over my skin, I am going to need a wash. Harry cleared his throat, crossing his arms over his chest. Whatever look that he was giving the doctor, propelled him into opening a door and indicating that I should go through. "Please go through but not too long. She needs her energy, yes she does." With an ominous chuckle he repeated himself under his breath.

I glanced back at Harry, as I trusted him more than this guy. He waved his hand at me, as he answered a call. Passing by the doctor, as far away from his as possible. It was dimly lit, causing me to pause as the door closed behind me. I looked around, clocking a red light blinking camera in the corner. Hmm, not private. There was an empty hospital bed, which I stepped towards. "Daisy?" I whispered, as it seemed appropriate. "Its me Olivia." Hearing a rustle from the side of the bed, I continued to step around so that I could see between the bed and the wall. Daisy was slumped on the floor, her back to the bed, her head in her hands. I pulled the blanket from her bed and gently settled it over her, she was only in hospital scrubs. Sliding down the wall opposite her, I crossed my legs and waited. Though I was aware that I only had a limited time with her, making me glance at the door.

After another couple of moments, not looking up, I heard a soft hesitant "Olivia."

With relief, "Daisy, I am so glad to see you. How are you doing?" As if with a skittish animal, I kept my voice soft and low.

"I should have listened to you Olivia. I should have left with you, I thought that you were being so boring. That I was being so cool, that something amazing was going to happen." There was a choked sob, her voice broke.

It was hard to listen to my bright vivacious friend sound so broken. I could feel anger building against those that had done this plus guilt that she had been picked because of me.

"Its not important, we all make mistakes. I am glad that I have you back."

She raised her tear-filled eyes to me, "I knew you wouldn't let me go. There were some terrible things, then a really dark sleep. I was fading, almost gone and then you were there. I felt you bring me back. I was filled with light, it was incredible and then I was here. Alone." There was no accusation just confusion in her voice.

I leant forward, "Daisy, they won't let us stay together, I am not leaving you though. Know that I will get us out of here."

"That doctor is scary but they were worse, so much worse." True fear threaded through her voice.

I held her trembling hands, making my voice firm. I looked at her in the eye. "Daisy, they have full security, guns probably. They wouldn't risk it."

Daisy's eyes dropped and she pulled her hands away to place them over her stomach, protectively. My gut clenched at the conclusion I drew. "They want what I have inside me, what the put in me." She started sobbing, carefully I moved to her side, feeling my own tears start. She put her head on my lap, and I hugged her, my tears falling onto her face. We sat like that for a while, crying for the past and for what the future might hold for all three of us.

We quietly sobbed, so I heard the door open and I tensed at us being seen like this. No-one came in but with relief I heard Grayson gently call me. "I am so sorry Olivia but we have to go, the doctor is pretty insistent.

"Okay," I turned wondering how I was going to let her go now. With some cowardly relief I realised that she had fallen asleep. "Grayson, can you come and help me get her onto the bed?"

He gently and with reverence picked her up and lay her under the covers, that I arranged carefully over her. As I looked down at her, the stress and trauma had fallen away. She looked years younger, I realised that she had lost so much weight. I kissed her forehead, smoothing her hair back and let Grayson tug me gently out of the door.

I turned and came face to face with the doctor, I couldn't hide my start. Despite my revulsion, I attempted a brittle smile. I was very aware that he was in charge of Daisy, "Thank you for looking after her, can I come back later today?"

He looked like he was enjoying he power that he had, he didn't answer, making me ask again. I was trying very hard to to kick him somewhere soft.

"Well that does depend on so many things," he stepped closer and reached out to hold my hand. Grayson grabbed his wrist before he could touch me.

"I think she asked a very clear question," his voice was deceptively soft but his laser gaze very hard.

He pulled back and angrily bit out, "I will let you know soldier boy." Turning towards me, he tried to say in a more ingratiating tone, "I will be seeing you soon, Olivia." It felt like a threat. He turned away, dismissing us.

Grayson moved to hold my elbow as I would have moved forward to get a more definitive answer. He hissed, "He is toying with you, we won't get an answer. Come with me."

Realising that he was right, I cast an angry frustrated look at the doctors back and followed him out. Grayson led me back to the canteen which was very busy. Sunny and her friend were there with two loaded trays each. "We got you your food, let us go to the other room to eat."

I smiled gratefully at her, "I knew that I liked you Sunny but now I think that I love you." I squeezed her arm before taking a tray, my stomach growling at the food smell.

Laughing, "I thought the saying was, they way to a mans heart was through his stomach."

We moved to an older looking area, I sat and unapologetically dove into my food. After half the plate had disappeared, I looked up into everyone staring at me, with their forks suspended in mid air. Except for Grayson who was just eating.

The guy next to Sunny, said "Thats like watching an eating contest. I was not expecting that." He said it with a smile and no sting in his voice.

I shrugged unapologetically, "I am really hungry." I leant over to shake his hand, "Hi, I am Olivia."

He smiled, "I am Matt, I am a friend to these two, though they don't seem to always appreciate me enough to introduce me."

Sunny pushed him with her elbow. I could tell from her slight blush that she liked him. I smiled into my food, as I demolished the rest. I quickly finished, as I sat back and sipped my water. I sighed and patted my stomach.

"What do you do here Sunny,"

"I am IT, following the data trails, finding Information. All the stuff that came in, was full of leads. There is a lot to work on." She seemed quite happy about the extra work.

Turning towards Matt, his black skin shone in the fluorescent lighting, he looked fit. He beat me to it, "Before you ask, I am not one of the soldiers, though I know that look the part. I am a lawyer and I am setting up various blocking litigations and the ultimate court room face off." I was impressed.

I had to say, "I know that there must be stories as to why you are here, I am glad that you are fighting this evil."

"Damm right," Matt said, "We are like super heroes." Sunny toasted her water with his, Grayson chuckled at them but joining in. I lifted my glass too, no that's me I thought. The mutant, without a Professor X to help them.

As they all talked together, I looked down at my empty plate. I didn't know why but I was thinking about food again. Grayson nudged me, "Walk first then I promise I will get you some more food." As he stood, he said bye to Matt and Sunny. I waved at them, as I took my tray.

I took a deep breath as we stepped outside, I had not realised how trapped I had felt inside. I just stood and appreciated the outside. My breath misted in front of me. A cough from behind me made me turn, Grayson stood holding out two jackets. "Thought you might need this," holding one out.

"Thank you," he held it out for me to slide my arms into. I smiled as I turned my back to him and slid my arms in. He didn't let go but held the front closed for me. I stood in the circle of his arms, it felt nice. It felt for just a moment that it was all going to be okay. I turned in his arms and took a step closer, so that we were touching. He looked at me, intently but strangely, there was something that I couldn't recognise. He stepped back with a shake of his head.

It felt cold without him as close, he pulled his own jacket on. I puzzled about what had just happened, was I looking for something that wasn't there. Too much was happening. I had to keep my head together.

He led off walking around the building, aiming for the sculptured hedges. Shaking off my thoughts, I followed smiling at the strange and fanciful animals. We walked in silence for ten minutes or so, I had relaxed. We were out of sight of the main building now, Grayson stopped. I drifted to a stop near him.

"It should be safe enough to talk here." His tone was neutral, his face in shadow.

"Where is your sister Grayson?"

"She is stable, so they tell me but they don't know how to get her safely out of that thing." His frustration was obvious and he fisted his hands. Was he wondering how Daisy had got out, of course he must be but I couldn't see his eyes. I started tugging on my chain, unconsciously comfort. My hand was stilled by Grayson's, "You reach for this when you are stressed, sometimes it is around your neck, waist or wrist." He ran his fingers over the links and the rings, he stepped closer.

Now I put my hand over his. "My father gave it to me, it's something that comforts me." As I looked up, all I could see were his eyes, glittering in the moonlight. His lashes were long, as his eyes were hooded. His gaze on my lips, I wet my lips and his eyes avidly tracked my movement. I could feel heat throughout my body, everything seemed to centre on his eyes and lips. I swayed towards him, knowing that it was a bad idea. So this is what butterflies in your stomach felt like.

It felt like slow motion, as he leant forward and our lips touched. Though it was soft and felt exploratory, it soon ignited. He lifted me up, my arms around his neck. He held me firmly around the waist, my legs wrapped around his waist. He backed me against something hard. Our mouths had were fused and it was amazing. I was light headed, I moaned as I felt his tongue play with mine. I rubbed against him, trying to get closer. I felt so hot. Slipping my hand under his jacket, I felt his muscles, he moaned and pushed harder against me. His head dropped to my neck, kissing and nipping, as he pulled my jacket zip down. I gasped, feeling like I couldn't breath.

As I felt his hands fully invade my jacket and run over my

breasts. I arched up against his hands, feeling his erection against my belly. He groaned more and pushed more insistently against me.

A small voice of reason that was drowning in the sea of sensation, tried to say 'stop'. There were so many reasons why this was not the right place or time. I pushed at him, he didn't seem to feel it, lost as he was in his own sensations. "Grayson, we have to stop."

He held me tightly as he fought to get under control. Our harsh panting breaths were loud in the quiet of the night. Slowly, so slowly he lowered me down. He still held me but took a small step back. He hadn't said anything, "Grayson, I am sorry."

He actually growled at me, "No you are right but just give me a moment." As I pulled further away, I clenched my fists, so that I would not grab for him. Embarrassed I met his eyes, they were really dark, pupils dilated and intense. They made me take a shuddering breath, looking away before I swayed forward.

"We need to talk but please don't look at me for a while. At my puzzled look, "You look lovely, your lips are swollen from me and I know that I could have you."

Annoyed at his assurance, I arched my eyebrow and looked down at his obvious arousal. He adjusted himself, grimacing which made me smile.

He stood turned away from me, in a still deeper than normal voice. "Marcus is not to be trusted. He will do anything for the cause. Your room and any devices given to you will be bugged. You can't trust anyone here."

"Then why are we here, why did you call them?" He ran his hand through his hair.

"They have resources and the medical care that my sister needs." He turned back to me, "They can also protect you. I know that you are not exactly what you appear to be." He raised his hand, as I started to protest. "No, I understand and I hope that you will trust me with your secrets soon." He came over and ran his knuckles over my cheek, "Trust me Olivia, I want the best for you, you have charmed me. Now, we had better get back, they will be watching for us, we have taken too long and you distracted me." He grinned, having recovered his swagger.

As we held hands and made our way back, I was surprised to realise that I felt recharged. My headache and fatigue had completely disappeared, I felt full of energy. The best that I remembered feeling since this all happened.

As promised, he took me through to grab some sandwiches. He led me to a room a couple of doors down from his. He opened the door with a flourish and let me walk in first. It looked like his, except that there were my washed and folded clothes on the bed. Remarkably my fathers jacket was there too. Most surprising was that my phone was on the table, It was fully charged, the screen showing multiple missed calls and texts.

I looked back at Grayson, who had stayed just inside of the door. "Why would they give me back my phone?"

Sighing he shrugged, "Try to get some rest. You still have the tour tomorrow, Marcus won't be happy that you didn't get it today." He paused and then walked out, shutting the door really quietly.

I closed my eyes and flopped down on the bed. I was bursting with restless energy. I wondered how private this room really was, could I find out. Putting my hand on my chain, I centred myself, reaching out in my immediate vicinity. I just felt, not knowing what I was looking for, with all my energy it was actually easier. There were three areas of wrongness in the room. With careful focus, I sat up and opened my eyes. There, my phone, the lamp and the window. I was relieved that there was nothing in the bathroom.

I got up and went to the bathroom, showered and changed into the thoughtfully provided nightwear. I placed my sweatshirt on one of the lamps, closed the curtains. As they had already gone through my phone, I guessed that they already had Louise's number. So I texted her that I was okay, lying low but nothing else.

There were several calls from the trainer that had contacted me. Detective Seymour had left me multiple messages and texts, he sounded really worried. I texted him back, saying that I had lost my phone and the charge was dying. I would be in touch. I then restored my phone to factory settings, and broke the phone. Looking through my bag, I also broke everything with a chip.

I switched the lights low, ran through some yoga to centre myself more. Seated with my legs crossed, I swept through the building, settling first on Grayson's room, where he was pacing. Then the rest of the building, there were lots of people. I could not sense Daisy or Grayson's sister. Marcus was in his study, I did not focus on him, he scared me. There was a flash of someone, near him, but they were hard to focus on. It was as if they were shielding, gifted like me. Concentrating and pulling on the energy stores that I had, I felt that it was Harry. Did Marcus know? With that in mind, I focused back on myself. Seeing myself from the outside, I weaved a virtual net around me, as a sort of protection. I moved my attention away from it and came back it collapsed. With some frustration, I kept at it and finally had one that lasted after my attention had moved away. Though it was probably a little late.

Feeling tired, I pulled my consciousness back and opened my eyes. I leant back against the bed, there was no headache but all the energy that I had was depleted. Pulling the chair on the room, I wedged it under the door handle and got into bed.

As I lay down, I knew that I had to stay and find out as much as I could. They had access to resources that I didn't have.

I turned towards Grayson's room, thinking on what had happened between us rather than worry about everything else. I feel asleep surprisingly quickly and with a smile.

CHAPTER 13

The bright light from my window, with the unclosed curtains, woke me.　It felt early, I stretched feeling rested, despite all that had happened. I lay there, resting my arm across my forehead.　I thought about what I should so today.　At the core, I really needed to make Marcus to trust me or at least need me.　I would be able to learn more that way, though I shuddered at getting closer to him.

I also worried about Cecilia, trying to wake her would expose me too much but remembering Grayson made it harder.　I sighed, sometimes doing the right thing was hard, I could not decide now but I needed to see her and then decide.　Though I was also not sure that I would be able to replicate what I did, looking back it was all a bit of a blur. If I did need to run, it would probably be at the drop of a hat.　Louise could help but I was going to need to be able to contact her and access my accounts. Lots to do, despite the fact that it would easier to close my eyes, I had better get up.

With reluctance, I got up and stretched while looking out of the window, it was sunny and clear.　It lifted my mood, as did the fact that I could wear my own clothes.　I twisted my chain around my waist, tucking them under my trousers.

I opened the door, pausing as I involuntary glanced towards Grayson's room.　Despite the fact that I was drawn to him, the warnings of not trusting anyone echoed within me. It would be better if I was more independent, my steps away were slow but setting my jaw, I speed up.

Smelling food, I headed down to the canteen and helped myself to breakfast. Feeling relieved that it wasn't too busy yet, I got my food and sat at a table near the entrance.　I wanted to check out as many people as I could, there was no knowing when I might need to recognise these people. As I ate and sipped my coffee, which was happily strong, I tried to smile at everyone who glanced at me. It always paid to be friendly, though from the responses, I wasn't sure that my smile was all that welcoming. Some smiled back, some ignored me, some women gave me the evil eye. I did roll my eyes at them, seriously were we at school.

As if called, Marcus strolled in, a coffee in his hand. I smiled pleasantly at him, he nodded and made his way over. Along the way he greeted people, before sliding in opposite me, "Morning."

"Morning Marcus. Thank you again for letting me stay, but I need to help, I know that I can." I tried to project confidence but also deference, while leaning back, sipped my coffee, keeping eye contact. Out of the corner of my eye, I saw Grayson walk in and spot me but I continued to watch Marcus. I waited, I knew that he would want to talk but he seemed to want to make me sweat. He continued to look me in the eye, a smirk appearing on his face, looking as if he had all the time in the world.

Knowing that I was going to have to give, I leant forward. "I am late to this but here is what I know so far." I took a breath, "They are an abomination, they take and despoil the innocent, creating things that should not exist. They need to be stopped but they have money, international connections. I have brought you information and survivors. I can do more."I made myself stop, my heart was racing, I felt impassioned, the pressure that I had to get Marcus on side. I waited, my breath felt loud in the apparent silence between us. I clenched my nails into my palms, to prevent me fidgeting or speaking again. Marcus continued to stare at me, not blinking, just obviously weighing me up in his mind. It crossed my mind to try to push my needs over but again I didn't know whether he could recognise it.

Finally a supercilious and superior smile appeared on his face. His hand patted and then rested on mine as it lay on the table. I fought the urge to pull it back, "You, have indeed helped the cause and will continue to do your duty. As you have a unique perspective and can help me overhaul certain aspects of our organisation here, as this base." He paused, waiting for my response. I didn't try to hide my relief, and nodded enthusiastically. "I will be keeping you close, my dear, I think that you are very special." The way that he lingered over those words, made me shudder internally.

Standing, he turned imperiously beckoning me to follow, sweeping up his assistant who appeared suddenly behind him. It was working that I had not even noticed him appear, I had been that engrossed with Marcus. I could not afford to be unaware of who was around me. We walked by Grayson who was just standing in the doorway, he made to move forward and join us, but Marcus lifted his hand. He stopped, his eyes trying to lock onto mine. I didn't trust my resolve, so I kept my gaze ahead. After we had swept past him, I could still feel his accusing eyes on my back. I straightened my shoulders back.

We didn't return to Marcus's room but went beyond what I had already seen. It appeared to be an operational type of area, we entered a computer filled room, large screens were mounted on the walls. Glancing around, as I stood back I saw Sunny. We did no more than smile at each other, Sunny casting nervous looks at Marcus.

Marcus in his element, walked to the centre of the room and raised his hands. I saw the satisfied look on his face as the room became silent. He obviously liked power and control. A middle aged guy with glasses stood up and welcomed Marcus. As Marcus asked him for an update, he stammered, pushed his glasses up and began. There were a lot of information, negative leads that had been followed. It was all very boring and not helpful at all. As I started to loose interest, my eyes shifted over to Sunny. She was bouncing slightly on her chair, almost raising her arm. I hesitated but then realised that I had to make a mark, so I stepped forward into Marcus's eye line. "Olivia, do you have a question."

I nervously cleared my throat, "I can tell that this is an experienced and focused team but we have little time before this information becomes obsolete. I am not sure if this is how you do it, but I would like to hear the positive, potentially actionable leads. I trust that the team would have gone over the others." Marcus's face had gone blank, going all in, I pointed to Sunny. "She seems as if she has something to share," I could see the man that had been talking, going to red in the face.

Marcus flicked his eyes over to Sunny, then to me. He turned and graciously inclined his head. Gulping audibly, she stood, smoothing her hands nervously over he clothes. As she stood, she continued tugging on her top. "Well, I found a shell corporation, based outside of Switzerland that paid for the shipping crate. I have checked and they have an address in London."

Marcus looked intrigued, encouraged I thanked Sunny, who collapsed back into her chair. Addressing the room, I asked loudly, "Does anyone have anything else?"

A couple of hands raised uncertainly. I stepped back to Marcus's side, allowing him to take over. The surveillance tapes that I had taken, had generated names for their people but also another ten missing peoples.

Though obviously contained, Marcus had an air of triumph, excitement. "Nick, I would like a word with you later, I see that we have a lot of talent that is going unrecognised." Marcus tone was chilly, Nick who was the first man that had spoken looked pale. "And I trust that all these leads will be followed up on with only the best support and encouragement."

Though Nick was left speechless, the rest of the room was excited, lots of conversations bursting out. I did feel sorry for Nick but from the glaring look that he sent me, he knew who he was going to blame.

Outside the room, Marcus continued onwards, without looking at me he said. "That was useful and exactly the kind of shake up that the group needs. Some people have been here since the beginning and their methods have not changed. I now see that things will have to change." He nodded at Harry. "Harry, take Olivia to all the other sections, see what she suggests but no changes until I have approved." From the tone, I would be unwise to do otherwise. We both nodded respectfully and stood back as he glided back towards his office.

"Well, I guess it is just you and me now." Harry looked down his nose at me, he sniffed, showing that he was not impressed by me. As I fell into step next to him, "So, why are you here Harry?" He walked faster. Damm, curse all long legged men. Embarrassingly I settled into a sort of jog, "Marcus has said that we are going to spend time to together, for the greater good, don't you think that we should come to some sort of agreement?"

He suddenly stopped, not anticipating it I ended up ahead. Blowing a frustrated breath out, I turned. He stood still, forcing me to walk back to him. More games. As I stopped by him, not looking at me but the air above me. "Marcus is my father, he is a general in this war. My middle name is William, after our enemy." As he said it, I realised that the nagging feeling I had had, was that he looked very similar to Professor William. Now he directed his eyes at me, stalking towards me so that I ended back into the wall. He leant down, "You had better focus on helping us, I know that you have another agenda but I will not allow you to bring harm to my father. Do you understand."

"Yes." What else could I say? He had rattled me, I was shaking. He was going to be a problem. After staring into my eyes a little longer, he strode off again. I sagged against the wall and the pulling myself together followed on.

"Lets get this done, we are to meet father at 6pm to discuss any changes."

That set the tone for the rest of the day. Harry William, I thought I would give him his two names, worked our way through the different sections. Though he wasn't as scary as his father, he had presence and they were all used to giving reports to him. There were many small departments that had probably been set up soon after I was born and not changed their organisation since. Multiple reports, filing, a strange version of human resources, lawyers, IT and the most unsettling were the security. They were more para-military. As we walked in, I did find that I walked more closely with Harry William. I noticed that Grayson was checking equipment but now he avoided my gaze. Which Harry Williams's eyes noted. I ignored them both, cataloging all the weapons. Odd to see so many in England, I was more used to seeing such things on TV. From the report, they were following our trail back to see if there was anything additional to be discovered. which was really strange seeing as it was England.

Though that was the most unsettling, the strangest was a dark room, smelling strongly of herbs, containing odd looking books and a group of people who refused to give their report in front of me. I couldn't contain my relief as I left, it had made me feel uncomfortable. I could not shake the feeling that these were the ones, who would know what I was. While I waited outside, I reinforced my shielding.

Harry William came out, to see me leaning, apparently at ease, against the wall opposite. "Should I take that personally?"

He shook his head, "No they are very secretive, it took a while before they would talk to me and that was only because Marcus insisted. I think that they are worried that we could turn against them for their knowledge, it is similar to that of the enemy."

I was reassured by the answer, there was no lie but also by the fact that he had answered in a more neutral tone, compared to the hostile of that previous.

We fell into step together, as we moved on, he also walked at a more normal rate, which I appreciated and took as a good sign. Wanting to try for more bonding and hopefully information, I asked, "Any chance that we could grab some food before we start brain storming."

He looked as if he was thinking of a reason to say no, okay so more business focus then, "I thought we could sort through some initial impressions, I want Marcus to have a great report." I saw that I had him then, his shoulders slumped.

We grabbed some food and just ate at first, with Harry studying his iPad and me studying him. I had a feeling that they iPad had all the information that I could possibly need. My immediate hunger dealt with, I attempted to make some small talk but all I got in response were one word answers. I gave up and finished my food. As soon as I laid my fork down, he was up. "Shall we meet in thirty minutes, come to my office, ask anyone for directions." And he was gone.

As I reflected on my poor subterfuge skills, Sunny appeared in his empty seat, "Why are you having lunch with the robot?"

I smiled with some relief, raising what an effort it had been hanging with Harry. Though Sunny's bubbly personality would make anyone smile, a stark and welcome change from Harry's dour manner.

With little conviction, I replied with a wry smile, "He isn't too bad."

Sunny wasn't letting that fly, "Are you joking, he hasn't eaten with anyone here, he only eats and talks with Marcus, unless we are giving direct reports. He is really odd." She looked to where he had disappeared to, then turned back with a mischievous smile. "It was so cool today though, I have been so frustrated with the way things were being done. I am now the new boss of the unit, can you believe it." She squealed, as I congratulated her. "Nick was a dinosaur, stuck in time. He never seemed to like us to actually find anything out. Its a big responsibility though, what if I screw up?" Then her eyes went wide, "Oh my God, this means I will be giving the reports to those two. Damm."

I leaned over to grasp one of her now flying hands, "If they picked you, you are that good. Trust in what you can do and remember the people you are doing it for. You are going to save lives. Now go kick some ass. Meet you after dinner? I have to go to a meeting now, wish me luck."

Sunny gave me a salute and bounced off, I shook my head, she was irrepressible. It was nice to have a sort of friend.

As I was wondering out, I saw an open door and could not help slipping outside. Feeling the weight of the situation, slightly lifting. I took some deep breaths of the crisp cold air, restoring my energy and clearing my head. As if waiting for the chance, Grayson popped into my head. I had missed him today, funny considering that we had only just met. There seemed to be something, that could be something. It was all so complicated.

With some reluctance, I turned in and walked towards Marcus's office, I thought that William's wouldn't be that far from it.

William was waiting stiffly by the door, a frown already on his face. I signed deeply internally but smiled brightly at him. He just stared at me and led me to, what looked like, an unused library. It was nice, though dark, until I drew back the heavy drapes and opened a window for fresh air. I turned back, catching William staring at me oddly. Not knowing what to make of it, I decided to ignore it and sat down. "Shall we?"

He sat, "Olivia, tell me your ideas?" I was a little surprised that he asked me but was happy that he did.

"These are just ideas off the top of my head, so just listen and then tell me what you think." At his nod, I took a deep breath. "You need everything to be feed to a central group, obviously headed by Marcus and supported by you. With all the best will in the world, Marcus can't micro-manage these groups and retain oversight. This central group needs include the heads and deputies of all the units. Working together, they might have insights. Also the ..occult group need to integrate, there may be things that the other groups won't look for, special supplies or such. They would build contacts between the units." I stopped, all of this made so much sense in my head, I just wasn't sure whether I had explained it well. William, I was going to call him that, as his moodiness reminded me of the Professor more.

I jumped, startled at the slow clap behind me, I turned to see Marcus emerge from one of the shadowed corners. "Excellent my dear, William get started on this, you have two hours, then I will review and we will present to the units. I want to get this restructuring done as soon as possible." Without looking at me, William gathered his stuff and walked out.

Still taking deep breaths, I tried to slow my racing heart. I needed to get myself under control but the fact that I had not realised that he had been there in the shadows, that must have been why William had been staring at when I had flung open the drapes. I remained sitting, trying not to show my fear. Marcus was more wily than I had thought, this was a good lesson. "This is like a reality show except I don't know the trials."

"My dear," sitting down next to me, it took concentration not to lean back. "You will be an important error in my bow. You through away your phone, not many people would do that and I am aware that you spotted the cameras in your room. Are you angry about them?" As I said nothing, he moved on his eyes glittering. "You are still here because I believe that you want what I want, to stop the people who hurt your friend and threaten you. You are only safe here, with me. I know that you won't tell me everything and I understand that a woman needs her secrets but do not doubt that I will know. I can see that you will be a powerful tool for my war but I will have no hesitation in tempering you first."

Fear flooded through me, there was utter truth and focus in his voice. Needing to respond, I uncoiled some of my power feeling it strengthen me, as I infused some compulsion into my voice. I wet my dry lips, as I thought fast. "Marcus, I recently learnt about Professor May, I was warned to avoid him. My father trained me, enhancing my intuition, and ability to sense lies. I don't understand everything that happened but I know that these people have to be stopped. I know that if you had not given me sanctuary, they would probably have me now. Do not think that I am not mindful of that but also I need to learn who to trust. You would do the same."

Marcus was sitting back, arms folded and pursing his lips. There was no expression, he had, a fucking great poker face. I felt sweat start to pool between my shoulders. I kept my breathing steady and settled to wait him out. I knew that this was yet another test.

Marcus suddenly sat forward, "How did you learn these things?"

"A letter was delivered to me, I don't know who sent it. It was short, more of a warning from my father, than anything else. It said to destroy it after and that I would receive more, if I need them."

"You destroyed a letter from your father? Why would you do that?"

"I got scared."

"Why did you go to the police?"

"Why wouldn't I?"

"I need a demonstration of this lie detecting. How do you do it?" His eyes were glittering again but the intensity that had been present earlier was less, I could breath a little more easily.

"Its like I can taste the lie, it tastes sour."

"And the intuition?"

"Its just a really strong feeling, a sense. Though I have never felt it as strong as when I found Daisy and Cecilia. To be honest before that it would be just choosing the right route home or knowing that the phone was going to ring. But in there, I knew that I had to find them, that their lives depended on it."

"These aren't the sort of evil powers that they are developing, these are more natural. Without you knowing I had you scanned by people who can detect evil, they found nothing suspicious." He nodded as if to himself, "Yes indeed, this is a gift."

"I am glad that you choose to tell mw this. You must always be honest with me. We are family now, we are all that you have." Despite the wrongness that the statement generated in me, I smiled dutifully.

Marcus stood, patting me on the shoulder. "Olivia, I would like you to rest before dinner. A word of advice, Grayson is a good solider but I don't think that he feels the cause like we do? It would be best if you try not to be so close. William is someone to trust, he is true." I nodded again, realising that these were more orders than words of advice. I bit my tongue to prevent me from responding impetuously.

Marcus left, obviously happy with the way that things had

gone. After I was sure that he was out of earshot, I let my breath out, and slumped back in the chair. I was shaky, sweaty and definitely felt like I had survived something.

CHAPTER 14

Overwhelmed by the need to escape, I staggered to the open window, looked over my shoulder and then climbed out, landing softly in the flower bed. I realised that I had no jacket but I kept going. Needing it, I touched the trees as I passed. Focusing on the feel of the bark, I approached the largest majestic tree. I reached out and hugged the tree, feeling the uneven bark through my clothes. It was worth the discomfort, with my eyes closed, I could feel the tree's energy. It was clean, natural and I could feel it washing away the negative energy and recharging me.

A cough startled me, it was a day for that apparently. I opened my eyes, feeling as if I had been asleep, everything was brighter, clearer. As my gaze settled on Grayson, my heart stuttered. He looked broody, angry, dangerously handsome.

I just stilled, our gazes locked, I felt like his prey. The intensity of his dark look. As he slowly stepped forward, looking at him, as he stood looking at me. Slowly he stepped forward, a step by step and my breath caught. I pushed myself further back into the tree. Instinct told me, that to run would be a mistake in the mood that he was in. He was in front of me, our chest almost touching as we both breathed in deeply. He reached out slowly, caging me in my his arms. I had to look up, he was looking down, his eyes hooded. I continued to hold still, my breathing not settling, I was feeling increasingly lightheaded. I had never actually had butterflies in my stomach before.

Grayson shuddered, groaned and leant down to rest his forehead on mine. We stood like that for a while, our breathing settling. He appeared in pain, I reached up and hugged his chest. His hands moved down and hugged me back, his head resting on mine. As I involuntary shivered, he rubbed my arms and swore when he felt how cold I was. He took his jacket off and placed it around my shoulders, ignoring my protest and hugged me again. Without thinking about it, I just accepted the comfort.

Naturally, our mouths found each other. As I gently kissed him, he resisted for a moment. But then as if a dam burst, he pushed me back again against the tree as he took control of the kiss. It was hard, possessive and demanding. It was amazing, the only think that I could feel, heat built as his hands roamed under the coat. Suddenly he stopped, still holding me but panting hard he groaned out, "No, we need to stop."

As if not trusting himself more, he pushed away and leant against the tree next to me. Despite wearing the coat, I felt suddenly chilled, from the cold and the rejection. My face flushed and I was filled with embarrassment. Had I just thrown myself at him, I must have been looking for a distraction, as I gently touched my sensitive lips, it had been a good one.

"I am sorry Grayson, are you okay?" I turned and traced his bruise with my eyes. Without thinking, I lifted my hand to follow my eyes.

He grabbed my hand to stop it, while harshly bitting out. "You didn't even look at me this morning but you want to know if I am okay?"

I flinched and turned away from him. "Marcus has answers, I need to get on his good side. He warned me away from you, why did he do that?"

"I don't blindly follow him, that's why."

"I am probably being watched all the times," looking around. "There were cameras in my room and my phone was bugged." I banged the back of my head gently against the tree. "You know that if you were a little more charming, you could make this easier."

He laughed naturally, gently holding my hand, "Not in my nature."

"I had noticed," I answered wryly, turning my head towards him, "So it will have to be up to me." He didn't answer and and

I took the opportunity to absorb his face. "He also wants me to spend time with William."

This got a response, his lips thinned as he scowled. Suddenly he was growling into my ear, "That's not going to happen." The butterflies started again and I shivered at his possessive tone. "But I warn you, I am trouble for you too." Before I could process that, he kissed me deeply.

I touched his bruise and raised my eyebrows. "Part of the job, we met some resistance at the club but got more information and prisoners."

"How is your sister?"

"A really odd doctor let me see her, to get rid of me but she is still in that pod." His frustration was obvious. "They don't know how to get her out, did they ask you about Daisy?"

I glanced at him, guilt coiling in my stomach, he didn't look suspicious. I fought against the wish to tell him everything. "I don't know but I want to tell you what Marcus knows."

He listened intently, brushing my hair back from my face, "Thank you for telling me, you can trust me you know. I know that you are important to me. I know that this is all really fast and the timing is not good but I can not shake the feeling that we were meant to meet." At my look of even more guilt, he laughed softly while cupping my face, "Don't panic, I am not asking for forever or even talking about love. Just know I am there."

I was glad that he had interpreted my look that way, needing to have some distance I moved away. It helped and to prevent any further talk. "Marcus wants my help in redesigning the way things work. William is helping," I didn't look at him, "It would be best if he thinks that I am useful, for the moment anyway."

He continued to lean against the tree but said nothing, which expressed his disapproval well enough. I shrugged, "Well what would you do?"

"Lets do it your way, I will try to fall in line more. Though it will look odd, if I change too much. We will need to meet and inside doesn't seem to be possible. Why don't you let Sunny be our go between. She is trusted, and you can tell her that we just

want to spend time together. She is a romantic, so she will help."
As I nodded, he stepped forward and warned in a low voice.
"But Olivia, William doesn't get to touch you." On that note, he
walked off, whistling softly under his breath with his hands in
his pockets.

I was reluctant to take Grayson's jacket off, as I discreetly
smelled it, I felt calmer with his scent. I turned and walked back
to the main building, slowing as I came into site of it. I did feel
more centred and happier than when I had left. Even better, was
that I saw no one I knew on the way to my room.

Entering, with my back against the door I sent out my senses,
the cameras had gone. Hmm, was that a sign of trust? There
were some new clothes on the bed, fitted pants, underwear and
sweaters, plus a black dress. I held it up, I think that this was
for dinner, int seemed a very Marcus thing to do. There was
more, a tablet and phone sat on the desk, as I touched them, they
had all been set up and I couldn't sense anything from them.
Checking the time, I decided to shower and get ready for the
dinner, Marcus wasn't one for lateness I think. In the bathroom,
I saw that I had been provided with some quality toiletries, hair
products and make up. Obviously being in Marcus's favour was
good, though I wondered about what would happen if in his
disfavour. After a lovely hot shower, I changed into the dress,
that was fitted and some thoughtfully provided ballet flats.
Light make up and then I was left where I would put my chain.
Loath to have Marcus see it, I placed it around my upper thigh.
It seemed to hang well but as an extra security I placed my hand
over it, willing it to stay. To check, I jumped up and down a
couple of times, it didn't move. It was time, so I went out of the
room. Grayson was opening his door, his eyes took me in and he
winked but then for anyone watching, slammed the door behind
him. Pretending to be annoyed, I angrily turned to the stairs and
on to Marcus's office.

Where as always, William was already waiting, looking
handsome in a suit and tie. It did cross my mind to ask if he lived
there but it was unlikely that he had a sense of humour. He was

holding a smart long coat, which he held out for me. I turned as he slipped it on, feeling vulnerable to turn my back. He then held his arm out and smiled, which was extra freaky. But I forced myself to smile back. As I placed my hand on his jacket, I noted with some internal revulsion at how cold he felt. I was led to a side door, to a long blacked out car. As I slid into the backseat, Marcus was waiting there for me. William slid into the front passenger side and there was a driver. "Ah, you look lovely my dear."

"Thank you for the clothes," smiling despite feeling like a doll.

He smiled complacently back, happy to receive his due, "William, doesn't she look nice?" William who had been looking out of the window but dutifully turned to me, nodded, then looked at his father. "William has given me a report and I am really excited about how we are going to move forward. So I thought we would welcome you properly and celebrate with a proper dinner."

This I could smile more naturally about, I wanted to see more of the surrounding area. With no encouragement, Marcus spoke for the next forty minutes, as we drove through dark country roads. He spoke about himself and his vision. I had to work hard, to appear interested, nodding and murmuring agreement at the appropriate times.

At last we arrived at what looked like a stately house, Marcus came around to help me out. I was a little unsteady from sitting for so long and he grasped my arm tightly. I pulled away as soon as I could and as politely as I could. Allowing him to precede ahead, I walked with William, finding him less stressful.

We entered the large and impressive dining area, I gazed at the opulent setting. With speed we were seated in a more private table at the back. Marcus, unsurprisingly ordered for us all, the meal was out if this world and accompanied by some lovely wines. Aware of my precarious position, I did not partake of the wines freely. Marcus had no such reservations, he freely indulged and certainly became more relaxed. William was the opposite, quietly sitting and listening to his father. He was almost colourless in comparison. Despite the company, I enjoyed the meal, something I had never experienced. Suddenly like the ice-berg appearing before the Titanic, with shock I saw Detective Seymour appear.

I stiffened immediately, unsure of what to do. Marcus, despite appearing a little tipsy, immediately noticed and turned. Unexpectedly he simply tutted, "|Ho0w unexpected." His tone was not unsurprised and I turned sharply towards him but he simply smiled at me.

As the Detective approached our table with a determined air, William stood up, "Can I help you?"

Seymour ignored them both, leaning across the table to me, "I have been looking for you, are you alright?" There was apparent concern in his voice and expression.

Not sure of how to play it, I tried to smiled reassuringly. "Detective Seymour, how unexpected. As you can see, I am fine. After everything that happened, I needed to get away and my friends were happy to help."

William answered, "As you see, Olivia is fine. She is safe with us and I don't want you to upset her. Though we appreciate your commitment to the job. Above and beyond really." He made it seem as if he was in the wrong, from being in the background, William really had presence. He appeared commanding, with my sight, I realised that he had loosened his tight control on his power. I could feel it coiled and ready to be let loose.

Marcus picked up his wine glass, swirling his wine in the glass, appearing as if this was of little importance. "I think that you have been reassured that Olivia is safe. I thank you for your concern, I shall note it." Though the words appeared innocent, there was an underlying threat in the innocuous words. Apparently Seymour heard it, as his face became dark with anger.

Wanting to deescalate the situation, I placed a hand on Marcus's arm, leaning over I softly spoke, realising that what ever I said couldn't be seen as challenging him. "Marcus, I saw him talking to one of them, It might be worth trying to see what he knows."

"Perhaps, you should be allowed to speak to Olivia tomorrow? Would that assuage your concerns Detective?"

Realising that this was better than nothing, he nodded stuffy. Smugly Marcus said, "How about here for lunch, 1pm?"

As we watched the Detective leave the room, Marcus patted my hand. "Olivia you handled that well, I am sure you noticed that William can be quite forceful."

"What shall I say to him tomorrow?" I chewed my lip, as if worried. I did text him, to reassure him but he came anyway, if he knows then they know where I am." Now the worry was genuine.

"Perhaps you underestimate your charm, you must expect men to be a persistent. I will have someone drive you here tomorrow, Daisy should perhaps come with you. Then there is be no reason for the police file to remain open. Then we shall have him followed and see who else is involved. This may be another opportunity, you are a gift that keeps on giving." He laughed, seemingly very pleased by it all.

I was too busy thinking, to be irritated by his proprietary tone. The opportunities for accessing a phone must be better here than at the house. I smiled, "If you are sure."

William looked over and said, "You don't need to worry, I will ensure that it is safe."

"He will try to follow us back?"

"Yes but we know what to do. William sort it out, let's give the Detective something to waste his time."

We left soon after coffee, through the kitchens before getting into a smaller, different car. I said good night, as soon as we were through the doors. Though Marcus pressed on me that we are to meet after breakfast.

Exhausted I collapsed onto the bed. It felt as if all this was happening to someone else. My mind was spinning with everything that I had to remember and hide. I curled up on my side, with my eyes closed. I just wanted to sleep and wake up to life as it was before, however lame it had been.

Reluctantly I swept the room, it felt okay. Pulling myself up, I pulled off the dress, grimaced at it and threw it into the corner. Managed the minimum of ablutions and cried into the now dark room.

As I lay there, I realised that if the Detective was here then perhaps Louise was at risk. Biting my lip, I grabbed the phone off the table and rang her. She picked up after the first ring, "Oh my God, Olivia are you alright?"

"Yes I am alright, alive and well. I have found Daisy, she's pregnant. I am with some people who want to help stop the society, aware that someone could be listening to this.

"I need you to keep safe too, maybe shut up shop for a while and go somewhere but don't tell me."

"Don't worry about me, I have my protections. You stay safe." As she signed off, I whispered 'I miss you' and then with some tears in my eyes I fell into a deep sleep.

CHAPTER 15

Already dressed, I was having breakfast as William walked into the canteen. Unexpectedly he came straight over, after grabbing a coffee. He slid in opposite me, I was glad that I had finished eating, having a sip of my own coffee as I subtly checked my warding. Behind him, I saw that Grayson slipped into the seat behind him.

I was glad that William wasn't more like his father, it had been an exhausting evening, I had needed two cups. William looked depressed. While looking down at his coffee, he sighed deeply. "I should have seen what you saw, made these changes earlier. I just didn't think that my father would want the change." He met my eyes, more directly than he had ever done before. His eyes moved over my face, I couldn't help the blush that rose, "I am glad that you are here."

From the corner of my eye, I saw that Grayson had stiffened. Despite that I smiled back and leaned forward, speaking softly. "I am here because I am not allowed to leave. You understand that right?"

He looked wary and pulled back from me, in a more stiff voice, after glancing around the room. "Shall we get going, Marcus is charing the new rental unit."

It was a little crowded, everyone was awkward and settling into their new roles. Marcus with skill led the meeting through, breaking ground and surprisingly it turned into a productive meeting. I had stayed quiet and just listened.

Before I knew it, it was time for my lunch. As I waited by the front door, Marcus came and patted me on the shoulder. "Olivia, one of our men will drive you and Daisy but on medical advice she will have to remain in the car, he can see her there. So you don't worry, I will have people in the restaurant, so don't worry."

Out of curiosity, rather than to receive instruction, I asked, "Marcus what should I say to him? I do not think that he is one to just let go of this, he is too invested."

"That is what we want, it does not matter what you say, you won't be leaving in him and the more unsettled he is the better. That way he will make a mistake and I want to see who he reports too."

"So this is a test for me?" I was annoyed and didn't think my response through.

Marcus eyebrow raised in rebuke at my tone but he didn't deny it. Frustrated with it all, I walked outside, as a car pulled up. Excited to at least spend some time with Daisy, I pulled open the door and gave her an awkward one handed hug. Unfortunately she had that unsettling doctor next to her. So, even spending time with her wasn't allowed. With reluctance I got in the front passenger side.

Turning in my seat, I ignoring the doctor and smiled at Daisy. She glanced up at me, smiled but then ducked her head. Obviously she was uncomfortable. Taking the silence as an opening, the doctor leaned forward, "Olivia, I hear very interesting things about you." He licked his lips, "I have arranged some tests for you tomorrow."

I sat back, not liking his smile or the way that he looked at me, in a dismissive tone I responded, "Why do I need tests?"

"I think that your brain will be fascinating, Marcus agrees with me."

Daisy looked at him casting a distrustful look his way. I caught her eye and a small shy smile appeared. "The lengths you will go to just to get out of work?" It felt good to return to our old running joke, the far out excuses that she had come up with and dragged me into. Her smile appeared again and was more natural.

Knowing that if Marcus had approved then I didn't really have a choice, "So if you want tests from me, then I insist on having dinner with Daisy tonight, some time just us two together."

Seeing the no out to come out, I said quickly "We will stay in the canteen but not you."

He frowned but obviously also wanted me to agree. I really hoped that none of these tests would reveal what I was. Daisy was looking hopefully excited, "Fine, I will approve this but in return I expect full cooperation, from both of you."

"Both of us, yes of course, you and Daisy."

I turned around in my seat to avoid his triumphant expression, I am sure of he weren't there, he would be rubbing his hands together evil villain style. With relief we rolled into the driveway of the restaurant. As we slowed to a stop, obviously waiting for us, Detective Seymour stormed over. His expression was angry.

I pushed open my door, the doctor getting out as well. He came over to Daisy's door, opening it and crouching down in front of her. More softly that I expected, "Hello Daisy. My name is Detective Seymour, I have been looking for you. Are you alright?"

Daisy smiled faintly and nodded a yes.

"Are you sure, do you need me to take you home or to the hospital." He had obviously clocked her paleness and timidness, different to both pictures and my description of her.

"I am okay, just recovering from being so silly. They are looking after me, here is my doctor. He can probably explain more." As if exhausted by this little conversation, she leant her head back on the headrest. Eagerly the Doctor stepped forward. Supercilious, "I am Doctor Dalton, Daisy is my patient. She has been through some intense trauma, I have recommended that she not be reminded of this trauma right now but when she is able to make a statement, I will contact you."

Straightening up, taller and broader than the doctor, Seymour faced off, "I am a police officer Sir and I know how to talk to trauma victims. You will allow me to speak to her, on her own or there will be trouble." As they were both ignoring me, I opened the door and sat next to Daisy. The driver looked at us but remained by the doctor's side. "Daisy, are you alright."

"Yes, I am alright better than I was. I just feel so tired and sick, all the time." She held tight to my hand, "I want to leave with you, do we have to stay?"

I hugged her, "I am afraid at the moment I haven't got a way out but we are together and know that I am on it."

"Well when you set your mind to it, I know that it gets down but be careful." She indicated the doctor, "Especially him," she whispered, "He is really keen to have access to you. I have heard him and that Marcus talking about you."

I shivered, feeling that it wasn't in my interests for them to be talking. Not knowing what to say to reassure her, I turned my attention outside.

"I really must point out that I answer to a higher duty, I must place the fragile mental health of my patient first. Without my permission you can not talk to her."

I squeezed Daisy's hand, "I am going to see if I can contact someone."

Knowing that it would be unlikely that someone wouldn't follow me, I got out, waved at the driver and walked in. Where I was met by multiple members of staff who had come out to watch the two outside. I said that I had a lunch booking and they waved me through to the dining area. On my way, I passed by an empty office. Quickly I ducked in and shut the door. Grabbing someone's abandoned phone, checking out of the window. The fight now looked to be escalating, the driver standing between the two. Good. I dialed Louise, who picked up immediately, "Louise, I haven't got long, I have borrowed someone's phone. I need help to get out."

"Go ahead," she calmly said.

Feeling so much affection, my voice caught, knowing that I wasn't on my own. "I need to money that I can access, somewhere Daisy and I can lay low."

"When do you need it, your father left something in case of this situation. Take these details, this is an account in a different name, here are the access details. Can you check that it works."

After casting another look out of the window, I focused on

the door and locked it. Accessing the computer I opened a private window and opened up the details that I was being given. Memorising everything, I repeated it a couple of times.

"Olivia, there is also a key and smoother stuff, I am going to leave it in a locker at your gym, and tape the key under the sinks in the bathroom."

I couldn't help it, I laughed, "How James Bond, how do you know where my rarely used gym is?"

"Don't ask and I won't lie but aren't you glad now?" While she was taking, I deleted the browser history. "I know that you feel alone but you arent, you have got this. Now get yourself and Daisy to safety, we can catch up then. Be safe."

"I really love you Louise, thank you again." She logged off. Feeling sorry for who ever phone this was, I took out the SIM card and broke it.

Unlocking the door, I slid it open and peeked out, then with forced casualness continued into the dining room. I was greeted and shown to a table, I ordered a drink feeling that I needed it. I had only taken eight minutes, it had felt longer. As I sipped my drink, I looked around to try top identify the men watching me. Some men in black, caught my eye. One gave me a short nod. I enjoyed this moment, closing my eyes.

Realising that I could hear raised voices still, I opened my eyes, there were people looking out of the window. Were they still at it, I would have thought a police officer would have better deescalation techniques. Probably realising that this was not the down low that would allow me an easier escape later, I hurried out. I approached the driver, pulling him away by the arm. I hissed, "You need to take us back now, leave them. The other men can sort this out, they are getting ready to call the police in there." He still looked reluctant to leave, "I bet Marcus will not be impressed, if we get taken away."

That settled him, "Get in."

I got in the back, grabbing hold of Daisy's hand, who grasped it back as tightly. We moved out, both men realising after we had pulled away. Twisting back, I giggled at the looks on their faces. I whispered out of the corner of my mouth, "Daisy, we need to get away as soon as possible, I don't like the sound of those tests." She clutched my hand harder, which I took as agreement. "Be ready but are you sure that you will be okay to make a run for it."

She touched her stomach and a serene smile came over her face, "You bet."

We arrived with a squeal of wheels. Obviously news travelled fast, people were waiting for us. William ran to my side and yanked the door open, unceremoniously puling me out. Daisy was more gently whisked out the other side. We locked eyes before we were separated, I tried to communicate my silent promise. Now to see how much trouble I was in.

Allowing William to pull me away, his anxiety was radiating out. I was pushed into an empty room, crowding em against a door. "Are you okay, what happened?"

Pushing him away, I frustratedly said, "This getting pushed and pulled everywhere is getting so annoying. Nothing happened. Your doctor apparently thought picking a fight with a police officer was a good idea. Aren't doctors meant to be calm. Seriously what the fuck William!"

He relaxed a little, knowing that I was unharmed but ran his fingers through his hair. "I can not imagine what he was thinking, he never behaves like this. Marcus is going to be very upset."

I had a feeling that Marcus being upset was akin to a volcano erupting and that he would get the fall out. Despite knowing that he was one of the people holding me here, I felt sorry for him. I approached him carefully, needing to reassure him. Without warning, he suddenly launched himself at me, he grabbed me by the neck and slammed me against the wall. I clawed at his hand and saw that his eyes were unfocused. To add to the physical assault, I felt a sudden spike in power from William. Like a blow torch his power punched through the now flimsy wards that I had put up. Completely frightened and overwhelmed, I fought, both physically and mentally. Wildly I thrashed, my heart pounding out of my chest. After what felt like ages, as my vision became dark at the edges, warning me that I was about to pass out. I gathered everything that I could and threw it all, including kneeing him in his groin.

I was dropped abruptly to the floor, gasping in deep breaths, pulling myself back against the wall. As my vision returned, I dragged myself up the wall. Holding on for support, I looked wildly around for William. He had been thrown across the room and was groaning on the floor. Confused as to what had happened, I just stood there in shock. Listening to William now crying plaintively and pathetically apologising.

With a loud bang, the door burst open and Marcus stormed in. Calmly, considering the scene, his eyes went to me first then to his son. Emotionlessly he gestured to the two men behind him, dragging William away. Disorientated and confused, I was still trying to process what had happened. I started to slip down the wall, I had drained myself of all energy. Hands grabbed me, holding me upright. Marcus approached me, he was smiling widely, a fatherly proprietary smile that chilled me. "Well done Olivia, you will have to forgive William. He has power but not as much control as you. You threaten his control, I am sure that we can avoid a repeat of it later, after all you have a lot in common and I know that you will make a fruitful team."

I thought that we would not. Quickly, aware that I was thinking sluggishly. "I thought that you would protect me Marcus. We are a good team but I can not work with William." I shrugged off the hands that were holding me up, needing to stand on my own.

Marcus rubbed his chin, as he stared at me. "This will obviously have to all be processed but I really must insist that you consider the long term relationship between William and yourself. I know that he is keen."

"I need sometime to myself right now Marcus." I flatly responded, seeing only madness in his eyes. So I stepped unsteadily forward and he graciously moved to the side. I left with sheer force of will holding me up.

Around the next corner I stopped, I pulled my chain with shaking hands and wound it around my wrist. I closed my eyes, feeling the pain around my neck and whole body. I pulled in energy from around me, from everything that I could. After about five minutes, I could open my eyes without seeing stars. I needed sleep but I needed food more.

Continuing onto the canteen, I pulled my jacket up to cover the marks on my neck. I loaded up food and looked around. My throat was sore but I persevered and ate all of the food that I had taken. Sunny was on a table nearby, she say me and excused herself to come over. As she slid in opposite her eyes fell to me neck. She stood and moved my jacket collar out of the way. "What happened? Are you alright?"

I was glad that she was subtle about it, I didn't want any more attention. But her kindness was going to start me crying, "I would love it if you could pretend that I was, until we get out of here."

She reluctantly nodded, worry still in her eyes but talked to me about her day and work. It was reassuring and soothing. As we both finished, I stiffly walked out, having got more stiff while sitting. She helped me once we were out of sight, as the stairs were hard. I was reeling from the realisation that Marcus knew of my abilities and that he wanted them. Was the lack of control that William had something that would happen to me. There was so much that I didn't understand.

I collapsed onto my bed, leaving Sunny to close the door. I was exhausted, Sunny didn't say anything just sat on the chair at the desk. I rolled onto my back, there was obviously no time for resting. "Sorry Sunny, I need some help. Can you show me on this device the leads that have been found."

Sunny dutifully started up the tablet, "I can do you one better and give you an untraceable link to all the info that we have."

"Sunny, won't that be traceable?"

With a knowing and mischievous smile, "Not the way that I do it." She kept tapping away, "Can you memorise well and when I say well I mean amazingly well."

"Sunny, I am great at that."

"Perfect," she leant over and showed me her tablet with a long IP address. I motorised it, confirming it before I nodded at her.

As she sat back, she leaned forward, I know that you want to know and I want you to know. "My sister was taken, I had argued and I have never forgiven myself for that. Maybe that's why, I am here. The guilt. But I am not blind to the problems here. I have a strong sense that you are the one that I need to follow." She put up a hand, "I don't know why but I know it to be true."

I felt tears gather in my eyes from the force of her emotion, I didn't feel that I deserved it. I hadn't done anything yet. "Thank you Sunny, I count you a friend." Carefully, "If I have to leave here, I will need a way to contact you." Without saying anything, she gave me a mobile number and an email account, which I again memorised.

Thinking that we have had enough serious talk, I slyly asked, "So how about you and Sam?"

To my delight she blushed, but she came back fighting, "What about you and should I say Grayson or William?"

I grimaced, "William is defiantly out," as I showed her the bruises on my neck.

She gasped, covering her mouth. "What happened?"

"I don't know, it was like he lost control. He was so strong. It was really hard to fight him off. If his father hadn't come in, I am not sure what might have happened."

Sunny looked shocked, "His father?"

"Marcus is his father. You don't know?"

"No, are you sure?" She looked genuinely shocked, so she hadn't. I was a little surprised, I had not realised that it was a secret. I groaned and lay back on the bed, "I have a headache. Everyone is crazy."

Sunny claimed onto the bed next to me, lying down and looking up at the ceiling too. "I know what you mean and I am not even getting paid."

Another thought occurred to me, "Sunny, where does the money come from."

She sat up, obviously excited about the answeres. "For Professor May, private massive donations, from people they have placed in positions of power. For us, it is the fact that we are all working for room and board, personal donations but I know that underneath it all is a trust fund. We are not encouraged to look at that but I do wonder about who would sponsor Marcus."

"It should be simple, the good guys are the good guys and you have the bad guys. You could always tell the difference."

Sunny said dryly, "They are guys, what do you expect." We looked at each other for a moment and then burst into laughter, giving me the lightness that I had not felt for ages. We laughed and talked about guys and our lives before this. Sunny left after an hour or so, pleading that she had work to do and would meet me for dinner.

I had a short nap, to recharge. On waking, I knew where I had to go. I made my way down the heavily incensed smelling corridor and nervously knocked on the door to the occult section.

The door suddenly swung open, spilling out a lot of noise. An older women with an upturned nose had opened the door and proceeded to look down that nose at me. I smiled brightly, "Marcus thought I should understand more about what you do?" She continued to look me up and down, obviously not buying it. I held my smile, though I suspected that it was rapidly becoming more of a grimace.

Another face popped up behind her, a small round face with moon shaped glasses. "Ah, Olivia isn't it. Move over Margaret, this is the one who has given us more of a voice."Welcoming hands pulled me in, "Hi I am Oliver. Our names are vey similar, that's a good sign. Though your name means Olive tree, a sign of Athena. Mine means warrior or elf. What do you think?" Overwhelmed by the greeting, I managed not to respond, to be honest I could not think of someone less like a warrior. Oliver was short and round, with a friendly face and smelt like sage, I smiled radiating friendliness. The stern woman had moved to the side, standing with her arms crossed.

Ignoring her, "This is an area that I haven't understood at all but I can already tell that it is key. Can you help me please to understand more?"

Olivia, also glanced at the woman, pulled back his shoulders and continued proudly. "As the unit lead, I would be happy to. Please come this way." He led me into the main room, interconnected to several others. "This is the main room, we have three tasks; to try to reverse engineer what they are doing to produce, what I call mutants, my joke. To make offensive and defensive weapons."

Leaning gingerly against a table, I looked at the strange jars and books. Trying to look at an open book that had ancient writing on it, it slammed itself closed in front of me. Which sent a small cloud of dust straight up at me causing me to cough. The scowling woman suddenly appeared in-front of me, "I am Mrs Evans, I don't know you and I don't trust you. You feel wrong."

"Marjorie, leave her alone. You think everyone feels wrong." Oliver dismissed her and turned away, gesturing for me to follow him. We walked into another room, I could feel her eyes following me, burning into my back. I rotated my shoulders once I was out of sight. I was now in what was an old fashioned solarium, a room surrounded by glass. There were small colourful birds flying high above us and a perfusion of plants. It was full of life but also a calmness, that was working like a soothing balm. I sighed, feeling this replenishing my energy. As I opened my eyes again, there was a goddess ahead of me. Actually it was a tall thin pale young woman, her skin was almost translucent, with bright aquamarine eyes and long white blonde hair. She had energy that felt like mine. I straightened up, shocked and unable to look away. Oliver who had noticed nothing, introduced her, "Ah here is Maggie, she is our expert on everything."

Maggie continued to look at me, "Oliver, be a love and get the rest of the presentation for the unit meeting tomorrow."Apparently not realising that he had been gracefully dismissed, she happily moved off.

Maggie moved her hands, chanting something under her breath. Something bubble like expanded out of her, encompassing the room. Smiling she said, "We can now talk without interruption or fear."

"There are different types of fears and secrets that are not protected by a mere bubble." I answered, not sure of her.

"How did you know that there was a bubble." Maggie smiled knowingly. She spread the folds of her chiffon dress and sat on a chair, her feet tucked underneath her, her head tilted to the side. She looked the picture of a lady, I did not match her, as I fell into the chair opposite. She released the guards that she had up, I was bathed in her power. It felt different, more controlled and focused.

With some trepidation I lifted the lid on my own power. It felt like a whole body stretch, a relief, I had not realised that it had taken so much out of me, keeping it under wraps. As our powers met between us, they flared.

There was some similarity between them, "Are we related or something because this feels strange but familiar."

She laughed, it was like a fairy tinkling, like it should glitter. I couldn't help it, I laughed as well. "I have been so scared, I didn't know what I was. We are the same right?"

"I am an expert in the field that created me. I am hiding in plain sight, as it is the best way for me to learn. You would be surprised how many people like us there are here."

"Like William?"

"Ah, you have met all the sides to him, haven't you. Unfortunately I don't know what he is, something on a very thin leash."

"What does Marcus know?"

"I am really not sure what he knows, he is always so contained and for someone without powers he can close off his thoughts. He only lets you know what he wants you to know."

"Are we monsters?" Scared of the answer but who else was I gonna ask, Who else had I met that I could ask."

"Settle back Olivia, there is a lot that you need to know. I will give you some info." Settling in more comfortable, "We are not entirely human. There is a ritual that calls forth a demon during the conception, especially as they are treated to be hyper-fertile. Along with being fearful, that's important. There are three demons, who work with the society. Initially it was rare that it worked, something about the demons essence being too strong. Killing the women and the babies. I was one of those babies, like you I escaped. I had a family background of being gifted, so it was easy to let everyone believe that my gifts were non-demon. I think that our magic melds so well because we have probably the same demon father. It links us." She leaned forward, with interest, "So can I ask what your abilities are, you have masked them very well but amateurishly. I am presuming that you have had no training."

Feeling the criticism, "I have had to learn myself over the last couple of weeks." Her mouth actually fell open. Defensively I continued, "It has been a massive learning curve. I can move things, sense lies, cloak my power, sense the power of others. I don't know what this is but I released my friend Daisy from a coma and brought her back from the dead." Maggie breathed out, she was silent for a moment and then impulsively got up and hugged me. I held stiff for a moment but then relaxed into the hug.

Looking me in the eye, "Well now you have me. I am with you."

I laughed, trying to discreetly wipe the tears from the corner of my eyes, "I seem to be getting a team."

"You are going to need help with control, that will help you with your power."

"I need it but I need to leave. Marcus has plans that will turn out badly for me. I will be taking Daisy, she is going to have one of these babies and I can't let it be here."

She frowned, "Well I guess then I will be going with you, well I will follow you after. It would be safer if we don't leave at the same time, it would be better not to burn all our bridges here."

Surprised I sensed for any untruths, I was going to trust her.

Was I being naive? Probably, "This is my number, what's yours. I will have to send you a message about where to meet."

"I am so glad that I met you Maggie."

"So am I Olivia, now hide your power again." After I had done so, she lifted the bubble, all the noise from outside rushed back in.

Oliver was enthused to see me, starting to chat again. "I have received a lot of information, I am overloaded at the moment." I leant in conspiratorially, "She is giving me the evil eye, so I had better go." He deflated slightly but then went back to full energy.

I pushed out and went outside, to the garden and the tree where I had met Grayson before.

CHAPTER 16

I gratefully slid down with my back against, what I now thought of as, our tree. I didn't know if Grayson would come but what I wanted to have a moment of calm. Trying to work though my thoughts, it was like the story line to a movie. If I told anyone what had happened to me, there would be a lot of psychiatrists in my future.

Knowing that going around everything would just make me stressed, so to settle my mind, I felt for the tree's energy. Slow and steady, the thump of its sap. Putting all thoughts out of my mind, I relaxed into this controllable moment.

Checking my watch, after half an hour or so, I realised that it was almost dinner. In my new normal, I was starving also that I was going to see Daisy. If the doctor kept his promise. As I brushed off my clothes, there was the rustle of leaves, announcing someone approaching.

I ducked behind some bushes and peered out through their leaves. I was surprised to see the strange doctor, he appeared to be angrily muttering to himself and touching the bruise around his left eye. I thought that it looked good on him and no more than he deserved. He moved along the tree line, pushing aside foliage, with no thoughts to the noise that he was making. Looking up to the sky, I thought why not and followed him. I had little real concern that he would notice me, the way that he was walking but I still tried to keep a little distance. He was moving towards, what I guessed was the back of the property. This had definitely not been included on my little tour. Cleverly hidden was a grass covered large flat building. I kept down as he approached the entrance. I was close enough to see the code that he entered into the entry pad. He yanked it open and went in. I paused crouching in the bushes, sending out my senses and felt out the building. I immediately felt the heavy warding around the building, it felt oily and unwelcoming. So I couldn't get a sense of who or what was inside. Looking around in a more ordinary way, I noted the security cameras covering all walls and the entrance.

Biting my lip, I played with my glasses. This was so a bad idea to go in alone. I would need to bring someone else, I had a feeling that whatever was in there was going to change my direction. Creeping back, I returned to the main building. Entering the main entrance, I was greeted by a lot of activity. Grabbing someone seemed the easiest way of finding out what was going on. "They are storming a stronghold, talking lots of teams."

I let them go, stepping back from the crush. Turning I walked straight into William. Looking everywhere but at me, he mumbled "I owe you an apology, I don't know what happened but I am sorry." Not knowing what to say, I remained quiet, I was still a little wary of him. "I am going on this mission, Marcus said that you are to stay here." Abruptly he stalked off, while I bemusedly watched him go. This could be good for me, so I headed straight down to the infirmary. I called out as I entered the main door, walking over to Daisy's room. I blanched as I saw that it was empty and stripped. It was as if she had never been there. Biting my lip, I looked around but there was no one in, no records. My stomach was in knots.

I returned upstairs, trying to ask people questions. Everyone that was left seemed to know nothing, so now I was beyond frustrated. I had seen Sunny but she has been leaving and only managed to wave apologetically at me. No sign of Grayson. I went unto his room and loitered there a while, in case he came back. Finally I went back to my room, I had decided that I would go and investigate that building on my own. It was the safest time, they had probably also reduced their staffing. I would wait until later though, I took a nap and awake with my alarm, in the early hours. They had also probably less staff and security. On a hunch I packed the stuff that I wanted to take with me

OLIVIA AND THE SOCIETY

and dressed all in black. I decided that I wouldn't leave by the door and climbed out of the window, landing without too much trouble. Sticking close to the walls, I clocked myself and feeling out the security blind spots I moved to the trees. Outside the building I watched for a while, calming my breathing. Everything seemed to startle me and I was turning at every noise. Moving my chain I looped it around my right hand and pulled my hood up. Focusing on the camera, I turned it so that it didn't cover the door, not trusting that my clocking would work on it. Running over to the pad, I tapped in the number, while sweating. With relief the pad blinked green, he door soundlessly opened and I slipped in.

On silent feet I moved down the dark corridor, everything had the smell of a hospital or lab. When voices started to echo down the corridor, I pushed more energy into my cloaking. I was a shadow, nothing to see or remember. I slipped by lots of meeting. As they seemed to move towards me, I slipped into an empty rooms. Two men in lab coats walked by. "We had better get some food now, they are on their way back with some more subjects." Then silence descended.

I made myself move further down the corridor, I was getting a bad feeling again. I followed the sloped floor downwards, to a lower level. Knowing that I didn't have much time, I decided to focus on Daisy. She was ahead, I jogged on. Suddenly I stopped at a door, as I looked through I saw Daisy lying on a cot. As I looked closer, I realised that she was connected to multiple monitors. I tried the code from the entrance but it remained red, looking around I decided the speed was the priority. I placed my palm over the keypad and just blew it. As I entered the room, I realised that she wasn't alone. Cecilia was lying to the side, still in her tube. I tried to wake Daisy but she seemed sedated, I wasn't going to be getting them out on my own. I went to look for an exit and someway to transfer them. With a sense of urgency I moved faster, pulled to a loading bay. I was relieved to find some trucks, even better they had their keys in them. I reversed one back by the loading bay and pulled the back open.

Even better there were some trolleys by the side, I could use those. I got to work.

I moved them all, one by one all the sleeping people I found after Daisy and Cecilia. I had to use my power heavily, lying them side by side in the back of the truck. Securing them with straps. I knew that I had to move them, that I was saving them. It over-rode my worry about moving them, especially Daisy and a more heavily pregnant woman.

When I had finished, I opened the loading doors. I was panicking now, the urgency had built. As I did, Grayson rushed through. "We have to go, they are all coming back."

I didn't think how he knew, I was just happy to see him. We rushed back to the truck and I throw him the keys as we moved to the cab. He started it, and pushed heavily down on the accelerator. We literally launched out of the bay. I bounced around, as we sped down the road, hoping that I had strapped everyone enough.

Grayson drove fast and with real focus. "Where are we going?"

"I had a plan for two but not this many and certainly not unconscious. You got any ideas?"

He threw me an unbelieving look. "Seriously, you are lucky that I love your impulsiveness." I couldn't help it, I kissed him on the cheek.

"I might have an idea but first let us get some distance. We are going to need to swap vehicles, they have probably got some sort of tracking on this." He kept driving through the night, I tried to send some power to the people in the back for them to remain asleep.

We stopped at a lay-by with other trucks and vans, next to a pub and cafe. We pulled in quietly, we got out and checked a couple of nearest smaller vans. One was unlocked, I called Grayson over. It looked pretty beat up, so I didn't think there would be any tracker on it. "This okay?"

He looked it over, "It looks perfect but I don't know how to hot wire."

"Don't worry about it, I got it."

As quickly as we could, we carefully moved everyone into the back. Luckily they remained asleep and no-one saw us. Every time lights flashed by us, my heart would race, wondering if it was them. As Grayson got started on the last one, I got in the driver side. I should be able to drive it, if it started. I placed my hand over the engine start, thinking of the the power moving through it and what I wanted which was it to start. A little buzz passed through my hand and the engine started, louder than I had hoped.

Grayson shut the back doors and jumped in the passenger side, surprised "How did you manage to start it?"

"I tell you later, trade secret," I winked at him. "You need to rest up, just tell me where to head and catch some sleep." He looked like he was going to argue, but thought better of it. He gave me a direction and I headed off. Grayson closed his eyes. I kept going, trying not to think on whether I had made a mistake or not. As the lack of sleep and exertion caught up with me, I started to fight sleep. I was forced to pull into a small petrol station, when I came back with some coffees, Grayson was awake and stretching outside.

He took one of the extra large coffees, "Thanks, I needed that, you did good time." He looked around in the early morning light, "There is a call box over there, I am going to ring and see if we have a plan." As he walked over to it, he paused and then came over to me. He hugged me hard, "It will be okay." When he came back from the phone box, he was smiling and I let out my breath that I had been holding. "We just have to make it another couple of hours, then we can rest. Any chance of some more coffee to go." I laughed and went to get them, as he checked on our passengers. Then we headed off, it was a gruelling couple of hours, we took turns driving. Catching micro sleeps in-between, we talked about everything to keep our minds alert.

In an exhausted triumph we pulled into a farm. It was light now, my eyes felt gritty. I was in a daze really, the low dark sprawling farm house looked surreal. Grayson was on the last shift of driving and he was flagging. As we got out, the cold made me shiver. Grayson came to my side and stood shoulder to shoulder with me. In a low voice he reassured me, "Relax, they are checking us out."

"For what?"

"That we aren't a danger to them."

I laughed without humour, us the danger. Nervous with the wait, I stretched my senses out. I could feel people, their emotions anxiety, hostility and a flash of something else. Turning automatically towards it, I focused, someone else with a gift was feeling us, me out. In this there was no hostility but not a lot of friendliness either.

I turned to the van, slowly and opened the doors. "We have many people who need help here. Please can you help us."

After an excruciating delay there was movement near me and a women stepped out. I was startled, not by her appearance but by the uncanny resemblance that she had to Maggie, that same timeless quality. As we stepped towards each other, she looked into my eyes and I could feel her mental probing. With some trepidation, I dropped my barriers and allowed her in. She was surprised that I dropped my barriers but nodded in acceptance. With relief I lifted them back up. She held out her hand to me and I took it, we would find some relief and respite here. Thank goodness.

Then she stepped to Grayson and greeted him warmly, stroking a hand down his arm, with a familiar smile. Grayson tiredly smiled back and hugged her, though after a look at me he pulled away gently. She turned and looked at me appraisingly. I didn't like the way that she had touched him, definitely jealously on my part.

She looked into the back of the van, raised her hands and called over people to help unload them. As I stepped forward to help, she gently pushed me away "You are exhausted Olivia, you are dead on your feet. Come inside."

Gratefully I followed her and Grayson through, it was nice

inside. Everything was new, comfortable. "Grayson, you remember where you stayed last time. Both of you clean up, sleep, I will wake you in two hours. I really can't give you more time," she said with an apologetic look. "It will give us a chance to assess those you have brought."

I couldn't argue with her logic and I was led to a small room with a double bed and ensuite. Grayson grabbed some towels and brought them in. He put one in my hand and pushed me towards the bathroom, "Have a wash, Catherine will look after them all. There is nothing that you can do now." The shower was calling to me, I wanted to wash off the drive but the entire Marcus thing. It was glorious and I would have stayed there longer but I didn't want to use all the hot water. Reluctantly I got out and left with my towel wrapped around me. I hadn't even thought about it, just that I didn't want to put on my dirty clothes.

Grayson was sitting on the bed, with his arms on his legs. He looked up, his eyes traveling up and down me. I heated and shivered, from the look in his eyes but also my response. He slowly stood up, his eyes hooded as he stalked towards me. Stopping just in front of me, with a hairsbreadth between us. His voice was gravely as he told me, "Leave your clothes on the chair and someone is going to wash them for us before we have to go down. I will have my wash now, otherwise we won't get any sleep." He stiffly walked to the bathroom and slammed the door. I took a breath, having not felt that I could have when he had been standing so close.

I might be a coward but I was too tired to deal with anything like that right now. I put my clothes on the chair, my chain on the bedside table with my glasses. With thankfulness I lay down, still with my towel under the blankets and surrendered to sleep.

I awoke later, feeling warm and comforted. I didn't open my eyes, I wanted to relish this feeling. As I burrowed into the blankets, I realised that I was being held against a warm and very male body. I went hot all over but didn't move. He whispered in my ear, making me quiver. "Did you sleep well?"

"Ah.." I found that I couldn't complete a sentence, all my focus was on him.

He chuckled against me, I could feel the vibrations. "I would like nothing more than to do something about you naked in my bed. Believe me but I think that I need to know what it is you aren't telling me. I am with you what ever but I can not help you with this unless I know."

I still hesitated, I was trying to remember that it was not safe to tell him but I was finding it difficult to concentrate as his fingers roamed over me. I half turned to look at him and he caught my mouth in a deep, almost punishing kiss. After my head was properly spinning, he gentled the kiss and his touch gentled. It allowed me to gather my thoughts, scattered as they were.

I pulled back and looked into his eyes, he had proved himself to me. I wouldn't be here without him. I pulled out of his arms and sat against the headboard. He let me go and positioned himself the same. Nervously I grabbed my glasses, playing with my chain. He didn't rush me, he just sat there.

Knowing that once I started, it would be easier. So I haltingly told him everything. Everything. It took a while and though his breathing changed, he didn't interrupt.

After I finished, there was silence. It felt a huge relief but I was scared about what his response would be to me. Or would he think that I was crazy. I picked at the blankets, as the silence stretched out.

Finally I turned my head to look at him, he was resting his head back against the wall his eyes closed. Should I consider it a good sign that he hadn't jumped out of the bed and the room? He finally opened his eyes and blew out a breath of air. He smiled crookedly, I smiled back at him a little nervously.

He dropped his other hand around my shoulder and pulled me to him. "It's alright Olivia, I have to say that I have suspected something." Seeing my anxiety, he leaned over and kissed me gently. "I am not going anywhere."

I dashed to the bathroom, when I opened the door Grayson passed me my washed clothes. Great. Grayson followed me after and we were both dressed quickly.

As we stood by the door, I put my hand on his arm, "Catherine is like me, did you know?"

He closed his eyes, "No but it explains a lot of things. Does she know?" At my nod, "Don't tell anyone else."

With his hand on the door handle, he kissed me briefly on the lips and opened it. We went down the stairs into the kitchen area. There were a couple of people, who Grayson nodded at. He grabbed two cups of coffee and handed me one. "Now you can defiantly deal with anything," and winked.

I smiled into my coffee, it was good not to feel alone. I had more confidence that I could do this.

CHAPTER 17

Catherine was definitely one to get stuff done and obviously didn't want us hanging around. As we looked outside, there was a beat up car outside, boxes were being loaded into the boot. As Grayson went outside, a man handed him some phones, cash and keys. I had stayed inside, grabbing another cup of coffee but went out when I saw Daisy. She was being helped into the car, supported as she appeared weak. I knelt beside her, she gave my a tired smile. "Thank you for getting us out."

"A little unplanned but I get there in the end."

"Yes you do." She put her head back and closed her eyes.

I stood watching Grayson walk into the door that Daisy had come out from. I presumed that he was seeing to his sister. I felt that it would be a bad idea if she joined us, I didn't know why.

Catherine came out and also gazed at Grayson's back, She came over, smiling softly at Daisy, she continued onto me. "I have instructed the men to prevent Cecilia from leaving."

"Thank you, I can't expect him to make such a choice but why are your reasons."

"The right choice is rarely the easy choice. I just made it easier for him to follow his heart but there is something else. Like you I sense something upsetting from her." I looked at her, I wasn't sure what I should be asking. "To business, I have ensured that our numbers are preprogrammed into the phones, the boxes have some IDs and the information that I have on the Professor. I would suggest that you read them and then destroy them. Again be careful who you trust." She looked towards her people, "They don't understand why I am trusting you, giving you hard earned information. I am going to trust that you won't do us wrong." She started to walk away, half turning her head to me,

"Stay alive and don't let this bite me in the arse." Turning back, she hugged me and then was gone.

I rubbed my eyes, feeling all the unknowns that lay ahead. I was also worried if Grayson choose to stay, after he looked at his sisters knowing that he was leaving her. Hedging my bets and to avoid disappointment I took the drivers seat and turned the car around. I smiled nervously at Daisy, she smiled equally nervously back at me. Suddenly, making me jump the passenger door was wrenched open and Grayson got in, "Lets go." His voice was gruff and he was obviously keeping his emotions tightly wrapped up. I realised that this wasn't the time to probe, I nodded and drove off. As I drove, I stayed within the speed limits, sticking wherever possible to the smaller A-roads.

There was silence, I concentrated on the drive for a while. When I couldn't take it anymore, I switched the radio on. Grayson gave me a look but went back to staring moodily out of the window. Gradually the tension in the car relaxed, lulled by the monotony of the drive. As I swerved slightly, I turned the radio on. It was strange and odd, how distant the news stories felt. Remote to what I was going through.

We stopped after a couple of hours, swapping over. Grayson doing nothing more than, grunting. Setting off for London. Daisy had been on and of napping. My eyes felt gritty and heavy with sleep but I couldn't help casting glances at Grayson.

Obviously feeling my eyes on him, he sighed deeply and finally looked over at me. "You need to stop looking at me."

"I can't help it," my voice dripping with worry. He grabbed my hand and held it tightly over his thigh.

"Its not your fault." He paused and looked towards me, his gaze intense. I can't help my sister. I can help you." He away, repeating it under his breath, "I can help you."

Not knowing what to say now, I decided to text Louise. 'Change of plan'. I got a quick response, 'Who is this'. Of course, I had forgotten that this wasn't my phone, she wouldn't recognise the number. 'Your troublemaker, I am on my way to collect key. Didn't want you to worry.'

"Grayson, we need to go to this address. Then we need to contact Sunny and Maggie."

Puzzled, "Maggie?"

"Yes, you don't know her. She is like me." I didn't mention her similarity to Catherine, that I wanted him to see for himself.

With a chuckle, he gripped my hand, affectionately asking, "Have you been setting up a team?"

"It seems that way." I leaned back in my seat, hoping that this was all going to work. "I think that we need to plan what's next."

We continued to drive, well into the evening. Stopping only for fuel, for the car and for us. Daisy seemed to be holding up better than I expected. Grayson was very gentle and protective. His reward was that she relaxed around him. I was happy as we entered London. As the streets became familiar, I tucked my hair under a baseball hat, pulling it forward. I didn't think that anyone would be looking for us, let alone here but I couldn't help but feel paranoid. I concentrated on making myself unnoticeable, I wasn't sure that it would work.

Grayson looked over and then looked again, "Olivia, why am I having trouble seeing you there."

I sighed thankfully, "That's great, it works. It's hopefully an additional protection." Biting my lip, I gently banged my head against the headrest. "I am still wrapping my head around all of this, I really don't know what I am doing."

He laughed at me, holding my hand tightly. "You are doing fine."

As I glanced in my mirror, I caught Daisy making kissy faces. I shook my head at her.

Finally we pulled up, I peered around the pretty empty car park, there didn't appear to be anything unusual. Grayson looked around too, tension in his hands on the wheel. He didn't switch the car off. As I placed my hand on the car door, he leaned over. "I don't need to say be careful."

I swallowed but responded, "Your job is to keep Daisy safe." Looking like he wanted to say something, he bit it back. Leaning forward, I pressed a kiss to his lips and got quickly out. Shutting the door, seemed to make a really loud sound in the car park. Taking a quick breath, I zipped up my jacket and walked forward. As I walked in, I kept my face turned away from the cameras, I slid my card along the automatic barrier. The bored looking teenager at the desk, didn't look up engrossed as he was in his phone. I entered the womens changing room and through into the toilet area. I checked all the stalls, to make sure that they were empty, then crouched down to look under the sinks. It was under the fourth one along, a key taped on. Pulling it free, I found the locker and opened it up. I could feel sweat starting to bead at the back of my neck. My breaths short, just as I was about to turn the key, I heard a noise. Someone entered, singing under their breath along to the music in her headphones. Without looking at me, she grabbed her own stuff and went to the showers. As soon as she was out of sight, I opened it and took out the gyn bag inside. I double checked that there was nothing else inside and went out to the car. I tried not to run but was walking at a fast rate, as I left and darted into the car. Grayson pulled out straight away. I blow out some breaths, as my heart rate returned to normal.

Driving for a couple of streets, Grayson carefully pulled to a stop. Turning towards me, with his hand behind my car. Daisy leaned forward to grab a look as well. I opened the bag, with my audience. Inside carefully sealed was a large brown envelope, containing a letter, some cash, new mobiles and some keys. Underneath this were some clothes. Pulling the letter out, I opened it. It contained simple an address, directions for using the keys, Grayson looked up the address. "It shouldn't take that long," he looked with a question in his eyes.

I looked at Daisy, she gave small nod. "Lets go then."

I awoke with a start, my eyes gritty and a headache developing. As I looked at my watch, I saw that it was after midnight. I looked over at Grayson, feeling embarrassed that I had also apparently drooled, hopefully I hadn't snored. He looked focused and tired.

"Sorry, I didn't plan to nod off."

"No problem, you needed it. Great timing though, here we are."

I scrubbed harder at my eyes, in an effort to wake up. I grabbed the letter out and followed the instructions. There were a couple of gates, each with a different code. As the car pulled in, I did feel more secure with all these gates. There were stairs that led up from the parking area, I took the bag and helped Daisy out. She stretched, grimacing at her stiffness. I smiled tiredly at her and indicated the stairs. Grayson took the keys and instructions, going up ahead off us. He indicated for us to wait, as he checked the building over. After a while, he nodded his head for us to come on in. Gratefully we entered, Grayson went down for the stuff from the car. I let myself feel out the area, nothing.

I led Daisy to the kitchen, where she grabbed a cup and had some water, rubbing her back. I moved on to look around a little.

I came back, noticing the blank look on Daisy's face. "Are you hungry?'

"Thirsty and hungry."

I opened the fridge, there were some staples in it. "How about some toast and scrambled eggs?"

Grayson answered for everyone, as he put down the boxes on a nearby table. "Amazing."

Though I knew that perhaps we needed to look around, I also realised that we were all exhausted and this was needed energy. Sitting back, I smiled feeling safe. Daisy got up and started to clear up, I stopped her, smiling, "No, bed for you."

She didn't resist and Grayson showed us one of the rooms. It was near the bathroom and the kitchen, shyly he said, "I thought that this one would be good for you, you are near food and the toilet." Daisy laughed and patted his cheek making his flush.

I bought some of the clothes that Louise had given, "Wash up and sleep, we will talk in the morning." Hugging her tightly, she hugged me as tightly back. Going back to the kitchen, I cleared up.

Grayson came in wet from a shower just wearing pyjama

bottoms. I turned and just stood, taking in how good he looked. He grinned and pulled on my hand. "Come on you need rest."

I followed him, a little shy. He led us to a room, two doors down from Daisy. The bed looked very welcoming and comfortable. I swayed towards it, not even listening to the voice that said, there is one bed. Grayson caught me before I could face plant on the bed, "Wash first, you will be grateful after. Here are some clothes and everything else is in there."

Slightly resentfully, I entered the bathroom. Begrudgingly, I had a lovely, hot shower. I stood under the spray for ages, feeling my skin lose a layer. Emerging, I did feel much better, towel drying my hair as I left. Grayson was already in bed, his hands behind his head. I stood, looking at him, "So we are bunking together? I am sure that there are more bedrooms."

He continued to lie back, grinning at me. "Are there, I feel for safety that I should not let you out of my sight. You attract trouble."

"I really can't argue with that, I wish I could but I can't." I throw the towel onto a chair and got into bed. Immediately he pulled me into him, back to front. I wriggled, I had never been in bed with a man before.

"Relax Olivia," he grumbled in my ear. I shivered and let my tiredness overwhelm me.

I stretched as I gently woke. I snuggled, pulling the sheets over my head, knowing that when I got up I would have so much to do. Slowly I realised that there was a warm, very male body next to me, I shot out of bed, getting caught in the sheets and hitting the floor. "Ow." Graysons laugh erupted, his head popping over the edge.

"You alright, that was quite an exit."

I lay back on the floor, "Don't ask." Gathering my tattered dignity and feeling his amusement I hurried into the bathroom. When I came back out, my cheeks still flushed, I was thankfully alone. I got dressed and came out to the kitchen.

Grayson was on the phone, sipping a coffee, thankfully also

fully dressed. Daisy didn't appear to be up yet. I popped my head into the room and she was sleeping, looking young and carefree. I carefully crept out, closing the door softly.

I helped myself to a big mug of coffee. As I sipped, I took the time to look around more. The wide windows appeared to be mirrored, meaning that no one could look in. The surrounding area looked industrial, no noisy neighbours. I retrieved the phones that Louise had given us and rang her. It rang through, I hoped that everything was alright.

Settling down, I pulled out some of the other papers out of the envelope. Spreading them out, Grayson came over to join me. Apart from the codes, there were schematics of the building. I found them confusing. Grayson pulled them over and whistled, "There is some fancy stuff here. Security failsafes, escape route, internet security. Reading this, this is a safe house. Pretty impressive."

I was confused, how did she have this ready for me. Then I saw the deed, it had been my fathers and now in a company name, with my name as a director. What the hell. I sat back, furiously thinking. So my father had known that I would need somewhere like this and prepared for it. So man things that I don't know.

Looking at Grayson, "Want to look around properly?"

He jumped right up with a huge grin, "Hell yeah."

Thirty minutes later we sat down, literally stunned by all we had found. In a shocked voice, I summarised, "So to recap, we have a weapons room, training room, additional cars including a hum vie! Computer surveillance and medical room, that appear fully stocked."

He laughed hollowly, an odd expression, "You have your own fortress of solitude."

I smacked his arm. "You realise that now I am going to think that you are with me only for this."

"No, I was with you before. Glad that this turned up though."

We glanced at each other at the same time, the stress causing us to laugh hysterically at the same time. Daisy walked in on us and her confused expression, kept us going. "What happened?"

We managed to stop after a while and filled her in. She looked at me, her mouth open, "Why were you working again?"

"Because I wanted to and you were there." She hugged me, "I expect great baby shower gifts."

"Of course," I crossed my hand across my chest.

Grayson stood up, "I am going to check out the local area, grab some more supplies. Daisy, do you want to come?"

She nodded, rubbing her stomach, "I am going to need things that I need to get myself." Appreciating that I would have some time to myself, I handed over a card that had been in the envelope.

"I am going to catch up with our other team members and then start on the files. Be careful."

After the had left, I carefully moved all the papers to the surveillance room, as well as the files that Catherine had given to us. As I looked around, I could not help but imagine Sunny's face when she saw it. Sending messages to Maggie and Sunny, I got an immediate response from Maggie. She was all set to leave, I sent her a location that I thought Grayson could pick her up from.

I split the files up a bit, into more manageable information, then scanned them into the computer. Uploading them to the account that Sunny had sent me.

Worried, I rang Louise again and again there was no answer. I knew that something was wrong but I didn't know how else to get in touch with her. Distracting me, a message from Sunny popped up. I opened the link and Sunny's face appeared. Really happy to see her, I smiled broadly, she said, "Where are you, I can't locate you, which is great."

"Some where quiet for the moment, I have lots of toys here if you decide to come."

She tilted her head. "I would love to but there is so much going on here, I think I would be more valuable here. I am sending you some drop files, with some more information. I don't know what you did when you left but there is a major lock down. Luckily I am in charge of all the IT, information comes through my team, meaning that I know they haven't found you." She looked around her, "I don't think that they suspect me but there are some eyes on me, as we spent some time together."

More worry for me, "Are you safe?"

"No, everyone likes me and most importantly I am very useful. I promise, if that changes I will let you know. In case, I will touch base at least twice a day. If I don't then come looking for me."

"That's a deal, I promise."

"Got to go, be safe."

"Sunny before you go, can you pin point a mobile for me?"

"Sure, send me the number, I will email you a location. I really have to go." With a wave, she signed off. With some trepidation I forwarded Louise's number, glad that at least I was doing something.

Full of anxious energy, I left the files and went down to the training room. It was like a small school sports hall, located a level below the garage and entrance area. I stood in the room, realising in the mirrors that I was still in my sweats. As I stood there, I pulled my chain out. As I ran my fingers through them, focusing on the rings and they felt. I then looked up breathing deeply in and looked to the weights in the corner. I focused on one, the heaviest and pulled at it. I pushed more and then I saw it lift and I threw it against the wall. I repeated that, feeling all the negative energy leaving me. Again and again. Finally I dropped to the floor, feeling completely drained but lighter. After moments of pure panting, I looked over at what I had done. The concrete wall had multiple holes, the ground below filled with rubble. I blew a breath out, satisfied that I was stronger, that I was not weak anymore. Though I was glad that no-one had been there to see this lose of control.

Pulling myself up, I went and showered. As I came out, I heard Daisy call out a hello.

I smiled and quickly went to help them. They appeared to have stocked up, my card must have dent in it. Working together we put everything away, lots of food but also clothes and pregnancy things. Exhausted, Daisy gave me a hug and went to have a nap.

"How was she?" I asked Grayson.

Grayson leant back with a sign, "I hate shopping, your turn next time. Daisy was good, she is strong. You don't have to worry that she won't manage. Though I think we need to think about preparing for a delivery."

I sighed, "I know, another thing to add to the list." Maggie's text come through, she was ready to be picked up. I gave Grayson the details. He was happy to pick her up, though "How will I know what she looks like."

With a secretive smile, "You will absolutely recognise her but if there are any problems give me a ring."

He looked at me puzzled, then with a sigh, "This is going to be something that blows my mind isn't it."

I laughed, "See how well we know each other." I got some sandwiches, then as I was clearing up, I turned seeing Grayson right behind me. "Oh you surprised me."

"Good, I am glad that it isn't one sided, just before I go." He gently but firmly held my chin and slowly lowered his head, I held my breath. His kiss was soft initially but then quickly became more demanding. I pulling him close, as he pressed me against the sink, his arms caging me in. He gentled, slowing and placing soft kisses at the corner of my mouth. As I panted, a dazed look in my eyes, with great satisfaction he grinned and kissed my nose. Then sauntered off, grinning smugly.

I stood there for longer, trying to pull myself together. Texting Maggie, I let her know that Grayson was on the way. Then checked my emails, Louise's phone showed that her last location had been her house but was now not transmitting. Worried I downloaded the rest of the files she had sent and sorted them.

I then had a thought, thoughtfully I went back to the training room. Turning the lights off, it became completely dark, carefully making my way to the centre of the room, I sat down.

Holding my chain in both hands, I focused, tapping that well of power. It was becoming easier and easier to do that. I thought of Louise, her friendship, how she made me feel. Letting images of her flow through my thoughts, focusing on the need to find her. Suddenly I felt that I was above London, hovering. It was difficult but I focused. I looked for the energy that I associated with her. I felt an echo, like an after image. I moved towards it, coming down to her house and then onwards to her cafe. I called out to her mentally. Quietly, faintly I heard an echo, I turned towards it in my mind. A whisper, "Don't look for me. I am safe for the moment. You must not look for me. Be strong." The voice faded away but the emotions were strong, a warning. Collapsing back onto the ground, I opened my eyes in the dark. I didn't like it but I needed to hold onto the belief that I would find her and I would.

I was glad of the distraction when Maggie arrived with Grayson. She was very excited about it all. We showed her a room and as she settle in, Grayson urgently pulled me aside. "Does Catherine know about her?"

"No, I didn't know about Catherine but they have to be related. I mean they look so similar."

"I agree but this is going to be interesting."

CHAPTER 18

We seemed to settle in a bit of a routine, though it had only been a couple of days. I knew that it could not last but it had been nice. I had gotten used to sleeping in the same bed as Grayson, though we had gotten heavy nothing had really happened. I still didn't feel that it was the right time, I was trying not to think about how Grayson felt about it. Though it has getting harder and harder not to go all the way.

As my phone rang, I immediately I felt a cold shiver run through me. I pulled out of Graysons arms and lunged for the phone. "Hello."

No answer, just static, I pulled back looking at the caller ID, Louise. I said again, "Hello." The phone line went dead.I through it aside and grabbed my clothes. I redialed as I dressed, nothing. Grayson, "I'll tell the others to lock down."

I literally flew out and into the car, literally vibrating with the need to go. Grayson rapidly joined me, looking at me doubtfully. "I know that you are going to go anyway but I need it on the record that this is a bad idea. It has got to be a trap."

I looked him the eye, knowing that he was right but also knowing that I wouldn't forgive myself if I didn't try. "I know." Shutting the car door, "Can you drive a couple of roads away, then we can check it out." I knew that I was going to go but I also understood the need for caution.

It all turned out to be unnecessary, as I already saw the smoke in the distance. As we got closer, there were fire-engines and blocked roads. Grayson indicated and I pulled over. He got out to look around, I leaned my head back against the headrest. Carefully felt out but with shields in place, grateful to the extra practise I had done.

With trepidation I felt the presence of, at least a dozen gifted nearby. They appeared surrounded by a swirling dark light. There were varying degrees of darkness, which I suspected that there were different energy levels. I moved on towards the cafe, could not feel the energy that I associated with Louise. My anxiety spiked, I used that burst to rise my sight higher. Finally I felt the softest brush of an echo. I breathed more easily, assured that she was still alive, though not nearby.

Grayson had been right, this was something to draw me out but perhaps I could take advantage. I got out of the car, I had an intense curiosity to put faces to some of these gifted. Cloaking my presence, I moved towards the one that felt lightest and I presumed the weakest. I pulled my baseball cap lower, making sure that all my hair was tucked in. Taking advantage of groups of people standing and staring at what was happening. As I tagged on behind a group of girls. Between them, I located a girl about my age, wearing all black. She was scanning the people nearby, not looking anywhere towards the fire-engines. She appeared confident and I had no doubt, better trained than I was. So I was careful about shadowing her. I was nervous, wondering how to track her, when I felt something flipped into my hand. I looked around and saw Grayson moving away, I opened my palm and looked down at it, it looked like a small disc with electronics in it. I realised that it was a tracking device, I turned back to the girl. I closed my eyes and focused on hiding it from feeling and sight, then I focused on the woman's pocket. Visualising the small disc being in her pocket. The pressure disappeared from my hand and hopefully into her pocket.

Moving on, feeling a little more confident,I gradually made my way towards the strongest signal. I localised it to an older, tall thin woman in her forties. She looked like she was in charge, her cold eyes hungrily scanned the people. As she stood there, her foul deep black aura was making my skin crawl. An involuntary shudder shook me, earning me. Strange look from the woman next to me. I tried to smile at her and moved further away, into a nearby doorway. In time too, as I felt the woman's gaze pause at the group in front of me. Hurriedly I envisioned multiple layers of protection around me. Cursing myself out for heading for the strongest one. I felt the edges of my chain digging into my palms, as I was gripping them so tightly. At last, with a slightly puzzled look her laser like gaze moved on.

Panting, I fumbled and pulled out my phone, taking some shots of her and the surrounding people. On shaky breaths, I moved my attention to Louise's shop behind her, a silent gasp as I saw there only remained a smouldering pile of rubble. It was a shock, realising all the memories that I had there. A little like losing my father all over again. Tears gathered at the corner of my eyes but I firmed my jaw, not allowing them to fall. Too scared to move on, I didn't want to take the risk of moving. Instead I allowed my anger to bulid, at their destructive arrogance. After, what felt like ages, something caught their focus and she led them away. As I moved out, I heard a scream. As I tried to move towards it, people seemed to get in my way. As I breached the ring of people and shocked voices, I saw a blacked out SUV suddenly pulled up. Someone was bundles in and it drove off with squealing wheels. People nearby were calling the police, so knowing that I couldn't do anything, I reluctantly my way back towards the car. Grayson dropping into step beside me, his hand caught hold of mine and it calmed me. I had had a thought that they might have taken him. We didn't talk, just got into the car.

As the doors reassuringly slammed shut, Grayson sat in the drivers seat, his hands on the steering wheel. "I was wrong, it wasn't a trap for us."

I pulled my hat off, shaking out my hair with some relief. "I feel sorry for who ever it was. I don't know where Louise is but I bet that they have something to do with it. Did you see their people?"

"All in black, blank faces, military bearings." I looked over to me, as he started the car. "I did and I got some photos to help us."

"I am tired of all this. I want to know more, to be ahead of them."

He smiled grimly, "I like that plan." As we drove back, I texted Daisy. He glanced over at me, "You are worried about your friend."

"More like family, really," and shared some my fond memories. I didn't think that he would look kindly on the lies that she had told and secrets that she had kept from me. "We wouldn't be here without her."

Daisy hugged us, as soon as we arrived back. We pulled her and Maggie though with us, as we uploaded the photos that we had. They didn't recognise them, Daisy apologetic. "I really don't remember faces, I was out of it. Though that scary blonde looks familiar, she gives me the creeps."

I patted her reassuringly, "Don't worry about it. Upload them to the shared account, Sunny can run some facial recognition thing." I completely agreed with her, I could still feel that oily stickiness from her aura.

Grayson then pulled up a tracking programme, the tracker that I had placed seemed to be pinging in stronlgly. "Well done Olivia."

"I am glad that you had one, where did you get it." I indicated the room, "From here of course. It looks like North London, Camden I think?"

Sunny appeared online, looking tired and stressed. It alarmed me, "Sunny, you okay?"

"I have sent you some info, but things are kicking off here. I don't know what has happened but I am bailing. Somethings is wrong, you got room for me?"

"Of course," Grayson responded. "Do you need us to come for you?"

"No, it will be easier to get away by myself." She looked over the screen, we could hear some muffled shouting. "I am going to grab some things and then I am out of here, I will explain more when I get there."

"Grayson will send you the pick up details. Be safe." She smiled tightly and signed off.

Maggie stood briskly, "You have a burner that I can use. I think I need to check. I don't know what could have happened to cause this but we might be able to gain some intel."

It made sense and I showed her the well stocked drawer.

Daisy rubbed her baby bump worriedly, "This is all too exciting for me, I am going to lie down."

As we remained there alone, Grayson moved behind me. His hands rested gently on my shoulders and finding them so tense, started to rub them. I hadn't realised how tense my shoulders had been. He leant down, "Try to relax, she knows what she is doing."

Relax he said, how did he think I could do that. Seeing that the pep talk hadn't helped, he mischievously whispered, "Come down to the training room, we can spar. You can get rid of some of this, otherwise you are going to explode. If you are worried, I promise I will go easy on you."

Huffing but smiling, I followed him as he laughed.

I stretched as returned to my room, feeling better and indeed more relaxed. Grayson had smiled smugly and given me an amazing kiss in the training room before leaving to pick up Sunny. He didn't take it easy on me but I had held my own without using any gifts.

Towel drying my hair after a hot shower, I ran into Daisy who was loaded with sheets. I grabbed some off her, "Ah there you are, I have got a room already for Sunny. I am looking forward to meeting her."

In a scolding voice, "You didn't need to do that Daisy, I would have done it."

"Not a problem, I wanted to feel useful." Her eyes dropping.

"I am sorry, thank you Daisy."

Brightening up, she continued, "It is the nearest one to the computer room anyway, I thought that she will be spending a lot of time there."

"If she doesn't actually try to sleep in there, she might." Laughing, she led us into the laundry room. She put the old sheets in as I pulled out the load to be dried. Carefully, I did point out, "You aren't to be the maid."

"I know but it's useful and I think I am nesting."

"We had better get some baby stuff in then."

Daisy paused and put her hands on her rounded belly. Frowning, "I don't want to jinx it," as she rubbed her stomach. "I might wait a bit." Looking away from me, she whispered "I am worried what this baby will be." She put her hand up, stalling any reply I was about to make, not that I was sure what I would say. I was worried too. "I know that you will be there and will help me. But what if it has ..gifts but can't control them. I love this baby with all my heart but I am scared."

I hugged her tight, "We have each other and we can do anything together."

She sniffed and rubbed at the tears that had gathered, "I know." Then with a sly smile, "Why don't you tell me what is going on with you and Grayson. I need the distraction and you should never piss off a pregnancy woman." As she watched me blush, she pressed on, "He is gorgeous, totally into you. He had proved himself again and again, he even choose you over his sister."

"Ah.." I swallowed, feeling uncomfortable, I had been avoiding thinking about what ever was between us. From experience, I knew she wouldn't drop it unless she went into labour. I sighed, leaning against the washing machine, as it rumbled. "He is amazing and I like him a lot," I heard Daisy give a snort of disbelief. "Okay, I like him a lot, he makes me feel safe, protected and he accepts me, all of me." I paused, biting my lip and playing with my glasses. "But he is almost too good to be true. I really don't know him."

Daisy frowned, putting a reassuring hand on my shoulder, "You always get in your own way."

"We haven't actually done it yet," I looked anywhere but at her.

Daisy covered her mouth, "What, oh my god, are you joking." She shook her head from side to side with disbelief. "What are you waiting for?"

"I don't honestly know, he has been really understanding." I laughed, enjoying the girl talk. We hugged again. As I went into the computer room to check the tracker, Daisy went off, taking about food.

The tracker had stopped and I looked up the location, google maps gave me a visual. It was an old Victorian building within its own grounds, in Hampstead. Sunny could probably find out more details.

Putting my feet up, I started looking through the files we had. I sat up when I saw that Sunny had highlighted, Professor May was coming to London for an event in three days. Looking online, there were tickets, very expensive tickets. With no pause, I booked five, knowing there was no better opportunity to get to him. Though we might have to work at fitting in. Though perhaps I also need to find out if I can cover more than just myself. I decided to make a list of what I thought we needed to do.

But then I heard Sunny's excited tones and left up. She was walking in to the living room, expansively talking nonstop. Grayson had an amused look, Maggie was laughing and Daisy looked a little shell-shocked. Sunny caught sight of Daisy and lunged at her, hugged her tightly. "I feel like you are family already. I bet that you have lots of embarrassing stories about her," and winked.

Daisy visibly relaxed. "You and I are going to get on very well." I shrugged, knowing that they were probably gonna be ganging up on me. When I got my hug, Sunny was quiet and the hug very tight.

I pulled back looking her in the eye, I recognised someone holding on by a thread. Waving at the others, "Give us a moment guys," ignoring Graysons questioning look. I dragged her to the computer room, "What happened."I folded my arms and waited, as she wondered around the room. Finally she stopped, shook her head and braced her arms on a table. I just waited.

In a hesitant and breaking voice, "It was a crazy after you left, but we were working. To be honest better than before. We discovered a safe house, we raided it and rescued some people." She pulled up the image of the blonde scary lady, "She was one of them, she played us. She played Marcus and William." She hugged herself, her speech becoming faster, "It was strange, like magic." I blinked, knowing that it was probably her gift. "William was smitten, she came to all the meetings. The occult team were suspicious of her, they made the mistake of telling Marcus. He did not take it well."She took in a shuddering breath, "The next night all we saw were nightmares. And they continued when we woke up, they didn't end. Awful, living nightmares." She started sobbing, heart wrenching sobs.

Standing, I took my chain off, settled myself and reached out with positivity. With great concentration, I pushed these feelings into Sunny. Again and again, I heard her sobbing slow. I kept going until I felt no more sadness, blackness from her. Then feeling tired, I opened my eyes and saw Sunny's shoulders drop, her face relax and she smiled a sad but genuine smile. "Thank god, I don't know what you did but it has gone." Crying afresh, she hugged me tight.

"Sunny, what happened to Marcus?"

"They took him and others. That bitch."

I leaned back, puzzled. Why would they have moved against Marcus, to be honest I had thought that they were small fry, unless.. "Did something happen before the raid, did you collect new info?"

Thoughtfully, "I don't know."

"I am glad that you are safe and we are going to talk about all of this later but now you need to rest." She wanted to argue but I led her to her room. "Rest and then we will kick arse."

I joined the others in the living space, there were a subdued atmosphere. Maggie was huddled on one of the chairs, tears drying on her cheeks. I sat down next to Grayson and pushed into his side, he lifted an arm and placed it around my shoulders.

"I guess that Maggie has filled you in a little. There was an attack, they took people and left the others tortured with nightmares."

Maggie sniffed, "I managed to contact two, one made no sense at all, they other told me the awful things that he was seeing and then…" she gulped, "..ended it." She dissolved into uncontrollable sobbing, full of anguish. "I left them," she wailed. Daisy sat next to her and stroked her hair.

Grayson leant forward. "Maggie, you would have suffered with them. We will get revenge."

I stood up, "Grayson, I am going to need you to call anyone you think can be trusted. We have work to do." He pulled out his phone to make the calls. I got up ands made sandwiches, so that everyone could eat them later. Then helped get Maggie to her room.

Daisy quietly hugged me, took a sandwich and went quietly to her room.

I sat in the dark, looking at the night sky. I sent out a sphere of protection around the whole building. Then I walked around, checking the entrances and alarms. Then I rang Catherine, to warn her of what had happened. She had heard of something like this before but not on such a scale. She said that they would avoid anyone new and double check the new recruits. At the end, I asked how Grayson's sister was. There was a long pause, "Olivia, she has run away, I had placed a tracker in her. It shows that she heading to London. I think that passed on her behaviour here, she is joining them, we will be relocating."

I frowned, "Can you let me have her tracking info and we will follow her."

She signed off, "Will do, be safe and give my love to Grayson." She sighed off with a chuckle.

I was left alone in the dark.

CHAPTER 19

I fell into a fitful sleep, my eyes gritty when I reluctantly blinked them open in the early morning light. Without disturbing Grayson, I crept out of bed to grab coffee. As I stood appreciating that first hit of caffeine, Sunny wondered out of her room. I was relieved to see that she looked completely different to how she arrived yesterday. The bright smile and attitude that I had come to expect was back, though the naivety that had been there before was gone. She had changed, but as I reflected we all had.

She was excited, like a child at Christmas, to see all that the computer room had to offer. I left her playing happily.

I thought that Maggie needed a distraction. I was right, she had dark circles under her eyes and a dejected air. Begging her for help in shielding, she reluctantly got up and came down to the training room with me. I showed her how I had been shielding, a spark of interest appeared. She excitedly lectured me on her version of it, I hid the smile and the boredom. We agreed that my way worked and we would stick with that, with a little trial and error we managed to expand the area of shielding. I wondered if we could do it individually and with no distance limits. This made her thoughtful and she tried to send me away while she thought some things through.

With some doubt to remind her, I told her what I had done for Sunny. She was shocked and was again surprised at the simplicity of what I had done. She admitted that perhaps the way that I naively approached things worked better. I had no limits to what I would try, as I had no idea of what didn't work. She pushed for more details about what I had felt, what I had thought. Trying my best I explained what I could, though I didn't really remember the exact details. This brought on a huff of exasperation, when I asked her what she would have done. She had a more complicated explanation, based on energies involving the speaking of certain words. I nodded my way through, scared that if she thought I wasn't following her, she would deepen the explanations.

I left with warnings ringing in my ears. As I acted instinctually, I left myself vulnerable. All the extra, what I thought of as useless were protection. They warded and allowed for inattention. I rubbed my neck uncomfortably, at the thought of the promise she had got from me. That I would train with her.

I came up the kitchen, hungry now that I realised I had missed breakfast. My stomach growled at the much Daisy was making. Though as I stole some cucumber, Daisy smacked my hand. Laughing I moved onto the living area, where I found Grayson checking emails. I leaned against him and again his arm pulled me into his side. I sighed at the comfort I felt. Playing with his hand, I told him of my morning.

He squeezed my hand, "Good, I have found two people I trust."

"I trust you. As an extra caution, perhaps we make initial contact somewhere and I can meet them."

He nodded in agreement, "Lets get that done today."

I paused, sitting forward and looking him in the eye. "There is something that I haven't told you yet. I have booked some tickets for this thing that Professor May is doing, it is in a couple of days. I thought that we should use this opportunity!"

Grayson pulled away from me and put his head in his hands. "I should be grateful that you actually told me, I guess." He groaned, "You do realise how dangerous that this will be?" He stood suddenly and started pacing, "Look at what we have to work with," waving his hand randomly. "You are going to get them hurt."

I surged up, powered by hurt, "You don't think that I know that? I know that it is dangerous but we have to do this, I feel that it is necessary and will be enlightening." I turned to him, looking him in the eye. "This is what we have to so, you are going to have to trust me."

He looked back and there was something in his expression, something that made me uncomfortable but I didn't know what it was. Before I could think further on it, he shook his head and said "Fine but we had better, I mean it really be prepared." He hugged me to him, "You are so special, I don't want anything to happen to you." I felt the sincerity in his words and relaxed into his hug.

"I thought that prehaps, it would be better if Catherine or at least some of her team were there?"

"You sure?" Again there was something in the tone.

"No, I trust her and she is ahead in terms of all of this. There is something else."

"Do I want to know?"

"Your sister has woken up and she has left." I pulled back to look at him. He had closed his eyes and was holding himself really stiff.

"Where did she go?"

"They don't know but they have tagged her with a tracker and I have the details, somewhere in London." He turned away, looking out of the window, "We will find her Grayson."

I waited, he finally nodded, "Good". Distracted, he said, "Why don't we try that tracker now."

"Okay," and I followed him slowly.

Sunny had pulled it up, "She is in London.. Hampstead." She is at that address that you looked up from the tracker you placed, she is with them." She looked up at Grayson, who's face had gone wooden.

"Grayson, she isn't herself. We can get her back."

"Sunny we are going to need everything on this place. Is that address?"

"Yes!"

"Its the place where the reception is for Professor May, where I want us to go."

Sunny covered her mouth and just stared at me.

Grayson's phone beeped, "The guys will be there soon."

"Here are the plans," I looked over at them. My stomach dropped with the realisation of how big it was.

"We are going to have to recon this place and then we can plan."

Grayson looking over my shoulder, "Nick and I will scout it and then come back. Send me some of these plans."

"We will need to be cautious, if Cecilia is there voluntarily, then we have to presume that they have learnt something."

Grayson came over and hugged me tightly, gently lift my chin and place a soft kiss onto my lips. I looked after him as he left, until Sunny none too subtly coughed. I rolled my eyes and turned back towards her. She waggled her eyebrows, making me laugh. I nudged her with my arm and pulled a chair along side her. "Lets have a go looking through all of the stuff that I left you."

"It was like homework," she groaned. Worried, I was about to apologise but then realised that she was trying to hide a smile.

"Stop it, you shouldn't tease me."

She grasped my arm, "You saved me but no, that doesn't prevent teasing."

"You sure you are okay, do I need to do anything?"

"No, I am feeling myself but I started to wonder whether you would be able to help others?"

"I should have thought of that. I want to help but they can't come here."

"I know."

"Also, I think that we should see whether Maggie can also do it. It will help spread it out."

As if we had called her, Maggie popped her head around the door. Seeing our faces, "What?"

"Come in. I was wondering if you could do what I did to Sunny?"

"I was thinking about it after you left and I think that I could, though I will approach it differently." She looked over at Sunny, "You think you can get them to meet us?"

"I will find somewhere and get a list of people."

"Maggie, I also want you to look over these plans. There may be some designs that suggest what they might have inshore for us."

"I can look at them but I think that they way to go, will be charms and talismans. They will work for everyone, it will also help with the shielding that you wanted." She glanced at the plans again, "You really look for trouble don't you."

Innocently I spread my hands, "These things just seem to happen to me." They both wore identical expressions of skepticism. I really couldn't blame them, "Well at least this is more planning than I normally do. You guys are bad influences on me." This caused them to laugh uncontrollably, I couldn't help but laugh with them, Grateful for them being there.

Daisy popped her head around, "What you all doing?"

"We are teasing her, join in."

"Oh, I am good at that, before this, it was my life's work." This led to them really letting go. I blushed, really glad that Grayson wasn't here. There should be some secrets between boyfriend and girlfriend, though to be honest I didn't know that we were that. We continued over a late lunch and it was fun.

After lunch, I went to read though some more stuff on bed. It felt like I had a plan and it was nice having a team. As I did, I felt something like a buzz in my mind. I nipped my head, absorbed in what I was reading. Then it happened again, I froze. Holding my chain, I closed my eyes and tried to focus on that feeling. It was a brush, a touch of something. The more I tried to concentrate on it, the further away that it seemed to go. When I realised that, I relaxed and let myself to be open to it. Slowly my consciousness rose, through the ceiling, through the room and I opened my eyes. I was suspended above London. As I looked around, I could see the glows of different energies. The lower intensity, that were normal people and the occasional flash of something brighter. Sudden a brush of air against my cheek, like someone had blown on me. Swinging around, I felt fear and realised how easily I could get lost like this, I had floated away from my building. I calmed myself and thought how my body felt and that I wanted to return.

I sat up, in my bed and in my body. I gasped, I still felt as if I could float away, opening my eyes I saw Maggie at the end of my bed. "Shit, what the fuck Maggie! I almost had a heart attack."

Continuing to frown at me, "Do you know how dangerous it is leave your body without an anchor? Of course, what am I talking about, you never know." She starting to pace angrily, waving her hands in the air. "Do you listen to anything I say! I can not believe that you would be so irresponsible, you are a child driving a car." She pointed at me dramatically, "You are going to start learning or I am out of here. I will not have you die or worse on my watch."

"Worse than dying?"

"There are much worse things," she said ominously.

Seeing how angry she was and that this anger came from guinuine fear for me. "I am sorry, really I am. Something called to me and I followed it." I held up my hand, "Yes, stupid. I got it and I will learn but remember that sometimes the fact that I don't know the accepted limits gets us results."

She glared at me, okay not a time for reason, she actually started an imaginative and resourceful wave of swearing. I had to cover my ears, I saw Sunny and Daisy crowding the doorway. Casting an imploring look for help, they vehemently shook their heads and backed away. Cowards, though I saw their point when sparks started to pop off Maggie. There was a massive release of static, my hair was standing up as was Maggie's. She was out of control. Tremendously I focused on calm, tranquility, peace, it was hard with all the distractions. Finally I released it out flooding the room.

Abruptly Maggie stopped, in mid sentence. Scrambling off the bed, I softly asked, "Maggie?"

"You are a shit, you ruined my self righteous rant." Then reluctantly, "Good work though, I might have been getting slightly carried away."

With the silence, the others popped their heads around the

door again. Sunny asked, "Everything alright?"

"Maggie was trying to keep me safe and was expressing her anger imaginatively."

"Haha, very funny," Maggie said. "But I am sorry if I scared you."

Daisy nervously giggled, "No it's alright, I was a little startled but I knew you had to under control."

"Really?" Sunny muttered under her breath.

Maggie obviously heard but choose to ignore it. We all made our way to the kitchen, Daisy making us all big mugs of tea. I looked at it but obviously realised that no-one was going to be offering anything stronger.

"Maggie you are right but I also got to follow my instincts. After all they got us here."

Maggie rested her head in her hands, "I know, I am torn between admiring your courage but your stupidity. It will get you killed." As we sat in silence, I thought on what she said, knowing that she was right. But knowing that I wouldn't be probably doing anything differently.

"Anyway I am off to meditate and I will leave some books for you to get started."

I was washing up, as I heard voices from below. Easily I stretched out, I felt Grayson's presence and one other. Looking at the clock, it was after eleven. Grayson's eyes immediately found me in the dark of the kitchen. He hugged me, "Everything good?"

"Yes, just talking to the girls. Who is this?"

His eyes watched me carefully but answered, "This is Nick, he has come to help our little band of misfits."

I held my hand out, "Thank you for coming Nick."

Nick was a stocky dark haired man, his eyes flicked over me and he smiled. "You are everything that Grayson said, he has been talking about you nonstop."

"You are French?"

"Oui, but I have been living in England a long time. I would like to join you on this journey. I need to help end this and I hear that you have more of a chance than most." He indicated Grayson with his head, "I trust him, so I trust you."Stepping forward more, I held my hand out again and after a pause he placed his much larger hand in it. I closed my eyes and felt. I could feel his strength, no deceit but a deep well of sadness.

I nodded and smiled, feeling reassured. "Sorry, are you hungry?"

"No, I will look around, familiarise myself with the layout, then turn in."

In my room, I shoved all the files that I had left on the bed together in a pile. Grayson came out of the shower, rubbing his hair dry, a towel slung around his lean hips. I could not help but look, feeling warm. Gulping, I licked my lips involuntarily. Grayson came to a stop, his eyes becoming hooded. My breaths came quicker and I couldn't look away from him, though I knew the danger. He stalked towards me, darkly intent. I stood and backed away. He came right unto me, backing me against the door. His arms came up and caged me in. He lowered his head, I could feel slow kisses over my jaw, refusing to meet my hungry lips, he moved back up the other side.

I let my own hands drift lightly over his stomach and chest and into his hair. He paused and then let go of control, plundering my mouth. Lost in a storm of sensations and feelings. I felt realised, he pulled me up and my legs entwined around him. He pushed harder against me and I welcomed it, it was overwhelming, wonderful and all consuming.

Without warning, pain lanced through my brain. I couldn't help but scream. Awful lancing pain, running along all my nerves. It wasn't helped by someone screaming, dimly I realised that it was me. Someone lay me down on a bed, Grayson holding me and calling for help. I rolled throwing everyone off me, every touch and noise made things worse. Vaguely I saw Maggie, talking in my ear. Arching my back, I panted with pain. Maggie shouted, "You need put your shields up, something is attacking you. I am going to ward you but I can't with you giving off so much energy. You need to share the pain with the others, so that you and I can do this."

Vehemently I shook my head, "No, I can't, I won't hurt them."

Maggie looked me in the eyes, holding my head. "You have to, everyone agrees, look at them." Looking around though half closed eyes at them all, they all nodded.

"Not Daisy," I bit out.

Maggie moved her head at Daisy, indicating the door. She reluctantly left, her worry and fear obvious.

I gasped again, closing my eyes against the pain. Maggie screamed at me, "Do it now Olivia, now!"

Reaching out to everyone, I pushed pain out to them. Suddenly I could breath, blessed relief. The pain was still there but I was able to think through it. As I looked around, Maggie was casting and the others had collapsed. I focused, feeling the wall that Maggie was building, I thrust all the pain and my anger into it. I pulled the pain from the others and pushed that in to. Collapsing back, I blew my breath out and swore colourfully. There were various groans and swearing from the others. Grayson dropped and collapsed across me, linking our hands.

Nick spat out, "I speak for everyone, when I say. What the fuck was that and why was this not mentioned in induction?"

Maggie, bracing herself against the wall, brushed her hair out of her eyes. "It was a psychic attack. It would ultimately have driven her mad."

Shuddering at the memory of that pain, that had been disgusting and violating. "Who and why?"

Maggie looked a little awkward, "Ah, I felt a huge energy surge before you started screaming. It was like lighting a firework in a pitch back night. It would have drawn unwanted attention."

I blushed and avoided Grayson's eyes. Everyone turned to look at me and I felt that my face was on fire. It didn't help that Nick winked at me, knowingly.

"Well, I guess that I had generated a lot of energy. I hadn't thought to guard it." At the looks, I whispered looking down,

"I guess that getting excited, or turned on gives me ebergy." I could not look anyone in the eye, it was so embarrassing.

Maggie was trying to hide her smiles, but failing miserably. I was so not amused but the corners of my mouth twitched. I groaned and covered my eyes, "I just can't catch a break."

Nick laughed loudly, slapping Grayson on his back. "Poor Grayson."

I had been trying to avoiding Grayson's eyes but now a looked towards him. He smiled and gave the back of my hand a kiss. "It's okay Olivia. We will get through this and when we do." He said while looking at me intensely. I felt goosebumps, summarised by Nicks whistle and Maggie's giggles.

Dismissing them, I turned back to Maggie, "Is it still going on?"

She closed her eyes, "I think so, but now it feels more like a search."

I sat up, pushing sweaty hair off my face and pulling my top down. "This is an opportunity, how about if I step outside, out of the barrier, with my protection up and try to locate the source."

Maggie had a huge frown, I tilted my head, pushing my eyes and gave it my best puppy dog eyes. "Please Maggie, you know that we need to."

Maggie pursed her lips and stood up, "No. Are you going to talk to her?" Looking at Grayson, who had also raised himself up.

"I really don't know why you are arguing, she is going to do it anyway, lets save time and just help her."

Maggie sighed deeply, looked at the floor for a while. "Fine, obviously nothing I have said yesterday, sunk in."

I smiled, grabbed my chain, gave a quick kiss to Grayson. I hurried out after Maggie, before she changed her mind. I grabbed a jacket and shoes. I put them on while hopping. I opened the door to the garage, looking back at Maggie who had her eyes closed and her hands out. "Now."

I stepped out and walked briskly to the building across the road. Just before I stepped off our property, I concentrated on building my wards. Despite what had just happened, I felt full of energy and power. Stretching out my senses, I built a protective bubble around me. I layered it again and again. Then remembering the pain, I added additional layers. As I left Maggie's protective bubble, I felt a slight heat against me.

Leaning against the wall, I let my consciousness rise up and over the building. Looking carefully back at my buliding, I could just make out a tenticle of pure darkness. Darker than the deepest black. It seemed to be moving around Maggie's protection, probing. Following it, I could see a long tail stretching out backwards from it. I flew, following it to the source. I was aware that I was taking a risk, my heart rate rising. The tail was thinning, but it was East. I sped up, feeling a sudden urgency. I sped up, though I was on a mission, I could appreciate how amazing that it all was. The thought did cross my mind, as to whether anyone could actually do this in real life. No stop that. Finally the trail ended in a quiet, green area outside of London. I hovered over a sign nearby, Epping. I had only heard of Epping Forest. I tried to memorise the building and area.

Then I visualised myself back to my body. It was a shock, I opened my eyes to find that the head of the thing was looking at me. Automatically I throw myself to the side at the same time to throw a power ball at it. Scrambling I ran back to my building. It charged at me but I managed to get in, it was primal and very angry.

I pushed more power into the shields, Maggie came out also chanting. "What do we do?' I yelled, quite freaked out at the moment.

She had gritted her teeth, "I don't know."

Well, I guess I was going to do something stupid then. I looked at my hands, pushing more and more power into them. They started to shine and grabbed on to the head, blasting it away. It recoiled back, howling silently and twisting angrily. Then it was gone, I sank to my knees as Maggie dropped her hands.

I heard Nick's voice behind us, "Well I can see that being here is going to be full of danger and excitement, I love it."

Maggie and I started laughing hysterically.

CHAPTER 20

"So what was it?" Daisy asked fearfully, as we came into the kitchen, a hive of food preparation. I cluelessly looked at Maggie, "Don't look at me, I am new to all of this." Then promptly stuffed some hot buttery toast in my mouth. As per my new norm I was famished, eating was also a welcome distraction from what I had just seen.

Nick, had stopped eating, I stuck my tongue out and kept going. He just shock his head with an amused smile and pulled his food closer to him. Maggie was nursing a tea and holding her head in one hand. "I don't know what it was and that really scares me. Ands the way that you got rid of it."

Grayson rubbed my tense back, "What do you mean?"

Maggie, "She blasted it away, so much power, so little control."

"Will it know what I did, where I am?"

"I am not sure," Maggie replied wearily. "It could have been drawn to you, but again I don't know."

"So I guess that the first priority is ramping up our magical and non-magical protection."

"I can get the regular security up," Nick said, with his mouth full of food.

"Say it don't spray it," Daisy laughed, throwing him a napkin.

Graysons hand stopped moving on my back, I looked up and he looked angry. His jaw was clenched, his eyes narrowed but then as he caught my eye. He ran his hand through his hair, "Maggie can you put us in touch with people who can provide the other."

"Once we help those suffering, they will be able to help us and will be falling over themselves to do it."

I thought, in case anything went wrong, I needed to do this.

At least I could help these people. "Maggie, I know that you are tired but let us get this set up for today."

Sunny said, "I can get started on that, I think I have found somewhere nearby. I am sure that people will come. I am actually gonna start now, then catch some sleep." Then casting a worried look at me, she smiled and left.

Daisy came over to Maggie, gentling pulling her up to her feet. "Come on Maggie, you look exhausted. Sunny can contact everyone, come and crash." Gently she led her out.

Grayson and Nick had made their escape and I was left in the empty room. I closed my eyes, tears gathered. I was so exhausted, battered by everything that was happening, confused by my emotions for Grayson and my fear for the future. It was all too much. I silently screamed into my hands, I was glad that I was all tapped out and couldn't produce any fireworks. I stood, leaning on the desk as I tried to get myself back under control.

"What are you doing?" Daisy's voice cut through my pity party. I didn't look up, not sure that I had it all locked back in. "Let it out, you don't have to be strong for us all the time."

I gritted my teeth, "I do. I make things worse."

"No, you have been thrown into an impossible situation and you are doing good."

I laughed hollowly, "You sure?"

"Oh my, you are deep in the pity party. Shall I invite more people, blow up some balloons?"

"Can I have five more minutes," I begged.

"Okay, I will just sit here. Me and my baby."

"Okay, you win. Are you joining in the party?"

"No and you have less than four minutes left."

I laughed ruefully. I looked at Daisy, "Are you alright?"

"I am content but scared. I have life growing inside me and I feel such a connection to it. I feel as if all my life has led me to this and that this child is going to be something great."

"How do you know?" I was fasciated by the glow that she had and the utter confidence that she had in what she was saying.

She looked mature, a Madonna in her serenity.

"I just do." She paused and looked at me mischievously, "Is it Grayson?"

Blushing, "No."

"Are you self sabotaging? Why can't you just accept the comfort he offers. It doesn't have to be more than that."

"There is something? I am not sure, it is probably all in my head." When did things become so complicated, ah yes when my life went up in flames. "I told him that I would be more careful and then I just ..didnt."

"No, you did what you needed to do, it is always what you do."

"That sounds suspiciously from Star Trek," raising my eye brow at her.

Laughing, she lifted her hands in surrender, "I won't deny but time is up. Go to bed, tomorrow is another day." Daisy raised my chin and said gently, "Don't worry, it will all work out at the end, an amazing story that you will tell my kid."

I stood and hugged her hard, "Thank you, you are the best."

She winked at me, "I know but I am sorry too. I took us to that party and I didn't leave with you. I just wanted to belong so strongly, have a family. I didn't realise that I had one with you." She looked down, I saw that tears silently falling. I hugged her close to me, offering what comfort that I could.

"No," I shook my head not feeling that I could let go of the guilt, "I left you."

She vehemently shook her head and pulled back, so that she could look in my eyes and said slowly, "It was not your fault." And then she hugged me even tighter, I let go and we cried together.

Finally Daisy pulled back, "There that's all you get, go." She shooed me away impatiently.

I entered my dark room, Grayson was in bed appearing to be asleep. Thankfully, I washed up and got into bed, falling into a deep sleep.

I awoke with a start, knowing that I had slept later than I

OLIVIA AND THE SOCIETY

thought. I stretched in bed, feeling refreshed and lighter in my spirit. As my hands slipped over the covers, I touched Grayson's side of the bed, it had a fading heat.

I jumped out of bed knowing that today was busy, In the kitchen I snagged some cold toast and taking another cup of coffee with me, I followed voices to the computer room. Pausing outside it, I could hear the voices more clearly and it was clear that they were arguing about me. Placing a hand on the wall, I listening intently.

Daisy, "I am worried that this is all too much for her."

"It was Olivia who wanted, no insisted that we do recon prior to the conference," Grayson insisted, "So it has to be today."

"Daisy, I think that we can do it safely," Nick's accented voice carried quiet assurance.

Maggie sounded exhausted, "She will do it anyway, let us be realistic, we need to help her."

Sunny cut through them all, "Her instincts were right because there is a lot of activity at the house today and your sister is definitely there."

"What about this place in Epping?" Grayson spoke, worry evident in the timbre of his voice.

"I haven't had time to do more but don't worry it is on the list." Sunny sounded tired.

Maggie, "I am going to check on Olivia." The door must have shut because I couldn't hear more. I pondered on what I had heard, it wasn't anything earthshaking. Missing the sounds of Maggie leaving, she suddenly appeared around the corner. Pausing she looked behind her and kept going, catching my elbow and pulling me in her wake. As I opened my mouth she put a finger to her lips. I promptly shut my mouth and went along.

We entered her room, which looked like a library, papers and books were scattered everywhere. The walls had writing on them, spells, some of which seemed to move when I peered at them. I turned towards the books, a mixture of old and ancient. There was a definite smell of mould from one of them. I turned full circle, taking it all before I realised that Maggie was standing, with her hands on her hips, her head tilted to the side.

"Impressive." Then I waited, as she obviously had something to say. Silently I waited.

"Are you alright?" At my nod, she then let loose "Do you have no concern for your life at all?"

I properly thought about it, "I do but I did what was a good idea at the time."

She shook her head in defeat, then pulled me in for a long hug. Not only did she embrace me physically but also blanketed me with her energy. "Lets go and help some people."

She let go but still looking into my eyes. "Right, let's grab Nick."

As I did my own grabbing, of my jacket, I paused in front of the mirror. I looked at this woman, my hair was in a messy ponytail, my body leaner than it had been, my eyes not as innocent as they had been. But there was also strength there. I had become someone different and better. There was a niggle though, something said this morning had made my on edge. As I turned, I caught sight of Grayson's bag that was lying half under his side of the bed, like it hadn't been kicked under properly. Quickly I glanced at the door and knelt quickly. Pushing aside some guilt I pulled it out further and looked inside. There was a phone tucked under some clothes. A different phone to the burners we had, he had said to get rid of our old phones. It was unsurprisingly locked. I frowned, then hearing some noise I shoved it back under and left. I didn't have time to think about this right now but my bad feeling had intensified.

Nick led us to one of the cars, I pulled open the back seat door. "You can have the front Maggie, I am just going to centre myself a little." Nick looked happy, I smiled slyly. Oh that was interesting and was something that definitely lifted my spirits.

Maggie and Nick chatted as we drove, I rested my head back against the head rest and focused on my breathing. As I drifted, I lost track of time and jumped when Maggie's voice cut in, "We are here."

We got out and went up the backstairs of building, that opened to a medium sized meeting room. It already about fifteen people in it. I stumbled, at the overwhelming tdespair and pain that was in the room. Nick came to my side and supported me, Maggie whispered, "You are going to have to shield yourself right now." Her face was also pinched, I visualised a shield over myself. Once that was done, the feelings retreated somewhat. Relieved that I could breathe easier, I pulled my chains from around my neck, wrapping it around my right hand. Nick noticed and raised his eyebrows but said nothing.

Deeper into the room, I could see that the people were in varying states. Some were crying softly, some were catatonic, some were moaning and rocking themselves. I allowed myself to be pulled towards a teenager standing at the window, staring out. "Hello?" There was no response, I repeated myself. Gently I turned her towards me, her eyes were bloodshot and empty. I could not help but be creeped out. "My name is Olivia and I am going to try to help you, you need to relax." Placing my hands on her shoulders, she stiffened at my touch but said nothing. Closing my eyes, I replicated what I had done for Sunny. Harder because I was shielded but pushed all the light feelings towards her. Hearing a gasp, I opened my eyes, she was standing there, crying silently, her eyes no longer dull. "Oh my god, thank you," she whispered in disbelief. Forcing myself to smile, I moved onto the next person. Maggie directed me, keeping me focused, as well as fed. Gradually she took over my shielding, as it became harder for me to do both, though as we worked through the room there was less and less.

It was the emotional load that felt the hardest, while I was cleansing them I was exposed to images of their nightmares. Ruthlessly I put them to the side, I was aware that I couldn't focus on them right now. My shoulders were very tight, up roundly ears, despite me stretching and rolling my neck out. It seemed that it would never end, more arriving to replace those who felt better. Nick had tried to protest but I wearily waved them in. I could not in all good conscious turn them away. I healed whoever I was put in front off, ate and drank what ever was given to me.

My headache had started to pound, made worse with every step that I took. Nick went to grab some painkillers. Blindly I reached out for the last one, just holding on.

As such I was unprepared for the voice that immediately resonated in my head. Opening my eyes, I found piecing blue eyes looking at me. There was a sharpness that I was not in the condition to meet. "What are you?" The voice was superior, cutting, unsympathetic, bringing to mind a scientist with a bug. It felt like blade slicing through my brain, I winced and with dwindling reserves I reinforced my shields. The pressure became more variable, straightening in my chair from the slump that I had found myself.

I replied out loud, to make Maggie aware, who had just turned back. "I think that it is impolite to ask me questions in my head." Maggie stiffened by my side and signalled Nick.

The woman sat back, "I apologise, was that rude? I am have never really cared about the niceties."

"You aren't catching me at my best.'

"I think that I am," she said as she looked around the room, at the people talking and laughing with each other. "You have eased a lot of pain," she sounded disappointed, "I like pain. No I have to wonder how you did it. I could feel that deliciousness disappearing and I had to come and see why."

I sat back, a horrible suspicion rising, "Did you cause their pain?"

"Yes, it was beautiful." She raised her hand warningly, "Don't try to tell them, I have so many wonderful such gifts."

"I can't say that I agree."

"Well, you are apparently entitled to your opinion. I will ask again, what are you?" Her voice had tightened, her long nails tapping on the table. "I am not used to waiting, it makes me testy.'

Not wanting to make her torture anyone again, "How about

we ask each other questions," I proposed, "We will take turns, I am sure that I can learn a great deal."

She sat back and crossed her legs delicately, I could not hero but note enviously her extremely high heels. I catalogued her outfit, designer short skirt and sheer blouse with a short jacket. Sitting near her, I was very aware of how I smelt and probably looked. There was no doubt that she was powerful and trained.

"Alright, how fascinating. I haven't been intrigued by anything in a very long time. Though to make you more comfortable, I think it safest that they all leave." Looking towards Maggie, I saw that she was too shocked to be any immediate help. Nodding at Nick, he began immediately and efficiently clearing the room. At last, only Maggie and Nick were left, "Nick, take her."

At her continued reluctance, I said "Please Maggie, just get things prepared in case."

As the last person left and closed the door behind them. I looked towards the woman who she nodded regally at me in approval. I pushed my glasses up with my left, trying not to draw attention to my chains around my right. Luckily I had been sitting with that angled away when she sat down. I wouldn't bet that she had not noticed, I had a feeling that nothing escaped her. With difficulty I gathered my tattered confidence and power.

"Who hired you to do this terrible thing to all these people?"

"You are like a little mouse that is looking at the cheese and ignoring the mouse trap."

"That was not an answer to my question."

"Very well, little mouse. He is known as Chen, a powerful man that help his friends. Your power reminds me of him, the friend that he helped."

She crossed and recrossed her legs, "Where do you come from?"

"I was born in the Society and I am not sure how I was made." I couldn't really give her anymore and I actually felt there was a plus in not really knowing.

"How and where did you get your powers and training?"

"I am a witch. Chen trained me, he could do that for you."

"I am okay as I am."

She laughed, "You are so sweet. You are naïve, there is no good or evil just power. I could just destroy you like that," and she clicked her fingers.

"Well I wouldn't like that, very Marvel."

"I like you, you are a feisty mouse. Why did you reverse my spell?"

"Because it was the right thing to do." I pushed my chin out.

"Hmm, that's not really a thing, as I have said. It is something that people say but they aren't the ones in power. I think that you are very young in terms of life experience. You have things to learn, I think that Che would like to teach you. You would be much more interesting."

"Is there any chance that Chen lives near Epping?'

She could not hide her start, she narrowed her eyes at me and hissed, "How did you know that?"

"I followed something there."

She sat back, pulling imaginary dust off her shirt as she recrossed her legs. "So that was you?" She paused, "How surprising?" She pursed her lips, looking me over again.

"How can I contact Chen? If I ever need to."

"I think that you will find that he will be contacting you. As a courtesy, here is my card." A card appeared between her fingers and she presented it to me. With hesitation I took it.

"Was Chen's friend Professor May."

"Yes," she smiled broadly, "For a newbie you are outstanding," She actually clapped her hands as she sat forward. "How did you know?"

"I have a score to settle with him? He threatens me and mine."

"He makes such trouble but often provides interesting recruits and subjects. I am not sure who would be the more valuable to Chen? You have the potential but he has the raw materials." She stood suddenly, "I really have to go back to Chen and relay this information. As I am intrigued by you, I promise not to harm you for reversing my spell." She waved by the door.

Nick and Maggie came running through as soon as she had gone and I once again slumped into my seat. They came closer and unloaded their hands, it was sandwiches and drinks. I grinned wanly and started eating. Maggie winked at me, "You could charge a lot quicker with Grayson!" I shock my head at her, my mouth full of food.

"Oh and these," Nick pulled out some paracetamol and ibuprofen.

"Thanks," I grabbed them and took them with a chug of water. Sensing that I needed a distraction while I ate, they started to talk and bicker. After twenty minutes I sat back and patted my stomach. "I needed that."

Nick said admiringly, "I don't think that I will ever get used to that."

Maggie asked, "How did you meet Grayson?"

"He drifted around a couple of groups while he was looking for his sister, seemed a good guy. He loves that sister of his, I didn't think he could love anyone more," winking at me.

I rolled my eyes, gathering the rubbish I put it in the bin. Now that my work was done, my stomach full and my headache gone. My mind was full of thoughts of what had occurred today. "Maggie, how is everyone?"

"They are alive, no longer tormented. I am still amazed by how you did it. You saved their lives, without any question." With tears in her eyes, she hugged me.

"We can talk about it later, I need to lie down, rest my eyes. We still have things to do today." Something was again niggling at the back of my mind, I also had a thought that I couldn't shake off.

We piled back into the car, with me at the back again and I closed my eyes, quickly falling aleep.

CHAPTER 21

When we arrived back, Nick had to call my name twice for me to rise like the dead and stumble in. Grayson's voice immediately raised in frustration, "What the hell happened now?"

I winced at the tone but only focused on getting to my bed. Maggie helped me off with my jacket and boots, I pulled the covers over and passed out.

All too soon from the darkness, my father called to me. Wearily but eagerly I followed. Suddenly I was there in our old house again. I looked around, touching and running my hand over my fathers' things. "Hey there," I ran towards him.

"You came back." My voice muffled, my head was buried in his sweater.

"Of course. I knew that this road was going to be and I am beyond sorry that I didn't prepare you. I should have." He looked me in the eyes,"You have done better than I could have hoped for."

"I have been stumbling from one thing to another."

"Maybe that is your way, thrust into a world that you don't know, how can you expect more. I need to tell you that you need to find Louise?"

"Louise? She told me to not look for her?"

"Listen to your instincts but you need to find her. Now I am sorry my love but you need to go.."

"But I don't want to," clutching at his sweater, breathing in his familiar scent. "I want to stay here, you can teach me."

"I wouldn't be able to help you, you are different."

I pulled back completely, looking him in the eyes, needing but scared to articulate my fear. "What am I? Am I human?" I whispered.

He put me away from him, a pitying sort of smile. "I tried to hide this from you for so long but you deserve too know." He took a steading breath, "You are human but also have some demon in you." He continued quickly at my sob, "You are my daughter, the most precious."

My heart was pounding and I could barely hear him. I refused to hear him. "No, I am a monster. I bring pain to those around me." I sobbed, kneeling on the floor. He just held me against him.

"Now you have to listen to me, I am not sorry about what you are. Do you hear me, I love you, so many people love you. You are my daughter. The demon does not define you." He hugged me tighter, "You are a fighter, a survivor and you are not for hiding in the shadows." His hands rubbed my back and his voice became hurried, "You need to go now, now!" I felt as if I was pushed away.

As I opened my eyes, there were tears streaking my face. My eyes swollen and gritty. A sob choked its way up, I covered my mouth, not wanting the others to hear. Pushing off the bed, I was entangled in the covers. Looking in the mirror did not make me feel better. There were huge dark circles under my eyes, which were blood shoot, my skin pale and dry. I looked awful, appropriate for something not human.

I had a job to do, so I had better look better. Maybe if I faked it hard enough, it would become true. Stripping off, I showered and put some effort into my make up. I went for the kick-ass look, dark eyes and all black. Finally, as I pulled on high boots and stood, I was impressed with how I looked. I decided that it would be better to hide my chain under my tank top, winding it around my waist.

Again in the mirror, Grayson's bag seemed to call to me. Kneeling I looked again through it and this time I used my gift. There was something about the phone, I pushed more and it was as if something shattered. His phone was black, scattered black areas over the clothes. I stood abruptly, a sick feeling in my stomach. Had I been this stupid and blind.

186

Someone knocked on the door. I stood for a moment, it wasn't Grayson and then answered. Opening the door to a surprised Nick, his hand still raised as if to knock again. I grabbed it and pulled him into the room, kicking the door shut as we turned. He stumbled but recovered quickly, "Nick, I need to check you, I need to know that I can trust you. It won't hurt."

He slowly nodded, I scanned him, there was a lot of pain, deeply hidden but a good heart and intentions. Very warm feelings for Maggie, I stopped. Relieved I hugged him and whispered with a choking voice, "I think that Grayson is not with us and is working for someone else."

He stiffened and then his hands came to rest on my hips. He leaned forward and whispered back in my ear,"I won't ask if you are sure because I know that you wouldn't say it otherwise. It would explain some things that have puzzled and I will admit worried me since I got here. But you realise that he knows everything."

I nodded and pulled away to pace, keeping my voice to a whisper. "To be absolutely sure, I need to scan him but I don't think that he will let me. I have developed this ability after we got together, he may also have some sort of resistance or protection to block it."

I paced, as Nick thought. "Let us do the recon, I think that something will happen there. His sister is there and while you were out he has been very pushy about it. Can you do your thing on his memory if we need to?"

Rubbing my neck, I thought about it. "I am going to have to talk to Maggie but seeing what I did today, there has to be."

"We will also have to tell Sunny, she need to check everything that he may have had access to and ensure that he has not done anything."

"You really think that this is real." I was exhausted all over again, my emotions running high. I did realise though that I wasn't upset, I was embarrassed but not heart broken, had I suspected.

"You do and we have to be prepped." He came over and rested

his hand on my shoulder comforting. "I know that this is hard, confirm it. We will go in two cars for extra safety. You okay?"

"I guess that I have to be," I straightened. Nick gave me a last pat on the shoulder and then left his face grim.

He paused by the door, "I am going to check everything again. I don't want any surprises. Are you going to be able to act as if nothing is wrong?"

"I will give it all I have." As he left, I sat on the bed surprised that I had accepted so easily that Grayson was a bad guy. How could I have never thought to scan him, I had left him closer than anyone. I rubbed my face, feeling another shower might be needed. He must have thought that me a complete idiot. At least I had not had sex with him, yuck. This was some bullshit. I brushed the tears that were at the corner of my eyes, fuck this.

Leaving the room, I found Maggie, looking fresh talking to Daisy. They both whistled when they saw me, "Wow, you look so bad-ass." I did a twirl, Maggie squealed, "Right I am changing."

Daisy laughed, "I wish I could join you but how about I feed you instead."

"Daisy, that's the way to my heart."

"I am already there."

"You know me too well."

Maggie pulled me into her room, I closed the door as she started to fling clothes around. "I know that this is recon but we can have some fun with it."

"Absolutely, I promise you alcohol when we get back."

"Yes, we deserve it." She pulled out in triumph a sheer black top and tight leggings. Impressed to her commitment, as she was usually in floaty dresses. While she was distracted I scanned her, all pure, true intentions.

I relaxed, I wasn't sure that I could take another one. While she was doing her make up, I touched her mind. Startled she looked at me in the mirror, her eyebrows raised. "Grayson is not a good guy, he is betraying us'. Her mouth opened into an O, her hand shook and I was glad that she hadn't anything near her eye at the time.

She closed her eyes, "I know that I shouldn't need to ask but are you sure?"

"Yes," I simply said out loud. "We are still doing this but we need to find away to return without him. I am going to need your help with something."

"Of course" and I explained what we might need to do. "Give some time to think on it, go eat something. You are going to need the energy."

I wondered to there kitchen, Daisy and Sunny were waiting. They joked about being left out while I scoffed the food down. As I finished off, I said that Nick had something to tell them before we leave and to do everything that he asked. Their smiled faded and they apprehensively nodded. I hugged them both together and then left.

In the garage, I found Grayson fiddling with the underside of one of the cars. He had nor realised that I was there, I made my steps softer. Perfect, very gently I scanned him. Like the phone and his bag, there was something that overlay him. That on a quick look would feel as if there was nothing wrong but now knowing what to look for I could see that false layer. I probed unsuccessfully for a chink in its layer, not wanting to make him aware I backed off.

He was humming off key, unaware of what I had done. I could tell that he was unusually happy about something, his excitement palpable. There wouldn't be such a good opportunity again, I focus laser like. Finally I found a minuscule gap, it showed as an extra deepness of dark. Slipped through I was hit with all the naked ambition at what ever cost. I almost vomiting in my mouth, I had thought he was someone special.

Not wanting to spend more time here, I backed off, knowing that I had my certainty. In time as he stopped whistling. As he pushed himself out from under the car he found me leaning against the car. He quickly slid a welcoming look on his face, which I might not have noticed before. "Hi, how are you feeling?"

Moving as if to hug me, I moved spinning around, as if to

show him my outfit. "What do you think?"

"I like it, it looks good," smiling appreciatively, I lowered my eyes so that he could not see the anger in my eyes.

"Are we set for tonight?"

"Yes, I know that I wasn't supportive before but I have changed my mind. We are all going to learn something." Now his smile looked creepy.

"I hope so Grayson, I need to get ahead of this."

Nick came down, and asked "You guys ready?"

Grayson said "Yes just waiting on Maggie."

"I will get her," smiling I ran for the stairs. At the top I found Daisy and Maggie. "Maggie, you thought about how I can alter his memories. I have my proof."

Daisy was looking shaky, "Olivia are you sure?"

"Yes, I am sorry. I know that you wanted him to be a good guy but he isn't and I can let him come back here."

"I know, I am just so shocked. Are you alright."

"I will be." Maggie told me a plan, "I will give it a try. Come on. You and Sunny lock up tight."

Nick throw me some keys once I got back, "You take that one," pointing to another car.

Grayson had already got into the one that he had been fiddling under. He opened his window, "Hey I thought that we were all going in one car!"

"No, Grayson. I think that this will be safer, we will be the point so that there are no surprises. That would be better, don't you think?"

Grayson looked as if he wanted to argue but pursed his lips instead. "Olivia, come with me and Nick can go with Maggie.."

Maggie appeared at my side, "No Grayson, we will have some girl time. You can't have her to yourself all the time."

"At least take my phone," as he tossed me a phone. I caught it and smiled, waving at him. As they pulled out, I took a good look at the phone, It wasn't one of our burners and was dark. I pushed power through it and burnt it, happy I put it to the side so that I could dump the remains further away from the others.

"Maggie, text Nick and tell him that we will take another route there. I don't think that Grayson will do anything without me there."

"I hope so," she whispered, her worry clear. So did I.

CHAPTER 22

We pulled to a stop while singing to a pop song. I felt that I had my game face on. Despite Grayson, I knew that we had a job todo.

We parked about three streets away, luckily it was free parking. Maggie had texted Nick as we arrived but I got out before we got a response. I needed to be out in the air, Maggie followed me out, "You got this?"

"What do you mean? About the man that I have been sharing a bed with, being a lying bastard. Or the fact that we are about to look around the enemies HQ?" I delivered in a dry voice and raised my eyebrow quizzically.

"Ehh."

"Don't worry Maggie, I have got both. I have to, how could I not with you guys at my side."

"Always."

"So we can do it, wipe his memory of our base?"

"Yes, it will help if he is relaxed and unsuspecting. Then do what you did before, get under his shielding and let yourself be drawn to the memories that you want to remove. Then burn them as you did the phone."

"Just like that!"

"Well for anyone else, there would be a whole ceremony, some chanting, some potions but hey you make it cheaper if nothing else."

"Well as long as I am value for money," I said with a wry look. She shrugged back, "What can I say."

Looking innocently at the ground, "So Nick seems really cool."

There was a pause, I glanced at her face seeing the blush that had appeared. "He seems okay."

Smiling I agreed. I focused on Nick and felt him nearby, there was the sense of suppressed anger about him. "They are nearby. You ready?"

"No but what the hell."

As we walked towards them, I was reassured by the amount of people out and about. As I passed my senses over them, they were all normal people, it would help us hide. Remembering belatedly, I stopped and concentrated on a shield around Maggie and myself. Once she nodded her approval, we moved on. Maggie pulled me behind a tree opposite the wall of the building that we had come to see. I rested my back and focused, easier now that I wasn't trying to walk at the same time.

The grounds were beautiful to the naked eye, expensively kept and maintained. With my other eyes, it was dotted with dark spots, lots of people, high levels of anxiety and a large under ground level that I was unable to sense fully. Disappointingly I did not sense Louise.

Opening my eyes, I told Maggie "They have over a hundred people in there." She frowned, seeing the danger.

"How many have gifts?"

"Maybe a quarter, if I am reading them right. Doesn't stop the others have weapons."

"Let meet the others."

I agreed, pondering what this might all mean. As we went around the corner she bent her head towards me, "Nick texted, Grayson is becoming a little agitated. I think that we have messed up a meeting or trap."

"Guess we better get this done then. Here is a good place, tell him to come here." I had spotted a perfect spot, a tree that had caused the wall to be built around it, with a small bench below. Due to the fact that it was in the shadows, no one was using it. With the branches, it would babe pretty private. Walking around the tree, I imagined building a shell of protection and invisibility. "What do you think?"

"Damm, that is impressive, here I brought these. They are stones that I have also imbued with protection for you. They will augment what you have constructed." She added, "I can't wait to see all that you can really do."

"Calm yourself. I am going to play nice to him, he will probably want to talk to me alone anyway."

"Yeah, talk."

I sat on the bench, a tingle form the stones that Maggie had placed at its foot. I leaned forward, so that my hair fell over my face. My heart beating a fast tempo, hearing mens voices just upped its beat. Then all too soon Grayson was sitting next to me, "Hey are you okay?" Gently pushing the hair from my face.

"I am just tired, I used a lot of energy today and we had to put some heavy shielding up to avoid some people."

"Its going to be alright, I think that the end is in sight." He held me close, lowering his mouth to my ear. "Won't it be fantastic when this is all over? We will be together and what a team we will make." There was a possessiveness that he was not trying to hide there.

I focused on keeping my body relaxed, "Tell me how it will all be alright. I am not sure that I can do this."

His smile was obvious through his voice, "You will have me. Nothing will happen to you, you are too powerful. They will do whatever you want. Imagine how powerful our children we will be."

Yeah, over your dead body. Oblivious to my reaction, caught up in his own fantasy, he pulled me closer into him. His grip hard and unforgiving. Tears of pure anger stung my eyes, as he lifted my chin, his eyes glittered in triumph at the sight of them. "Don't worry, I will be with you, if you follow my leave all this hiding and running will be over." Leaning forward with that ugly triumphant grin, he kissed me.

Letting it play, I ran my hands through his hair and sighed to alloy his fears. While he kissed me, I remained passive, which being the jerk he was didn't seem to bother him. While he was distracted, I pushed past the layers of self satisfaction and arrogance. Calling to me, any memories of us. Reassuringly he hadn't told anyone, he had hinted but wanted to hold onto this advantage. He had planned to bring us into the building, where they would take us. Rather than burn them out, I saw that I could smooth all the memories of us over, like disappearing footsteps in the sand. He would be left with gaps, I focused knowing that I needed to get them all.

My anger built at how amused he had been at my naivety, though also envy at my power. There was typical male arrogance and anger that I had not slept with him. Disturbingly vivid images of what he planned to do once he had revealed himself. This pushed me out, a rolling nausea in my stomach.

I came to myself, finding that he had bent me back on the bench and was obviously grossly aroused. I pushed him off me, my lips dry. Cluelessly he asked, in a deep voice "Whats the matter?" I realised with interest that I had not gained any power from his kiss, so I had to be emotionally connected for that. Something that had obviously just occurred to him, as his brows furrowed. Looming over me, his smile slipped, "What has happened?"

"Nothing, this isn't the place?" Fighting the urge to let him have it, my hands trembled. A confused look appeared on his face and he sat back, "Who are.."

He didn't get to finish as Nick slipped behind him and hit him. Shuddering with delayed reaction and disgust, I rubbed at my lips and stood. Maggie hugging me, as we both looked at Grayson slumped over. "You did well, I don't think I could have let him touch me."

I dragged my sleeve across my lips again, "He hasn't told anyone about us, not in detail, just hinting that he had a great prize. I am sure that they drew their own conclusion. He was scared that he wouldn't get any credit." I kicked his leg, "Dick."

Maggie smiled widely but pulled me back, "Let me just check." She stood forward and held her hands over Grayson, muttering under her breath.

Muttering under my breath, "You couldn't have done that before? Why did he have to stick his tongue down my throat." Shuffling around to Nick, so that I didn't disturb her. Nick was repeatedly looking at his watch. , though I really wanted to. Nick started to shuffled on his toes, as he stared at his watch. Maggie with sheer concentration ignored us, her muttering getting louder. My hairs rose on the back of my neck, there was a stickiness to the air. Unconsciously I stepped back, noticing that Nick did the same.

With fascination we watched as nasty boils erupted all over Graysons, without a word we stepped further back. It was probably petty of me but I loved it. Finally Maggie straightened up. She staggered and Nick was there immediately. He whispered something in her ear and despite her exhaustion she blushed. "What did you do? Though I love his makeover, the outside matches the inside now."

She grinned proudly, "That was simple, a really old fashioned spell. What took time was that I checked your work and messed more with his memory." She raised her hand, "I trust you but it is better to double check. I couldn't do what you did, especially with him like this."

Setting aside my annoyance that she had essentially double checked, it was better that she did, I could have missed something. "Lets go, Nick you got his keys?"

He patted his pocket and nodded, still with an arm around Maggie. She smiled wanly but gave me a thumbs up. It was lighter and fresher outside our little bubble, lifting my head I appreciated the air on my face. Feeling the cloud that had been bothering me lift away. As we moved away, I collapsed the protection that we had set up. Looking back, I could see Grayson moving groggily. Speeding up, we distanced ourselves.

Catching up with the others, I included Nick in the shield. Maggie turned, feeling it settle, nodding she held onto Nick. As we came around to the front of the estate, we paused observing the steady flow of blacked out SUVs. There was a lot of security, professional with the look of people who would definitely ask questions with violence. Moving closer to the entrance, we waited. No-one approached us, their gazes seemed to move over us without registering our presence.

Taking a deep breath, Nick and I exchanged glances and then pulling Maggie, plunged forward. Quickly keeping by the cars queuing, we diverted off towards the trees that line the driveway.

We observed, as the occupants of the cars got out they all had something in common. They were all wealthy, hard looks in their eyes and excited.

We moved along the side of the buliding, sneaking looks through the windows. Nick was noting everything, no doubt building his own internal layout. Coming upon a small room that looked empty, Nick paused and then picked the lock, so that we could hoist ourselves in through the window. Looking around the room, Maggie picked up a small booklet. I looked over her shoulder at it. It was high quality, pictures and blurb on the Professor and followers. Many of whom I recognised from TV and film. Pushing it into the waist band of my trousers, we joined Nick at the door.

Nick whispered, "I would love to get more of an idea about this place and what the security is like."

Maggie responded, "Are you sure we aren't pushing our luck."

They both looked at me, "Maggie are you sure our cloaking is enough?"

"Yes but here are some more charms, passing us each a little pouch. These are incase we get separated."

"Should we let the others know where we are," I asked while tucking my pouch in my pocket.

Nick shook his head vehemently, "They might be able to compromise that. They know."

"Okay then."

Nick listened again, then gently opening the door a sliver. He went first and then beckoned us through into a back service corridor. Following Nick, I boosted our shields more. Feeling a headache start, not helped by the aura of the building. Since we had entered I was very aware of the fear and darkness in its walls. Passing rooms, we could see the prep for a very posh party.

Maggie managed to grab a plate of great mini starters and champagne, which I drew the line at. At my look, she defended herself, "Its medicinal."

We moved on through to the main rooms now. Staying in a small alcove, as not to run into anyone, I caught sight of Cecilia. She looked very well, very pregnant but glowing. I printed her out to the others, her escort was Detective Seymour. "Do you thin we can get any closer."

"We really aren't prepped to do a full insertion."

"Insertion, who are you?"

"Lets stick to watching, I think I have seen enough."

"Give me a mo," pulling out my phone I took pictures of the guests.

We moved slowly back to where we had entered but I stopped and moved to another service corridor. Something was pulling me. Before I could move further away, there was a loud shouting from the area we had just left. Nick looked back, paused and then we moved so we could see what had happened. Grayson had arrived, looking awful and Cecilia was screaming at him.

This was the distraction I needed, everyone was staring at the drama. Quickly I ran back to the back, following my instincts. There was a door set as aside, a door that had oily tentacles of darkness oozing from it. I knew that this was the area that I had not been able to scan. Looking behind me, I had no doubt that there had been guards here and that they would be back soon.

With determination, I pushed my glasses up and touched my chain for reassurance. Holding my top in my hand, I used it to touch the door handle and turned. I was rewarded with a zap of angry punishing power. Gritting my teeth, I turned the handle and entered.

CHAPTER 23

As I moved further down the hallway. I followed it to the end, ignoring the doors either side. It was strangely quiet, with an oppressive feel. There was a choice of directions, as it split. I confidently moved to the one on the right. Carefully I moved forward, not wanting to make any noise. Again the hairs on the back of my neck were standing up, it was getting very cold. Each breath a white mist, fogging my glasses. Regretting that Maggie or Nick was not here, very aware that they wouldn't know where I was. If I got out of this, there was another lecture in store, I hope they got the chance.

No more doors appeared, just this dark cold corridor. Gradually a strange low pitched deep sound appeared, making my stomach roll. Pausing I pulled my chain out from under my clothes and wrapped it around my right hand. Stretching my neck out, I rolled my shoulders ready for what ever was coming. I had no doubt that something was. Pulling loose the knife that Grayson had given me, I held it loosely in my left hand.

With trepidation I walked forward, hugging the wall as I slowly moved forward. Without warning the corridor ended in a large atrium, that framed a black ornately carved door. Though door was a small word, for something twice my height. The door appeared to be sucking all the light, darker than appeared possible. Okay bad feeling was moving onto fear.

With great reluctance, I placed my left palm parallel to the doors surface. Gasping, I felt small pin pricks erupt, drawing small points of blood. The door wanted an offering, I could feel that, of blood and pain. Despite knowing that I needed to get through, I hesitated unable to bring myself to place my hand on it. I took a deep breath and then used my right to push it down hard.

I hissed as pain lanced through my hand, I had continue to push down with my right, as I fought my natural urge to remove myself from the pain. My powers localised, meeting the power of the door. Blood oozed from between my hand and the door, I gritted my teeth again to prevent my cries out. Tears fell but still I bore the onslaught. I pushed back with my power, fighting the power of the door. It became timeless, as my tears fell.

Then suddenly the door clicked open. I fell forward between the gap, I nursed my hand against my chest. I was scared to look at it, it looked like it been run over a grater. I pulled some of my top at the back and bandaged my hand. I bit back the whimper and angrily brushed away my tears. Casting a baleful look at the door, I moved on. I really didn't want to touch that door ever again.

The room that I entered was stale and smelt of death, a sourness that made me light headed. It took a while to settle my breathing, I had felt evil before and this was it multiplied. I could feel something watching me but when I turned there was nothing there. I was so out of my depth, I actually contemplated the thought thought of being sensible and leaving, slamming that cursed door behind me. Instead it slammed shut, with a boom that made me jump. My thudded in my chest, this was like a horror movie. I started to hyperventilate. I went down on one knee, holding my chain tightly. My father's voice came to me, 'Get up, get up now.'

I shook as I forced myself to me feet, my legs were unsteady as I staggered forward. I took more steps forward and I became steadier, the pressure lifted. I looked back and there was a wall of that darkness with something coiling around inside it. I realised that it had been a test of sorts or something to prevent entry.

Cradling my hand, I managed to pick up my knife and tuck it in its sheath. Though still dizzy, I felt better. Taking a steading breath, I looked around, trying to make more of my surroundings. It was again an atrium, the walls made up of darkness. Scattered around the centre were ornate chairs, covered in red velvet. Tall gilded lamps stood by them, casting a small circle of light. At its centre stood an altar.

It couldn't be anything else. Very reluctant to approach it, I stood cataloging it from the edge of the circle of light. It was big, the size of a single bed, it looked like it was made out of a dark rock, like a piece of obsidian that I had once seen. There were carvings along its side, I had no idea what they were. Snapping pictures of the sides, I made myself move around it.

Pausing, I cautiously moved a closer, as I did a simmer of light appeared above it. It was mesmerising and without thought I found that I had stepped even closer, my hand outstretched. I clenched my injured hand, the pain focusing my mind, I looked away from it. Not maintaining eye contact with it, I moved around it. I could feel the compulsion to look at it again but I averted my eyes and if it felt too much then I clenched my hand again. I took a picture of it without looking at me and I found that the colour had changed to an angry red. There was some awareness in there. Sitting with my back to it, I strengthened my wards. Then tentatively I felt out towards it. Nothing, then something slammed into my walls. They shuddered, cracked but held. Immediately pulling back, I was left with the feeling that it wanted me or something inside me, there was recognition. It was dangerous, something demonic. Backing off further, it seemed to be pushing out. I snapped more pictures of it and moved away.

Hugging myself, I could see why they would want power like this and the lengths that some would go to. I would have to think about the feeling of recognition later.

Thinking that there must be another exit from the room, I looked the walls ignoring the thing in the altar. There, a hidden in tiger shadows corridor. I stepped through braced for another test but there was nothing. Breathing a sigh of relief that nothing happened. Going though I looked forwards but it led to a simple room, bare of anything. Puzzled, I checked it all over but there was nothing. Knowing that I had probably pushed my luck enough for today, I made my way back. A little hesitant about going back through that room and door.

Well nothing for it, I had to leave, couldn't stay here forever. Briskly I walked through, pausing by the doors. I pushed at it with my power and it opened easily, making a mockery of my entrance. Typical.

As I passed it, it silently closed behind me. I made my way back out, as I pulled the door at the end open I peered out. Luckily there was no one there. I was lucky that we had chosen today. Focusing with the little power that I had, I pulled on my shields and left.

Hurrying away, I made for the nearest open door that led out to the grounds. Leaning against a tree, I took blissful deep breaths. It felt amazing, dusk had fallen while I had been inside. I drank in the peace of the grounds. My headache easing back, I connected with the nature around me. Helping to replenish my energy levels. Once I felt much better, I sent a thought out to Maggie letting her know where I was. I felt an answering echo from Maggie.

Relieved, I continued to stand there allowing me to relax a little. I did make sure that I was not easily seen, so that I could relax some if my shielding.

After a while I started to go through some of the photos I had taken, I got them ready to send as soon as we were out of here. I decided that I would not think about anything that I had found at the moment. To distract me, I felt out for Louise, focusing on her alone. I was not expecting to find anything but was doing my due diligence. Resting my right hand against the soil next to me, I left my body. For just a moment, this was not the best place.

Again I focused on thoughts of Louise, calling for her. Nothing, nothing.. there was nothing there. What was that, a whisper on the wind. Following it without thought, I skirted around the mansion to the west of the property. I could feel Louise, I marked the area in my mind and returned to meet the others. Returning I walked into Nick, pulling a giggling Maggie.

"Seriously is she drunk?"

"Unfortunately yes, I did not realise until it was too late." Nick sighed deeply looking torn between annoyance and embarrassment.

"Nick, I need to check out the west side of the property. You get Maggie to the car and wait for me, remember that we have two cars to go back in."

"I don't like that."

"I don't think that you have any choice."

As we looked at Maggie, she hiccuped and slumped against him. Managing to slur out, "I am so tired, Nick. Can I lie down?"

He closed his eyes, as if asking for strength and then looked at me.

"Hey, it is your fault."

"Fine but please careful." He then gave me a look that would do any mother proud, muttering under his breath, "Look who I am saying that to."

"I heard that."

"You were meant too."

I left him to his load and went back the way that I had just come, strengthening my shielding. I couldn't help but think that I was not going to let Maggie live this down. Getting drunk on the job. Passing an orchard, I rolled my eyes at how rich these idiots were. Pushing forward I felt an increased sense of urgency, starting to hurry. I came upon a low lying building camouflaged beneath a grass roof. Pausing behind a tree, I pushed out with my senses, finding a black hole. Gathering my shields, I moved slowly forward, on high alert.

Reaching the structure, I followed its walls, which were smooth and unusually cold. It was soon obvious that there were no entrances that I could see, so I started to look with my other senses. Pushing firmly against its barriers, I felt something changed. With increased force I pushed, a light appeared. I walked around to it, there was an outline of a door but no cracks. After some more power an opening appeared.

As it had taken some doing, I had to lean against the side for a moment. All this was taking a toll and I am sure that I was going to get a bill soon. Mindful of the time I walked in. Despite the light that had escaped before, it was dark, pitch black in fact. Why was it always dark.

Feeling my way against the wall, I continued to search for Louise. Trying to use my phone light failed, the light apparently sucked in.

Everything seemed to be a bloody test, of pain, strength and sheer stupidity.

I was getting no where, gathering my courage, tattered as it was. I recklessly dropped all my shielding and stepped away from the relative security of the wall. My trailing fingers slowly left the wall, as it did I felt as if I was falling. There was the strangest sensation of moving but also of being in the same place. I held on, my teeth gritted. When at last it stopped I fell to my knees again. Waves of nausea rolled through me and I dry heaved. Shakily I rose to my feet, as I did I saw that it had gotten lighter, Shadows appeared. Stumbling forward, I put my hands out and they touched cold metal bars.

Jerking back, I felt out the bars. As I explored them, I realised with fear that they were small cells. As soon as I did, I could hear soft shuffling and moaning.

I called out urgently "Louise?" Turning towards the gasp that echoed. "Louise?" I followed it down, it had gotten lighter but still not enough to see clearly. I peered into the cell but it was so dark. "Louise?" I whispered again, my hair started to rising on the back of my neck. My sweat chilling in the sudden cold. Glancing anxiously behind me, I turned back. As I did I was meet with a face, I fell back with a curse. As I lay there I realised that it was Louise. I wouldn't have recognised her, she was so thin, her eyes sunken in.

She looked at me as if I was an apparition. "Olivia." I pulled myself up, scrambling to my feet.

"Oh my god, Louise. What the fuck have they done to you?"

She started to sob and wail. Pulling frantically at the bars did nothing, pushing all the power I had into it did nothing.

Frustrated I kept on trying, blasting again and again. Finally exhausted I collapsed on my knees in front of the cell, tears rolling down my eyes. "I'm sorry, I'm sorry." It was all my fault. More tears fell, as I fallowed.

Then slowly they stopped. Deep anger started to fill me, rage at all that was happening. Louise's cries faded away and all I could hear was my heart beat, thumping like a battle drum. I fanned the flames, allowing all my pain to fuel it. I realised the dam that had held all this back.

As I rose to my hands they started to burn with a bright light. It spread up my arms, to my body. I felt so much pressure inside me, something had to give. Then I suddenly released it all at the bars. Pouring out of me, the bars resisted for seconds and then they melted like chocolate. Louise huddled against the back of the cage, covering her eyes.

I fought to pull it all back in, it wanted to be free. The fear that I saw on her face helped me focus and wrestle control back. Once I had it under control but not banked, I knelt before her. I knew what to do, I placed my hands on he shoulders, "Let me heal you Louise. Accept this power to heal."

At the back of my mind, I heard cackling and a voice welcoming me and this show of power. I ignored it focusing on healing. Blinking at me, her eyes opened and I could see her in them.

"No, Olivia that's enough. I am here, stop. You are calling to him." She shook me and I laughed at her. With a determined look she slapped me.

I fell back again, holding my cheek. "What the.."

"I am sorry but you had to stop." I couldn't speak, shattered, even breathing was exhausting me. The floor looked very welcoming. "No, you can't sleep. This is an oubliette." Silently I just looked at her uncomprehendingly. Sh pulled me, "There is a trick to getting out. You actually have to want not to get out of here, not just give up."

She grunted with my weight, I just managed to keep my feet stumbling along. As we made our way out, I felt that awful sensation again and thankfully blacked out.

CHAPTER 24

"Wake up Olivia!" Why was someone yelling at me, I didn't want to open my eyes, go away. "Olivia, you fucking wake up now," but this time it was followed by a slap.

I sat bolt upright, my eyes wide and holding my cheek. "What the fuck."

"Thank God," suddenly I was buried under an avalanche of hugs. Confused I pushed everyone back.

"What's going on, why is everyone here. What happened?" They all stood by my bed, hoovering over me. "Guys, what's going on?" Everything seemed louder, brighter, a cacophony of sound. Helplessly I whimpered, prompting the voices to move from excited too concerned. "I just need a moment."

Daisy shooed them out and closed the door on the noise. I put my hands down, pushed myself off the bed and stumbled to the bathroom. Everything ached, as if I had been in a fight. In the unyieldingly bright light of the bathroom, I stared at myself. I looked pale, tired, my make up all run and my hair a bush. Groaning, I washed my face and brushed my teeth, then made my way back to my bed and collapsed onto it. Daisy gently sat next to me and soothingly stroked my hair. She said nothing but sat there, her presence soothed. Without moving my face from the bed, "What happened?"

"We don't know, you arrived back passed out accompanied by a strange woman who looks like a cross between Louise and a scarecrow." There was a pregnant pause and then, "I am going to say this once and then nothing. I am sorry about Grayson, we were both wrong." It started a flood of tears.

Having cried myself out, I rolled onto my back and stared at the ceiling. Feeling more at peace, the last bits of anger having been washed away. "Thanks, I needed that."

She smiled warmly, "Well what are friends for, you needed to let all of that out."

"Is it annoying that you know me so well?"

"Not to me. Was the spell that Maggie did as awful as Nick described?"

"It would have made you throw up." We looked at each other and started laughing hopelessly.

"Still think you should have kicked him in the balls."

"If I see him again, I will bear that in mind."

"Do you think that might happen, that you would see him again?"

"He is there, so I wouldn't rule it out." At the worry on her face, "Don't worry he won't remember me." Then with a wink, "Which means that he won't see it coming."

She laughed and stood. "Come on, lets go."

"If I have to."

"Come on they are worried about you and there will be food."

"That's blackmail."

"I know."

I stood, then realised I was in the clothes I wore yesterday. "Let me have a shower and change. I will come out and you can come and get me if I don't."

"I will hold you to that and remember the longer you take, the less food there will be."

"Sneaky." I smiled fondly as she left, I was lucky to have her. Come on lets' see if I can make myself look more presentable.

Feeling more presentable, I went through to the kitchen. Where they had left me a plate of food, piled high. Gratefully I heated it up and then sat down with them all to eat. Everyone avoided asking me any questions until I had put it all away. They talked about silly conversational things, Daisy telling them stories. It was soothing again to listen to, free of that bad feeling that had started to plague me.

Is I put my fork down, feeling stuffed I realised who was missing, "Where is Louise?"

Maggie answered. "You did an amazing job but she needed more healing. She asked us to drop her off, with people who could help her. She left us a number and wants to talk to you soon." Preemptively, "I know that you would want her here but she said that would be two targets in one place. She was really insistent."

Though it felt wrong, I had to trust her judgement. "Okay."

"Well done on finding her and I am sorry that I got tipsy!" She looked away, her face flushing.

Well, I couldn't let this pass. "I wouldn't say tipsy, I would go with drunk." I tried to keep a straight face but at her stricken expression I couldn't and burst out laughing. Looking upset but then as everyone else joined in, she smiled and started laughing herself. Though she Nick got a half hearted smack. He pretended that it hurt and that set everyone else off. It felt good.

"I don't even know what time it is."

Sunny answered, "It's seven."

"That's not too bad."

"But we have lots to do, if you are up for it."

Patting my stomach, "Now I am."

"Any signs that they knew we were there?"

Sunny confidently responded, "No, I was up most of last night and there was nothing. I think that whatever magic scrambling you guys did worked. I also double, triple checked everything and Grayson didn't compromise anything. There was a virus that was coping everything we had but it had not sent anything and I took care of it."

I cleared my throat, "Grayson conned us all and I am sorry for that. I brought him into this group." Maggie and Sunny both hastened to reassure me, "I know, I had not realised the deviousness that they have. But now I know and I will not do that again."

Nick, "It happened and we managed it. It's alright."

"So, I have a feeling that this might be it, a confrontation tomorrow. If anyone wants to step back, I won't hold it against them." My eyes touching everyone, "I don't want anyone to feel that they have to be here."

One by one the others looked at each other and then stood. I followed, one by one they put their right hands in above the centre of the table. Relieved I placed mine on top, "Thanks guys."

Maggie and I caught each others eye, and we started instinctively to build our power. Strongly I felt the need to bless this friendship, this fellowship. I wished for this to last, for my friends, my family to be protected and for us to trust in each other. As Maggie whispered words, tingling light started to build around our hands. Everyone else gasped but I focused. The light faded, everyone pulling their hands away. As we all looked at the space between our thumb and the index finger, a translucent tattoo had appeared. It was a set of linked symbols, everyone was looking and touching theirs. As we compared we saw that they were all identical.

"How did you guys do that and why?" Daisy asked.

Maggie said, "It is a bond. We will be forever linked, know if each of us are in mortal danger. This is the Goddess's wish." She paused looking everyone in the eye, "I have never seen this before, only read about it." Nick was rubbing at his hand, a bemused expression on his face, she took his hand and smiled reassuringly at him. He smiled back and dropped his hand.

Rubbing my cheek absently, "Okay who slapped me because this is really starting to hurt." Everyone laughed and denied knowledge, moving back to the table.

"So what shall we start with?"

Sunny answered, in her element. "I think that Nick and I will need to go through all the data that you got yesterday, we will divide it up. Security for tomorrows event, identifying some of the pictures that you got. Maggie I will need your help in identifying some of the symbols that Olivia took pictures of. It would be better if we were a little more knowledgable."

Happy for her to take the lead, I put my hand up, it seemed appropriate. "I think that Catherine could help with that. I can contact her, I have to warn her about Grayson. I mainly focused on removing us, I'm not sure that I got all of his memories of her."

"Do that, maybe she might want to combine forces. Let me know." Ticking off jobs, "Daisy, we need some outfits for tomorrow, I think dressy but practical. Olivia will be getting into trouble." I tried to glower but I was unable to hold it, as I had proven it multiple times and was undeniably true. I sat back further in my seat. Nick patted my back consolably, trying unsuccessfully to hid a grin.

She looked at everyone again, "I think that tomorrow will be something else, I have a feeling of something big, that is going to make a bog difference to us all. So we need to do everything we can to prep." I was impressed, Sunny the leader and I couldn't help but felt proud. Pressure lifted from me, I knew that I could trust them to get things done.

I went to my room to make the call. It took a while to psych myself up, so it was a while before I rang. Part of me hoped for the answering message. No, she picked up on the second ring, "Hello."

"Hi Catherine, it's Olivia. I need to talk."

There was a pause from Catherine, "Give me a moment, let me go somewhere private. I have a bad feeling about this conversation." I heard her giving some instructions and answering some queries.

I could feel my heart beat picking up and sweat starting to build under my arms. I started to pacing while I waited, full of anxious energy.

"Go ahead Olivia."

"It has been a complicated couple of days and I want to fill you in. So here goes." I told her everything and she said nothing. I found that I was clutching the phone tightly, painfully I switched hands. Then I had finished and there was an answering silence.

Realising that I had given her a lot tho think about, I waited. It least the worst part was over.

Finally I heard a crackle, as if Maggie had shifted. "If I had not met you, I would be questioning your sanity." Pausing, "I am amazed at what you have done. Don't beat yourself up about Grayson, I was in your position but allowed him much more liberties." I had suspected that much, "What a devious bastard, I wondered why he had moved on. Coincidentally at a time where we seemed to go through troubles, something else that I can lay at his door." Clearing her throat, "Moving on, my team and I will be arriving tonight, Well after we vet everyone again, so don't send me your address. I will send you ours and my email so that you can forward me those images. We will need to combine forces."

"I know but I think that yours are bigger, I don't want mine to be overwhelmed."

"Your power itself ensures that won't happen."

"I will be coming tomorrow. If I see Grayson, don't try to stop me." Her voice promised vengeance.

"I wouldn't think of it."

"Good, try not to get into any more trouble until I get down there." Great, I had a reputation.

"Be safe, see you soon."

I went and updated Sunny, she took the address and started sending the images. She sent me away as I hovered, "Go away."

Wondering back to my room, I looked around and stared to remove anything that was Graysons. I emptied everything out onto the floor. Annoyingly the clothes smelled like him, reminding me of our first meetings. Nothing else, I turned the bag over, feeling along the seams and felt something hard. Grabbing a knife I cut the bag open, finding a memory card within the seams. Then I collected everything in a black bag and throw it out. It felt good.

Popping into Sunny, she looked very in control. I waved the flash drive at her, "I found this in Graysons things. It gives me a bad feeling." Sunny took it, turning it around in her fingers.

"I will have to use one of the older computers, give me ten minutes."

I nodded and went to get the others, we should probably all see what was on there. "Here goes nothing." She inserted the card and opened it up. We all crowded around, as she quickly checked it for viruses. Sunny busily tapped away, "Let's see what he thought was important." She whistled, "I thought he wasn't tech savvy. Its a lock box, lots of stolen data."

"From us," Nick leaned further forward.

"No, naughty boy was stealing from the Society. This has lots of useful info, something else I am going to have to work through." As we all remained standing there, she waved us off, "Go, you all have jobs to do."

I went down to the training room, I tried yoga but it was difficult to quiet all my internal noise. I kept going determinedly, gradually I slipped lower and lower in my consciousness. Images of the past floated by, I allowed them to pass by. Grayson, his smile at the beginning, knowing he brought me the people in this house. I was grateful for that.

Louise, the demon, so many thoughts slipped past me. I had been there long enough to get stiff but I felt balance in myself. I stretched and did exercises, amazed at how much better I had become. Moving fluidly, in tune with my body and powers. Had something been holding me back. Content and at peace, it took while for the shouting to register. I ran up the stairs and into chaos.

CHAPTER 25

A wall of noise and emotions met me at the top of the stairs. It was obviously because the link between us was wide open. As I had no shields up I was left wide open, I put them up, noting that I could now do that so easily. Breathing a sigh of relief, I moved forward wondering what was going in. Entering the computer room, where everyone gathered around one of the monitors and shouting at each other. I stood waiting for some enlightenment.

As it looked like no one was paying any attention to me, I clapped my hands and hollered. "What the hell is going on?"Everyone was rendered silent, though by their stunned faces, it may not have been voluntary. Oops, I might have augmented that request with my powers. "Oops. Sorry everyone but your emotions are coming through very loudly." Nick straightened up, "Sunny opened up Gaysons drive and it was shocking. He had so much information, on all of us. Details that we wouldn't share with our loved ones let alone our enemies. On that point, he had info on all our loved ones, I need to check on my family." Pulling out his phone with a rattled air, he went outside. It was shocking to see him rattled.

"Where is Daisy?" Worry lacing my tone.

"She went to call her mum, I am sure that she will share with you."

"Maggie are you alright?"

Maggie was pale, sitting with her head in her hands. "You said that Catherine was coming today?" I had a bad feeling about this.

"Yes?" Maggie looked up at me, some accusation in her glance.

"I think that you suspect why, as you have seen her and now I have seen a picture. According to this she is my mother and she has known where I am all this time!" She yelled.

I gestured for her to move over and then sat down, "I didn't know for sure, I suspected but I didn't know if that was enough. I didn't mean to hurt you and I am sorry." Looking in her eyes, I repeated "Really sorry."

"I know, its not your fault. I guess that I am a little shocked, especially as I am about to meet her. What will I say?" She rubbed her neck, "I just need a moment."

I let her go, as she walked off. Dreading it, I turned too Sunny, "How are you doing?"

She took a breath, turned to me with haunted eyes, "I really underestimated the lengths that he would go to. The details that they have here, it's unbelievable." Straightening up, "Lets hope that they have as much on their own members, it will give us an advantage."

I had to admire her determination, "Remember if you want to talk to me about anything, after this is over, then you can?"

"Thanks, I think that we all will."

"Do you think, you can let me have the info that have on me. Maybe I will learn something and it will give me an idea of how he thought I would react." As she nodded, "Are you sure that this info hasn't been shared?"

"As far as I can tell, he was pulling it all together but I can't be absolutely sure. He was good and I don't know where he found the time to do it."

"Do you think he had any info on the nightmare lady."

"Maybe, it would be a pleasure to send it on."

"Thanks, I am going to check on Daisy." I couldn't find her, then I saw that her jacket was gone. So I grabbed mine, it felt good to go outside. I sent out my senses, feeling for Daisy. Following her I set off, ending up after about twenty minutes in a park. It was cute though small. Walking through, I enjoyed the children carefree laughter. I spied Daisy sitting on one of the benches overlooking the playground.

I approached slowly, seeing the dried tears on her face. I slid in next to her but didn't say anything. I knew, that she knew I was there. After ten minutes, she spoke, still not looking at me. "I tried to call my mum, she actually picked up. She hadn't even noticed that I had gone. She was busy, too busy for me." Tears continued to roll down her cheeks, there was the info that they had on me, that they knew that no one would miss me. How sad is my life.

"I care about you."

"I know." Her hand drifted to her belly, as she absently rubbed it. "What kinda mother do I think I am going to be, I have never had an example of a good one."

Reassuringly I said, "You don't need an example, you are a great friend and mother me all the time. You are kind, trusting and have the strength to always make the best of it. Look at you now, helping me and preparing for the arrival of your baby. You gave me a family, you have always been my rock."

She looked a little shocked and shyly smiled pushing me with her arm. I pushed back and then hugged her. "You done with your pity party?"

She laughed, "You are going to be a bad influence on my baby."

"Since you were that for me, then I think it is only appropriate. I could teach them everything you taught me."

"Don't do that," she said, sounding shocked.

"Maybe, you will have to wait and find out then." We continued to sit, as she dried her tears. It was nice and a reminder of what I was looking forward to after this was over.

"In the old days, I would say that it now time for a drink but I can't do that." Daisy looked sideways at me, with a frown.

"Or you could just watch me have a drink?"

"You are a terrible friend." Laughing we got up. We arrived back in a happier mood than either of us had left it. "And remember I get to pick out you dress for tomorrow!"

My phone beeped, as Daisy went to her room for a nap. It was a text from Catherine, she was arriving in London and sent me her safe house address. There was some additional information about the symbols that we had been sent. After glancing at them and understanding little, I forwarded it onto Maggie.

I made a batch of sandwiches for everyone, taking some over to Sunny. She absently mindedly grabbed one and munched with her eyes glued to the screen. I grinned and went to grab a coffee and my tablet, going up to the roof with some cushions.

With some determination, I looked over the info which was confusing. The demon had been identified, I couldn't even pronounce the name. It remained on the plane by having part of its life force tied into that of certain people. If these people had their connection cut, the demon would be banished back to wherever it came from. That was a plan, any if we could find those people.

Though why these people would agree, I had no idea. How to identify them? There might be something in their aura. Hmm.

Moving onto some info on the hybrids. There appeared to be different amounts of demon energy that you could have. If the foetus survived, they could develop, inherit any number of gifts. But the rate of loss was incredibly high and I am sure would ensure that no woman in her right mind would agree. Those that survived would be valued highly and I was surprised that they had let me go. It would explain why Grayson thought that having me eating out of his hand would be beneficial to him. It also led me to believe that there wouldn't be many truly gifted there.

With great reluctance, I opened my file. It read like a medical report, with the info on my mother and the pregnancy. It looked like they had exposed her to a lot of tests, this pressure and the expectation had caused her mind to break. Apparently she had died during my delivery and I wondered what my life would have been like if she had survived. The scrutiny continued as I grew, Professor May had been personally interested in my development. Then nothing. A significant gap until I was in my teens. There was a long lease image of my father and I. They had thought that I had a predicted lack of ability. As insulting as I found that, it had worked to my advantage. They had found Louise and there was information on her.

Graysons personal notes were difficult to read, he had played a good game. He had not suspected my powers initially and had just thought that I was a nobody but then he became suspicious and followed a hunch. Well that had paid off, he carefully documented my powers and his excitement had grown with the more that I did. Insultingly of all, he had actually thought that if he got me pregnant he would ride my coat tails. As if, I had better taste than that. I got up and paced, the facts of my life being on record was disturbing.

However I got here, I now had a purpose in my life. I had people I could trust and love as family. What ever the bumps on my road, I was making my own journey. What ever the outcome, I was happy that I was on it.

Though the demon part worried me, I knew that I was not evil and I was confident that I could deal with this, with my family.

I took some more time to read more and then decided to start dinner for everyone. Looking through the cupboards, I found everything for Spaghetti Bolognese. The cooking calmed me, once everything was almost ready, I went to look for everyone.

I found Maggie in Nick's and from the embarrassed faces and sudden pulling apart, I suspected what had been going on. My smirk continued as I gathered Sunny and Daisy. At the table everyone was quiet, Sunny looked exhausted. "Okay, now everyone is not to talk about work, we are gonna enjoy this family meal. Though battles lie ahead of us, I for one want to enjoy us time."

They all nodded but didn't look convinced, slowly but surely with wine and food, the conversation became less forced. With a determined air, we shared stories and laughed. Helped by the game I made everyone play, where they had to tell us about something they had learned from life and something they were grateful for.

It was memorable and something that we had all needed. A time that I would always remember and I wasn't that only one.

After I had made the coffee, I brought them back reluctantly to work. "Sunny, you are the boss, you want to catch us up?" I was relieved by the fact that she looked more relaxed than earlier. With energy she went and grabbed her computer and a small projector. Moving all our chairs around so that we could see, jostling as if we at school.

With a school teacher air, she sighed at us, "Come on, settle down and listen up."

"So Nick and I have gone through the security for tomorrow. Here is a lay out of the building, the event itself is going to be held in the main hall. I have marked up the exits. I have also marked up the security routes that are likely, they are using their own security." She based us out paper copies, "Familiarise yourselves with these. Now here are some of the people that we have managed to identify."

The images came up, including Professor May, looking confident. "He is quite reclusive now, only attends certain functions. We guess that he has some abilities but mainly he surrounds himself with stronger ones. He has access to multiple bank accounts, personal and various shell companies. Money is not a problem for him. He has a simple strategy, he blackmails or blacklists people who are in his way. They then join his organisation or disappear. More working he has contacts in various police or government posts. I have put together a list, which will give us a heads up. Your Detective Seymour is there but it appears as if he has fallen out of favour. He refused to do some things, he could be a help?" Surprised I nodded, feeling more kindly to him. "Next we have some of the seconds. This is Amanda, she is the his right hand gifted, as it were. She is a bitch, a sociopath if I read this right. She was brought up only in the Society. They sent her out to the army, coming back with a dishonourable discharge for you can guess." Consulting her notes, "I think that she has some form of persuasion and can kill. My advice is to avoid her or disable her."

Well she sounded delightful, Nick agreed, "We are going to need something to neutralise her specifically. I would not like to take her on."

I put my hand up, "I second that, really strongly."

Sunny moved on, "These are the other gifted." As she ran

through them, I recognised some.

"I have seen some of these guys, my invisibility thing worked on them and I was new to it at the time."

"Great," Sunny said looking relieved. "Their security will be pulled from their followers, as they don't trust anyone else."

Nick stood and went through some of the security, he seemed happy that he and Sunny would be able to circumvent their traditional security.

Daisy brought up the point, "Can we record the people that come? You never know when it will come in useful."

"Easily done, good point."

With a long look to me, she asked, "Tell me again why you have to go there? It seems such a risk."

Everyone looked at me, "I know that you guys think that I haven't thought this through but I know that I have to meet the Professor, that this will be the turning point." I saw and appreciated their apprehension, making me appreciate all the more that they were supporting me. "I don't know how to explain this but this is a point in time, a fixed point that has to occur. I am sorry that is a bit Doctor Who."

Daisy nodded, "I was afraid that you would say something like that. Well you haven't really been wrong in all of this." She seemed to suddenly recall Grayson, especially as my eyebrow went up. "I didn't mean that, I am here because you followed your gut when anyone else wouldn't have been that foolhardy and look here I am."

Sunny coughed, "Well that is why we are going through and doing more research. So it is a little more organised than normal."

"I have to say that it would be a nice change, maybe less stressful." Perhaps it would be.

"You won't know what is going on, how's that going to feel?" Nick teased.

"How it feels to you all the time," sticking my tongue out.

Sunny took control of the meeting, "I was planning that we surprise him with you as he is in the green room, which is here," she indicated the plans. I suspected that there will be the most number of guards here, so we will need a distraction. Nick expressed some ideas for that. "We will take care of that, you go in with Maggie."

"I think that actually Catherine and her team would be able to provide a good distraction." Still uncomfortable, I avoided looking directly at Maggie, "She was part of the society and she will know how they work these events. At least it may put them off their game."

Sunny glancing at Maggie finished, "I think that we will need them. They up the numbers but I don't think I can plan until I have met her. She's an unknown." Maggie was looking uncomfortable again, Nick started to rub her back in an effort to reassure her.

Leaning over, "Well we are going to meet her today. Then you will decide if they increase our chances."

"I know but let me meet her first." I nodded reassuringly.

Sunny continued, "Once you are there, I will be able to sense via the bond but I have also adapted some ear pieces. They should not be able to intercept, if we use if only for emergencies. Looking at me only, she leaned over, "Nonot answering the phones."

"I promise," making everyone burst into laughter. More of a nervous relief.

"I am going to be outside monitoring, Daisy will be here with the backup information and systems. I don't believe I am saying this but Olivia tell us more about the demon."

I told them what I had learnt, the demon was contained and how we could destroy what held it in our world. Everyone sobered up pretty quickly.

Daisy breathed out, "So this is the plan?"

"Well, we need to identify the people who hold the bond. Ideas?"

Maggie, "I think that their auras will be polluted and we should be able to see that."

As they discussed it, I whispered to Daisy, "So you are going to be monitoring the computers and talking to us through ear pieces." We shared a look, as Daisy had never been known for her way around a computer.

"I have been watching and helping Sunny out," she touched her belly, "Actually I think that this one is sharing some of its gifts."

"Really?" and I put my hand over her stomach. With a gentle touch I felt an answering tingle of power but where initially it had felt dark, now there was light. I was glad and perhaps it was the environment, away from the dark influences that had restored the balance. So if the women left, these children had a chance. Something to think about later.

Sunny stood, "I am feeling a lot better about this plan. We have the invites, Daisy did you manage any fairy godmother stuff."

She laughed, "With Olivia's money, thank you." I bowed, "You will all have the right clothes tomorrow, you will fit right in."

"Excellent, I think that this has been good. Rest up until we know when the meeting is."

As we said goodnight, I went to my room.

As I tried to rest on my bed, I knew that I couldn't sleep. I sensed that Catherine was close and I worried about thus mother-daughter meeting.

CHAPTER 26

Despite my reservations I did doze off, drained by all the emotions. When my mobile rang shrilly in my ear, I shot up my heart pounding with panic. I grabbed for it, "Hello?"

"Olivia, it's Catherine. You still up for a meeting?"

"Absolutely, where?" Let her not say here, I held my breath.

"Come here, we don't have time for meeting elsewhere and if I can't trust you, then we are all pretty screwed. I have sent you the address, see you in an hour. Be warned that not everyone agrees with my decision." Beadily I looked at the address, it wasn't too far especially at this time. Wearily I swung my legs out and stretched. Before getting ready I looked around to see who was up.

Of course Sunny was up, her hair wildly sticking up in all directions. We spoke and agreed that Nick, Maggie and I should attend. She agreed that it would be better to get this meeting over tonight. I told her that she needed to get some sleep while we were out and that we would call if there were any problems. She looked dead on her feet and I walked her to her room, despite her protests. I may have pushed an overwhelming need for sleep onto her as I left. Looking in on a sleeping Daisy, I left her a note.

Making my way to Maggie's, I knocked and there was no answer. Hmm, trying Nick's next, I was almost knocked over by the speed at which the door opened. He was fully dressed, as was Maggie behind him. "So I guess that you guys are up for coming with me?"

Maggie came behind him, looking calmer and more settled than earlier. Dressed all in black and with a determined look on her face. "You going to be okay?"

"It's gonna be fine, at least I don't have time to obsess over it."

She asked with a barely noticeable tremor in her voice, "How do I look?"

"You look like you mean business." I could not imagine what her feelings were at this moment. "We are both here for you."

"I know but I don't want to put the whole operation at risk. I can not promise that I won't have a freak out." I pulled her in for a hug and as we did so our tattoos burned with our bond.

Nick raised his hand, "If anyone wants to know, I will try to behave too." The tension definitely eased.

"He is definitely a keeper," to my delight they both blushed and avoided looking at each other.

"Give me ten minutes, I'll meet you by the garage. I still need to change." I forwarded on the address, feeling lighter and definitely more awake. I also ended up all I black, as I swiped on some eyeliner, I thought about how far I had come. As I put my chain on I wondered whether additional power or protections could be added? Something to ask Maggie and Catherine. Just over a little late, I rushed down. Nick was in the drivers seat, watching Maggie pacing and muttering to herself. Pausing by the side of the car, I waited. She looked up, "I am trying to make myself calm, do you think that it is working?"

"No, did you really expect it too?" I slapped her on the back, "Lets get this over with." Nick spent the ride, reassuring Maggie. The affection running though every word. I day dreamed of a time when this was not my world.

I awoke again from a doze, got to stop doing that. I checked that I hadn't drooled. I had the sense that something was trying to get my attention but I was unable to pin-point what it was. Shrugging my shoulders, I leant forward and used the drivers mirror, to repair what I could. Nick had got out and I joined him, unspoken we didn't look to where Maggie was hunched over in the front seat.

"This a good idea?" I asked Nick.

"Well, it's an idea?" Well that wasn't reassuring, nor was the way that he was scanning the buildings. We had stopped outside a large iron gate, there were cameras everywhere, so that there was no doubt that they knew we were here. We continued to wait, the cold starting to seep through my jacket.

Finally, when my nerves had been suitable stretched, the gates creaked open. Nick and I exchanged glances as six men exited, looking suspiciously around. I shifted as I clocked their weapons, they surrounded us. One of them gave a nod and then Catherine joined us. As she walked confidently towards us, I let my senses spread out, feeling no deceit or danger.

Catherine held her hands out in welcome, "Apologies, my men are so cautious. Please all come in, will your friend be joining us?" Her eyes flitted over Maggie, a slightly puzzled look in her eyes.

"This is Nick, I guess our security and this is Maggie." She slowly opened the door and got out, with Nick and I moving to flank her. Catherine looking more puzzled, an involuntary stepping closer. Maggie pulled her hood down, under the lights their resemblance was marked.

As Maggie and Catherine's stared at each other, energy started to build up. Static started to build, I could feel it in my hair and clothes. Without looking at each other, Nick and I took a step back. Then another five or so.

As the wind whipped up between them, one of her men stepped towards us. "What is going on?", raising his voice which was cautiously concerned.

Raising my voice, "It's a family reunion, can't you tell?"

"Her daughter died?" he insisted.

Spreading my hands, as I closely watched them. "What can I say?"

As a gust caused me to stumble, he grabbed my arm holding me up. I glared at him but he pulled me with him. Calling out, "Inside now!"

Despite my tugging, he didn't let go and ignored my glares. Managing to grab part of Nick's jacket, I towed him along. "There is nothing you can do, get inside. They won't hurt each other." I hoped. Nick pulled away but two other men picked him up between them. As the last of us struggled through the main door, it slammed behind us and everyone crowded the windows for a view.

"Let go." He frowned at me.

"Didn't you think to warn her, this emption it makes their powers unpredictable. It's going to get worse before it gets better." He was well into angry now but pulled me again away from the others. "How can you be this irresponsible?"

"Stop pawing me." I spun to face him head on, "I didn't know that this was going to happen. What would I have said?"

"You should have prevented this." Opening and closing my mouth, I didn't know why I was taking this. Or why for some reason I noticed that his eyes were a dark chocolatey brown. Shaking this off, I remembered Grayson, guys were idiots.

"We only found out today, hours before this. You think that Catherine would have said no to meeting her, though as part of my team, she would have had to." Stepping toe to toe, "Now I am warning you to get your hands off me." I gathered my power, feeling Nick moving in behind me. How had this escalated so fast.

His eyes continued to be focused on me but he stepped back and slowly, deliberately straightened up. As he stepped back, the overall tension reduced. It seemed that they others were taking their lead from him. He stood with his arms crossed, annoyingly I couldn't help but notice his muscles. Nick gave a discreet cough behind me and I pulled myself together. Nick moved to my side, his hand on my shoulder. Bending close to my ear, "You okay?"

The man's focused with laser intensity on where Nick was touching me, causing Nick to move forward. What was going on, suddenly I felt a power surge from outside.

Spinning around I threw up a protection around the people, it shimmering and held, as the windows blew in. There was sudden silence and then we were moving outside. Nick leading us. There was a ring of destruction around them, cars thrown, covered in dents.

Maggie and Catherine were visible in the centre, holding each other. Moving cautiously towards them, I was relieved that they appeared unharmed. "Hey you two alright."

Maggie answered, "We are okay," as her startled glance took in the surrounding destruction. "Did we do that?"

I nodded. Catherine took a breath, though she still clasped hands with Maggie. The hold was tight, as if she was afraid that she would disappear if she lost contact. "How long had you known?" Her voice held reproach and anger.

"Today we knew for sure but I had noticed the likeness immediately." Spread my hands, "What would you have wanted me to say? I am sorry though but I am so glad that you have found each other."

The silence stretched uncomfortably, finally. "You are right and my anger should be directed towards others. They stole my daughter from me." She turned her gaze onto Maggie, smiling softly as she touched her hair. "But we will talk about it after."

"I look forward to it," I muttered.

As she also looked around, her look taking in the building, "Thank you for keeping my men safe."

"Of course."

"Now, that I have woken you all up, I need these vehicles checked, clean up this glass otherwise just leave it." She walked in, as they jumped to it. As I turned to follow her, I walked into my new nemesis. His hands caught my shoulders, I looked up. "Thanks." Well that was gracious, he let go and waved me on. Feeling uncomfortable with his perusal, I hesitated but went in. I huffed as I passed him and annoyingly I caught the ghost of a smile. Nick gave me a look and smiled, it was knowing and decided to ignore it.

We followed on into one of the inner rooms, that was undamaged. There were lots of computers, papers and was obviously the heart of the operation. I took a seat opposite Maggie, who was seated next to Catherine. Though there was no contact, I could feel their combined power. Nick pulled out the chair next to me but the guy slipped into it. Nick growled and remained standing behind me. A smug look rested on this mans face, I ignored him. An itch had started between my shoulder blades, something was wrong. I fidgeted in my seat, feeling pins and needles. My tattoo started to burn, Maggie looked down at her hand, then looked at me. "What's wrong?"

"Something is coming, can't you feel it?"

Catherine and Maggie closed their eyes, then Catherine suddenly stood. "We have been detected, my fault that power surge outside. We all need to leave now."

I stood, having sent my senses out more. "We need to leave faster than that, demon."

Catherine blanched, "Go now but Maggie stay with me."

Maggie looked torn, Nick apprehensive. "Maggie stay with them, you can be the link, we still need to share information. Come on Nick." I paused, "But Catherine, you need to keep her safe." She looked at Nick and I looked away from the raw emotion. Nick went around and hugged her hard, as I did. As I came back to the exit, the annoying man stepped forward, "I should go with them, then its equal."

I started to object, Catherine was looking at him oddly, her gaze drifting between the two of us. "If you think that is the best idea."

"We will be okay."

"Now you will be even better, let's go."

"No, we don't know you and you are going to throw us off. You stay here."

The pressure built in my head, I reinforced the shielding around the whole building. "We don't have time for this, Catherine keep him."

As she moved, "This won't work Reese. What ever you have done to piss them off, is the reason why you can't." She put her hand up, forestalling his argument. "Now get us evacuated."

He gritted his teeth, I could practically hear them grinding. He looked me in the eye, "Try not to get yourself killed."

I ran on without a come back, we left into our car that Nick reversed out with speed. Nick put a hand on my knee, as it bounced up and down. "Ring them," fumbling I pulled out my phone, They pressure was lessening as we increased our distance. No answer, I tried both Sunny and Daisy.

"Don't panic." I knew he was right but I didn't like that fact that I couldn't contact them. I pulled out my chain and wrapped it around my hand, in case. Then my phone rang, I dropped it in my haste to answer. Nick swore, as he had been distracted and almost hit anther car.

"Hello?"

"Olivia, what is it? Are you alright?" Sunny's sleepy voice came through.

"Are we alright? Oh my god, I thought that something had happened to you, is Daisy there with you?"

"No, why would she be in my bedroom. I'll go check. What's happened?"

"Just check on the security after Daisy, please. We will be there soon, especially the way that Nick is driving." I held on as we took a corner at speed.

I heard her calling Daisy, worry appearing in her voice,"She isn't here, Daisy?" She sounded wide awake now. I gripped the phone tighter. "Okay, I have the security feeds up. Shit, she looks like she sleep walking out of here. But I don't know that she knew how to disarmed the alarms and left." More typing, "I am looking at feeds from around us, see if I can track her down."

I had put the phone on speaker, Nick said, "Just see if you can narrow down the search area, after you have reset all the alarms."

"I got it, done. Ah I have her heading towards the park, she isn't wearing a jacket or shoes, something is controlling her. Her expression does look right."

"Could be something that the baby is doing?" I mused out loud.

"That possible?"

"Who knows but the baby has power."

Nick had dropped his speed and headed in the direction indicated, "Then feel for the baby, you can do that right?"

A brilliant idea, I knew and should be able to find them. I

brutally pushed down the worry about losing her again. There, no then they had gone again. Something was interfering with my search.

"Text Maggie, let her know." Nick ordered as we slowed.

Sunny yelled, "West entrance to the park," she yelled and we sped up, squealing around a corner. "Hurry, a van is pulling up."

I hadn't thought that we could go any faster but I was wrong and was pushed back in my seat. Nick was eerily quiet, angry and focused. As we rounded the corner, I saw a blacked out van ahead. Daisy was standing motionless, now that I could see her, I could sense them. The baby was preventing her from moving forward.

Nick took it in, "Brace yourself and accelerated aiming for the van.

"You aren't."

"I am," he grunted. I threw up shields around Daisy and ourselves.

Holding my breath, everything seemed to slow as we hot them van. Our airbags burst out and my seatbelt cut into me. Groaning, I pushed out my power to lock the van so that no one could get out. I knew that I was stunned and I could faintly hear Nick shouting. I blindly stabbed the airbag with my knife. My eyes stung but I peeled them open and with trembling hands unbuckled my seatbelt. I fell out of the car, onto my hands and knees. Something wet dripped down the side of my face. Blinking I slowly realised that it was blood.

Forcing myself up, I staggered to where I felt Daisy. Who still stood motionless, with one hand I pushed power into her. It burnt away what ever was controlling her, her eyes blinked at me, the blank look replaced by puzzlement and then horror. She grabbed her belly protectively, "What happened, where am I?"

"Its okay, come on, we have got to go." Gently but firmly I pulled her away, wiping my eyes again. I could see that we weren't going anywhere in our car. I staggered over, my ears still ringing to get Nick.

Some force pushed me to my knees, Daisy screamed. I turned

to look but could see nothing. Again, I kicked blindly back and connected with something. Who ever it was was invisible. I spun around and kicked out again, thank you Grayson. I was rewarded by a thump and the sudden appearance of a guy on the floor holding his bleeding nose. Nick appeared and kicked him unconscious.

"Come on, we got to go."

Together we ran towards Daisy and moved into the park. At least we had cover. Shit, I had dropped my phone, "My phone."

Nick continued forward, "Forget it. Sunny knows we got out, she would have seen us. We got to get back. Come on Daisy."

Daisy was whimpering, I tugged off my boots and Nick gave her his jacket. From a distance, we must have looked like a three of drunks on their way home. We moved as fast as we could, I was glad that I had think socks. I also clocked us with invisibility.

As we arrived home, with a teeth chattering Daisy, I could feel every bruise and bump.

"Well that could have gone better," Nick dryly stated.

As I looked at Daisy, "It could have gone much, much worse." He followed my look and grimly nodded.

Sunny opened the door and flew at us. Nick and I groaned as she hugged us hard, scolding us all the way. Which increased once she saw out injuries properly. "First I am going to reset all of the alarms and no-one will be getting out without me knowing. Then you are going to tell me everything that has happened."

With some trepidation, I quietly stated, "Sunny, Daisy needs looking after first."

"Of course, come on let's get you sorted."

"Olivia," she whimpered.

"Its okay, Daisy you get sorted first.'

Nick breathed a sigh of relief, "Thank you, now that was scary. I am going to check security and make sure that Daisy can't leave again, or at least that we know. Sunny will be busy for a bit."

Touching my head, he said, "You want help with that?"

"No, I will have a go first. As he left, I looked up and begged that tomorrow would be a better day. Actually, looking at the time, today. Groaning, I made my way to my room.

CHAPTER 27

As I walked to my room, my steps dragging I received a text message from an unknown number. Puzzled I opened it, 'I said not to get into trouble.' How dare he text me, about to reply I decided to let him stew.

Hearing voices from Daisy's room, I knocked but hearing nothing peaked in. Daisy and Sunny appeared to be facing off. "Hi, what's going on because seriously I can't take anymore excitement." This earned me a look of disgust from both of them. "Okay, I can take a hint," and I backed out of the door and left them to it.

I met Nick cautiously coming up the stairs, "Are they done."

"No, if I were you I would avoid them right now. Rest up you and get some sleep."

"I can't deny that I really need the sleep but I worry about Maggie," he looked sad and I felt for him.

"We can trust Catherine to take care of her."

He looked out the window, "I know but it has been a long time since I cared for someone like this.'

"I know and she knows, she has to have the time with Catherine."

"Yep," he turned and looking towards the raised voices, "I guess I will try to catch what sleep we can."

"Come on let's eat something first." Gesturing to the kitchen, I led him in. He followed slightly bemused, I heated up some left overs and we ate in silence. After we finished, I showed Nick the text that I had gotten.

He sniggered, "I thought that there was something there."

With that cryptic comment he sauntered off, "Boys." I showered and sank exhaustedly into bed, hoping that I would get some rest. Closing my eyes, I feel quickly in a deep sleep.

As morning came, I woke and I slowly blinked the sleep out of my eyes. I rolled back over, burying my head back in the blankets. I wondered if it was too much just to have a day off. I was sore and wrung out. Vaguely I wondered what would happen if I stayed where I was. No doubt someone would just come in and drag me out. Though it was obviously my own fault, tonight was my idea.

Groaning and swearing under my breath, I rolled out of bed. Sitting on the side with my head in my hands, I looked towards the bed longingly. An image of Grayson lying there popped into my head and the refuge it offered soured. I leapt up into the bathroom. Another shower, it occurred to me that I was going to a posh do and therefore I needed to prep. Being a woman was unfair.

A small thought also crossed my mind, it would be nice to make someone's jaw drop. Finishing off and feeling really smooth, I got dressed in sweats, wondering out. Despite my reluctance to get up, there was a feeling of anticipation.

Tonight something was going to happen, I knew it.

I started the coffee up, taking it unto the roof with me. Nick joined me, "How you doing?"

"Better now that I have spoken to Maggie."

"How is she?"

"Alright, I think that she is happy to have some much in common with her mother. She keep saying Catherine this and Catherine that."

"That's sweet."

"I guess but I would feel better if she was here with us."

"Me to." Closing my eyes, "So what the plan for today."

Nick laughed, "I thought that we had handed that off to Sunny? Myself, I am going to go over the plans for tonight and check the suit that Daisy got me. Hopefully it won't be too uncomfortable."

"Great, what about me?"

"You could practise not getting into trouble." He chuckled as he wondered off.

"HaHa," I yelled at his back.

Staying a bit longer, I then forced myself down to the empty computer room. Logging on, I checked for any alerts. There were some, I rang and left a message for Catherine. I tried Louise's number next, not expecting her to answer but wanting to touch base. Just before I was about to end it, she answered. "Louise!"

"Olivia, can you meet me." Looking around the empty room, "Yes." Pausing, "Should I be worried?"

As of old, Louise laughed, bringing a smile to my face. "Probably. Does that mean that you are not going to come?"

"No, just felt I should prepare myself." She gave me an address and I looked it up, an hour away. Dressing better I texted my plans and the address to Nick, Sunny and Maggie. Already more organised. Grabbing a car, I set off.

It was good to be out, I turned the radio on and enjoyed the music. Arriving at the address, at the edge of London I parked in the overgrown driveway. So thick that I couldn't see the house itself. A general air of isolation lay everywhere, I was grateful that it wasn't night because that would be really spooky.

I turned and sent out my power, I felt something on the right but I couldn't get a focus. I pulled out my chain in case. Cautiously walking through the undergrowth, I was grateful for the boots that protected me against the thorns trying to snag me. Making my way through I could feel someone's senses reach out to me. There was no feeling of danger, just curious probing. Pushing on I finally saw a small detached house. It reminded me of a house from a story book. I marvelled at the small turrets and gothic windows. Louise waited at the front entrance, she had lost the sunken eyes and sense of defeat. With a wide reassuring smile she came forward to hug me. "Oh Olivia, it is so good to see you."

I returned the hug hard but accusing said, "I was so worried. Why did you tell me not to look for you?"

She drew back, "Come in and I will tell you." I was led in, it smelt of spices and magic. She drew me down next to her in an ornate sofa, "I didn't think that anyone could get me out of there. Sending that message to you was the last thing that I had the energy to do. I didn't want you to get caught as well." In response to my disbelieving look, she continued "You would have done the same, don't say that you wouldn't."

I couldn't argue against that, I shrugged. "I won't say that you are wrong. I don't truly know how I did it either."

She closed her eyes, "My poor girl, your father and I did you a disservice. For that I am truly sorry." She held my hands earnestly, "I am so proud of the woman that you have become." With a sly look, she said "I know that your father would be as well, has he told you?"

Startled I stood, "How did you know?" Shocked but relieved that I wasn't going crazy, well more than I was normally. Relieved to be able to talk about it, I eagerly asked, "It has only been twice but I was so grateful. What is it?"

Wringing her hands, she stood. "I will try to explain, when he suspected that he wouldn't be there for you, he wanted to leave something that could help. He went to someone who could see the future. That's how he got the safe house and money ready. You have to know he loved you very much." Continuing "I think that he made some sort of deal to take part of his soul and merge it with you, so that he could come to you and hero you at times."

That sounded weird, I wasn't sure how I felt about having part of his soul with me. No time to freak out about that, "Can you help me?"

"I have always helped you, Olivia and now we will help you."

"We?" As I said this, two people stepped into the room causing me to stand. They were my age, with power, though a different sort of power to those that I had come across. My hands itched as I collected my own power defensively.

Louise stood between us, "No Olivia, these are my children."

"What!", I couldn't bring myself to relax as there was something about their power. I backed towards the door. They didn't appear to find me a threat, as they sat on the sofa side by side. Oddly they spoke in sync, "We don't mean any harm, we want to help."

"Louise, I am so sorry but I have had too many shocks recently. I didn't know that you had children."

Louise walked towards me with her hands out, "I am sorry but it was too painful. I didn't even tell your father that I had children." She covered her face, tearfully continuing, "If I didn't talk about them then it was less painful. As you guess they are like yourself." Her children, stood and came to rest a hand on each of her shoulders. It seemed to give her comfort and she fondly looked up at them. "After they were taken away, I left and I learnt what I could."

"After I was taken and placed in the oubliette, in an effort to make me betray you, they learned of me. They hadn't known who I was or where I was. Once they found out they came to me but couldn't get me out."

The man looked at me, "You rescued our mother and for that we will help you."

"I want them to know you, you have been like a daughter to me. I trust them, I ask that you trust them too."

I felt bad but I had to ask, "Sorry, Louise, why would they want to help me?" I came forward and held her hands, kneeling before her. "I have been naïve before but now the stakes are so much higher."

"I understand, I really do but they and I will help."

I worried my lip again, absently playing with my chain. The twins followed the movements of my hands in a snake like way, blinking very slowly. Way creepy especially in combination with their white hair, pale eyes and stick thin figures. Closing my eyes, I felt out towards the twins but their auras were nebulous. "It will help if they allowed me to see their intentions."

Louise looked towards her children as they stared unblinkingly at me. They looked at her and then each other, in unspoken agreement they dropped their mental walls. Feeling their essences, an outer shell of chaos with calm cores. Consisting of their love for each other and their mother.

Reassuringly they held no ill will towards me but a deep hatred of the Society.

There were images of their childhoods, the Professor. Painful memories that had made them into the heartless things that they had become. I was extremely grateful that my father had kept me away. Pulling back, tears in my eyes, "Thank you for your trust." Gently and in unison they inclined their heads, raising back their walls. "I should have asked, what should I call you?"

With a courtly bow, "I am Harrison, this is my sister Carrie."

Choking back a smile, I pursed my lips tightly. I had to suspect that someone obviously liked Star Wars. When we had more time, I would like to get to know them.

My phone chimed, I frowned as I saw that there were missed calls and a text. 'Where are you? I came and you weren't here. No-one will tell me where you are.'

Harrison leant forward interestedly, "Text him the address."

"Really? This guy seems a bit of an overbearing idiot." At his single raised eyebrow, I sighed knowing that trust had to start somewhere. Louise was also looking puzzled, until Carrie leant over whispering something in her ear causing her to giggle. When I caught her eye with a raised eyebrow, she turned it into a cough.

He responded back, 'On my way, stay there.' Well really, did I need babysitting. Deciding to ignore him, I filled them in about our plans.

They remained quiet though Louise was obviously worried. Harrison spoke, "Why do you need to meet him?" voicing his doubts.

Respecting that he knew him better than I did, "So then tell me about him." He looked unconvinced and worried about my sanity. Again, I tried to explain the unexplainable, what I felt in my bones. "I have to meet him tonight, it will make a difference."

Wordlessly he held one hand to him and another to his sister. Linking us, I dropped my walls for them to scan me. He held it for so long that I started to worry about what they were seeing.

Finally they released me, it felt strange to have been scanned. Harrison spoke solemnly, "She feels that this meeting is fated. She could be right, it will be the end for one of you. Are you ready for that because it includes those who follow you."

I felt the weight of his words, a chill running through me. He continued to stare at me, "I am not sure that you are the right person but you are the only one standing up." He turned his gaze away to his mother and sister. "My sister and I will help you but from outside, if they see us the game is up."

Impulsively hugged him, "I will be most grateful for that." A cough broke us apart, my new nemesis was standing in the doorway looking pointedly at us. Reese, that had been his name. An uncalled for blush stained my cheeks and I stepped back. Harrison held Reese's eyes and slowly let me go. Reese's eyes narrowed further and he crossed his arms with his legs wide.

Trying to prevent any testosterone driven escalation I stepped between them. "Reese, thanks for coming," though I didn't invite you. This is my friend Louise and these are her children, Harrison and Carrie.

There was a pause before he relaxed his posture. He smiled charmingly at them, coming forward and shaking hands. Other than a full top to toe slow check of my body, that made me want to smooth my hair, he ignored me. I resented this charming man, I hadn't gotten an ounce of it myself.

As I sat silently fuming, Louise came over. "He is a charmer," as we watched him talking to Harrison and Carrie. "I didn't get to say it before bit I am sorry about Grayson. He fooled me." I shrugged my shoulders, what could I say but as I opened my mouth I was interrupted.

Reese cut in, "Well I think that we have a plan. Let me just update Catherine." He pulled his phone out and towed me out with him.

"Catherine, I am with Olivia. She has found someone for the team, powerful." He didn't take his eyes off me as he listened. I couldn't help but fidget under his gaze. "Here she is."

I took the phone, "Hello. Yes, I have sensed them and their

intentions are pure. They would be able to distract and protect our backs. I know that I am putting us all on the line with this."

"She wants to talk to you again."

"I trust her and these people." Shocked that he had backed me up, I stared at him. He gave me a smirk and turned away. Fine, I walked back to Louise, who was watching from the doorway.

"You could at least pretend not to be watching."

She laughed, "You have your hands full there. Thinking back, that was what was missing with Grayson. He just let you lead the way all the time. It wasn't what you needed."

I shook my head vehemently, "We aren't like that."

"Reese will, I am sure give you more details. But don't put yourself at further risk for me. You have done more than anyone could have expected and I love you for that."

Reese came back in and addressed everyone briskly, "I am going to need to have your numbers, you probably don't need the plans. We are also going to send you some pictures, you can help identify what we might be up against."

I interrupted while he took a breath, "Do you know how to help us identify the people linked with the demon?"

Carrie nodded, "Their auras will be corrupted." Sh looked at me, "You should be able to identify them. The gifted weren't allowed to be linked or know who was." Well that was reassuring.

As Harrison, Carrie and Reese sat by a computer and started going over things, I couldn't help but feel anxious. Reese frowned at me a couple of times and pulled a chair next to him but I didn't sit. Louise rescued me by getting me help get some food, which we delivered to them. She didn't stay but took ours with her outside. "You need to be in nature."

As we entered a lovely walled off garden, with old tall trees that provided shade. Flowers were everywhere scenting the air. That felt better, "Ah, you noticed that this area is protected. It was to provide a space for my healing." She looked around proudly.

I sat on the grass, Louise settled herself on a bench. "I know that this isn't relevant tonight but I want to talk about Chi. He is something very different. Even the Professor is wary of him, respectful too. He therefore must be more powerful. Watch yourself. The Professor wants you. You are something that he always wanted to create, not just you but the children you could have."

Lying back on the grass, I closed my eyes which didn't help thoughts. They were all tumbling with thoughts, it was all too much. Determinedly I sat up, no just focus on tonight. What I had to do, so to that end I decided that I should meditate, build some energy. Closing my eyes, I felt for the centre that I had developed, that core of strength that I now knew that I had. Repeating that I could do this and I would do this.

I lost all touch with my physical body and surroundings, trusting in Louise and the others to protect me. It felt like something new, another plane. Drifting along, I found my father.

He smiled at me, and we were back in Louise's garden. He smiled at me sadly, "My Olivia, how strong you have become. I am so proud, you are going to have to be even stronger. Tonight he will tell you that I am not your father. I turned away, not wanting to hear this. "I am your father in all the ways that matter."

I had thought that I had it all under control but it explained something more, why Grayson had latched onto me. "It okay, you are my father. Thank you for keeping me away from him."

Smiling proudly but sadly he disappeared. His voice fading with "I love you."

I whispered back, "I love you too" as I opened my eyes, tears still on my face.

I lay for a little longer just wanting to hold onto those thoughts and feelings. They should have made me weaker but they just hardened my resolve.

CHAPTER 28

A shadow fell over me, removing the warmth of the sun and the tranquility of the garden, I knew immediately who it was. I could feel the self conscious prickling of my skin. I debated for a moment whether to ignore him. I sighed frustratedly as I reluctantly opened them. Already I could feel his annoyance bathing me. Raising myself up, I leaned back on my elbows. Squinting up I could only make out Reese's outline as he stood staring down at me. I fidgeted as I waited for him to speak, annoyed that I couldn't see his expression.

Finally caving, "Can I help you?" I said with a bite in my voice. Reese said nothing, continuing to stare at me. Feeling at disadvantage, I got up but ended up chest to chest. He didn't step back, in fact it felt like he had leaned forward. My heart raced as I peered up at him. He didn't appear to feel as I did, indeed he appeared to have flexing his muscles. I licked my dry lips, looking away in defeat as I stepped back. Crossing my own arms, "Problem?" He took a deep breath but still said nothing. "We are going to have to work together, you can't just stare angrily at me." Pissed with his attitude, I huffed and walked around him.

He grabbed my arm, "I know that we have to work together but I don't trust your naivety or inability to apparently control yourself."

I tugged my arm back angrily, ignoring the burn from where I could still feel his handprint. "I will not mess this up." I poked him in the chest, "How do I know that you won't? What are you bringing exactly?"

A wicked smile appeared, he stepped into me again and bent down to whisper in my ear, "Why Olivia, I bring me?" I was unable to hide the shiver and the goosebumps that appeared. He turned and politely waited for me, "Shall we."

I gritted my teeth, fuming at him and the loss of serenity that I had. Spying Louise standing by the door, I forced a smile.

Apparently not noticing my mood, she asked brightly "I hope that was useful?"

Yeah, until I was disturbed. "Thank you Louise, I needed that but I have to go now." At the movement next to me, "We have to leave now, you all set?"

Reese answered for her, "Yes. We sorted it while you were having a lie down."

"I was meditating and anyway isn't that what you came for?" Challenging I raised an eyebrow at him, "I will be sure to let Catherine know how helpful you have been." I turned away enjoying the scowl that had appeared on his face. Despite that he nodded politely to Louise as he said goodbye. Louise winked at me after he had turned away and I rolled my eyes back at her. Her laughter made me hug her harder.

He had already gotten into his undamaged, pausing by the back passenger door. He called out, "Don't even think about it." Grumpily I got in the front passenger, he didn't acknowledge me as he started off. I leaned back in my seat thinking over what had happened today, closing my eyes. I could feel him looking at me occasionally, the looks causing my skin to tingle. I was annoyed that I felt anything and sat up straight. I pulled out my phone seeing a message from Sunny.

In the theme of avoidance, I turned to the window and rang her. She picked up quickly, "You seriously have to stop wandering off. I know, I did appreciate the text messages." Guilty I apologised again, ignoring the laugh next to me. "You needed your sleep and it was worth it, tell you about it when I get back."

"You better, I am going to check on things. By the way, you are going to love the dress!"

She cut off me with my mouth open, I could already tell that I wouldn't like the dress. As I turned away, I caught a small smile that disappeared as soon as I saw it. He rumbled, "We might die tonight but you're worried about the dress that you might die in?"

"You don't know how bad it might be, guys never have to worry. So unfair."

He laughed, I was surprised by how relaxed he had suddenly got. I got distracted watching him drive, my eyes running over his face and body. I shifted in my seat, feeling hot again. What was going on. Annoyed at myself, I spoke. "I know the plan and I do my best to follow it but shit just happens around me."

I was almost relieved by the frown that appeared but he suddenly pulled over to the side of the road with a scream of tires. Horns blared at us as we sat there. I clutched at my belt that had bitten into me. He undid his and leaned over to me, angrily "You are a dangerous liability, I can not believe that Catherine believes in you."

Not really having a thought to danger I replied, "Why are you questioning her. I thought you were a good follower?"

He stared into my eyes, he had taken off his sunglasses and I was caught by his eyes. He was breathing deeply and harshly, my eyes fell to his lips and his to mine.

His next words, brought me back to myself, "You both made a mistake with Grayson. I knew he was bad news."

"Wow, you must be psychic."

"No, you are naive."

"So what does it matter to you, it was my mistake. It wasn't like you shared a bed with him."

He went completely still. I panted, he eased slowly back into his seat, rubbing his face. Then with speed, he turned the car back on and pulled into traffic. "Yes that was your mistake." There was something off in his tone and the way that he avoided looking at me. I turned my head away not trusting what I would say.

There was an uncomfortable silence in the car. I was angry with him and myself. I didn't know what his problem was but aware that he didn't trust me. That stung but I didn't know why it should.

"Seriously I will follow your instructions but we have to have a working relationship. I need to know that we have each others backs."

"Fuck it." With another angry twist of the wheel, he pulled onto the side again. He stared forward, "I know everything that you have done. Amazing, incredible things, shown strength that few others have. I am not going to be only having a working relationship with you." With that, he swung back onto the road.

"Ah...what?"

"I think that I was quite clear."

Stammering, as I processed his words, "I thought you didn't like me?"

"Well guess again." Looking over at my shocked face, he sighed. "Forget I said anything, just know that I trust you and I have definitely got your back."

"Okay?"

"Good, don't say anything else I am not sure how I will react."

We arrived back and I put my hand on the lock. "I will see you later and I am looking forward to seeing the dress." The cocky was back in his voice and I blushed.

I stumbled out and ran up the stairs without looking back, feeling hot and flustered. "Bloody man." Slamming the door behind me, I leant against it taking some calming breaths.

"What are you doing?" Daisy asked, looking at me with amusement.

Shrugging, I smiled wanly at her, "Nothing. So what's this about a dress?"

Immediately her look changed to guilty. "I don't know what you mean?"

I knew that I had her, as she avoided looking at me, "Daisy?"

"No time to change it, so you are stuck with my choice. I mean I would have shown you if you had been here." She smiled, knowing that she had me. "Don't worry, I know what you need, even when you don't." Turning away, motioning for me to follow her. "You can't be mad at me anyway, I am very pregnant and I don't get to dress up."

Oh why did she have to go there, I gave up and caught up to her smiling. "When you are right, you are right. You know that you won't be able to use that forever right?"

"Well a bit longer anyway," she giggled.

"Come on then, lets she what we are all wearing?"

She squealed in delight, "I knew one day I would get you to dress up." She pulled me with her, her excitement was infectious. Laughing I let her tug me forward.

We went to Sunny's room first, where Sunny was lying in the dark. Daisy slammed the door open, clicking on the lights while announcing, "She's back!"

Groggily Sunny jumped up and hugged me, then rubbed her eyes. "Olivia, you have to remember that you are the linch pin of this operation. Think bigger than just you from now on." I looked suitably admonished and then she smiled, "So tell me about these people you meant."

While we sat on the bed, I filled them in on what had happened. They were understandably a little apprehensive with all the new people. Trust was difficult to earn.

Sunny summed it up, "So they really are able to go against a life time of conditioning?" Nick had come in while we had talked, he seemed quiet and just took it all in.

I understood but felt that for this they could be trusted. As I opened my mouth, trying to think about how to reassure her, she closed her eyes. "So we are going with your gut again, aren't we."

I shrugged ruefully, "You know me so well."

Daisy was laughing at us, "I can't wait to see Louise, I bet she will be able to give me some tips on having a special child." That was something that I hadn't considered but we could both do with her help.

Turning, "Nick, you are being very quiet. What do you think?"

He considered me, "We have prepared as much as we can do. Let's try not to get caught or worse." His somber words caused all of us to pause.

"Neither would I, Nick, neither would I. Why don't we review everything again."

He talked us through, how we would arrive, exits in case. Sunny added, "I will be jamming any external communications, with Catherine's team. There will be no reinforcements. I need to be nearby in case." I frowned but knew that she was right. We ran through pictures of the members.

Nick suggested that we call Catherine's team, confirm meeting points and any extra intel. The conference call was another hour, with the lead taken by Reese annoyingly, I kept to the side of the camera, so that I wasn't seen. Maggie, Sunny and Nick. As I looked at them each presenting and reviewing aspects, I couldn't help but feel proud of this team, this family that we had become.

Catherine ended the meeting. "This evil will be stopped tonight and our names will be remembered, by a few. Our loved ones revenged. Olivia?" I moved into view, "You need to be guarded, Reese will be your shadow."

I opened my mouth to protest but she cut in, "This whole plan depends on you and I can depend on you for this?"

With everyone looking at me, what else could I say, "Of course." Ignoring Reese and his knowing smile.

"Reese and Maggie will come to yours, as you need to arrive together." This made me happier, and by the look on Nick's face he agreed.

I had forgotten that Daisy was about to live her best life through me. I was only allowed to eat because I insisted that I would pass out if I didn't. Then a quick shower, where she made me shave and scrub everything that she could get me to. Several lost layers of skin, I sat while Daisy plucked, moisturised, made up and pulled my hair. It was impossible to feel that she was getting revenge for something, as she couldn't possibly be my friend. I was questioning my looks, as really should it take this long.

Nick popped his head in while I was swearing and snorted with laughter. All he had to do was wash and shave, on his own. Men! Daisy, while doing her own muttering about ungratefulness, pulled the dress out. Making me close my eyes, She slid something slinky over me. "Ta da!"

Taking that too mean that I could open my eyes, I did. I stood in silence as I looked at myself, turning around. I knew that no one would recognise me.

In the mirror was an undeniably beautiful woman. I touched my hair had been taken up in an undo, a few strands floating by my face. The makeup, was stunning, my eyes, even behind the glasses were highlighted. I had cheekbones and a lovely dewy glow, I kept turning my face and touching it. The dress itself was sexy, thin spaghetti straps held up a light weight dress, made of some shiny sky blue material. It floated when I moved, and ended by my knees, which I appreciated. The back dropped, exposing my back. It was surprisingly non-restrictive, I could run and Daisy held out some boy shorts to put underneath. They had artfully concealed pockets that I could place my knife and other things. My chain would fit nicely into the design around my waist.

Daisy was bouncing on her feet, her earlier irritations forgotten. "I love it and I love you."

She blushed and "I love you too, this is how everyone sees you, you just never realised it."

"I think you work magic."

She continued to blush, "These are the shoes, heels but so comfortable, you could run a race in them." As I continued to thank her, she shrugged it off. "I need to catch up with the others."

She rushed out of the room and I could not help but look at myself in the mirror some more. Smiling, I wondered if I could get some pictures because I was not going through that again. The plus side was that I had not had times for nerves.

I put on the shoes and they felt so comfortable, wow. I added my chains as a belt, easily accessible. I added my knife, I could not see it or its outline.

Stretching out my neck, I stole another glimpse at myself and went out to meet the others.

I heard a car pull up and decided to get coffee ready. I heard Maggie before I saw her, "Olivia, I have so much to tell you. Oh my god, you look amazing. Reese, you have to see Olivia."

I turned fully, as Reese came around the corner. He looked amazing in an evening suit, very handsome. As my eyes moved up from my involuntary perusal, I caught him looking stunned. Shuffling self consciously, I couldn't break eye contact. Maggie had stopped, staring between Reese and me. "Ah, well I will go and check in on the others."

Reese shook his head, "Olivia you look amazing," he stepped towards me with a heavy tread. I didn't, couldn't move. As he stopped in front of me, he gently touched my cheek. As he leaned forward, the others came to join us. I stepped away, busying myself with the coffee. I felt him move to my side but facing the others. I needed to get this butterflies and racing of my heart under control.

As I offered around coffee, I belatedly looked over my friends. They all looked amazing. Maggie and Nick were holding hands tightly, their eyes not leaving each other.

Everyone had nerves, waiting for the time that we were to leave. I escaped with my coffee for just one moment alone on the roof. Looking across London, I thought of the millions of unaware people. Hopefully they would reap the benefits without any of the worry.

I had a purpose in my life, I was proud to have helped the people that I had helped so far. I wanted to finish it, I had to trust that I could do this. I wasn't on my own, I had support.

Someone came up and I could sense that it was Daisy. She stood by the rail with me.

"We have come a long way haven't we." It wasn't a question, it was a statement.

"That we have."

"You have grown, you aren't the girl that was waiting to live, to experience life. It was like you were on hold."

"I was, I can not believe that all this has happened over a

season, it feels like more."

"I know what you mean, I can't wait to meet my baby though. It feels different now, the baby feels different. I will try to be an amazing mum. I am not alone."

"Just you survive Olivia," Daisy looked away still, over the houses. "I can not do this without you, so you have to come back."

"I promise you that I will fight with everything I have." We stood and stared at the sky, as it darkened.

Sunny called from below, "Time to go."

CHAPTER 29

As we gathered downstairs, ready to go, Daisy insisted that she take a picture. It crossed my mind that it was incase some of us weren't going to return. Something that had maybe crossed other minds, as we all stood awkwardly in the kitchen area. It was certainly quiet, everyone lost in their thoughts. It reminded me of soldiers going into battle. Though they certainly dressed differently.

I hugged Daisy but refused to say bye. As I turned away and came down the stairs I felt fragile, vulnerable. Reese stood there, I slowed, not wanting a confrontation. He took my hand and led me to the car, opening the door. As I got in, he leant over helping me in. "Don't worry, it is all going to be fine."

"Thank you," I whispered, looking at him seeing only sincerity. I placed my hand over his heart, pausing for a moment, he covered my hand with mine and nodded consent. I felt, finding strength, passion and a soft centre. Strong feelings for me but I drew back before looking to hard. Letting go, I tumbling back into myself.

He grabbed my hand before I could pull away, "Do I meet your approval?"

"I am not sure but I do believe that you have my back. Enough for now?" I smiled softly at him and pulled away. After a moment he let me go.

With a wink, he nodded as if to himself, "Yes, for now." |with that promise, hr closed my door and got into the driver seat.

Intense. I turned, watching the others come down. Embarrassed I looked away as Maggie and Nick shared a private moment. Reese looked knowingly at me and I shifted.

An unexpectedly quiet Sunny got in next to me, her usual

buoyancy subdued. I held her hand tightly, as we shuffled over to make room for Maggie. Nick sat up front with Reese. We set off.

Closing my eyes I decided that I would be useless, unless I centred myself. With the butterflies it took ten minutes or so before I was there. Once I had achieved my calm, I projected it onto my friends. Helping to centre, reinforcing our bonds. Suddenly the car swerved, jerking my eyes open. Reese was gesturing at his hand. Nick was trying to explain something but as he held his hand up we could all see that he had received the tattoo.

Nick laughed, "Olivia must have decided that you are part of the family."

Reese grinned broadly and I ignored his eyes in the mirror. Blushing, I realised that I had unconsciously included him. I ignored the knowing smiles from Sunny and Maggie.

Finally we arrived, I had found my zone and felt powerful, Reese got out and was by my door to help me from the car, his hand lingering on mine. I could feel his strength and confidence flowing to me. I smiled at him, causing him to smile back, as I stepped forward his hand fell to my lower back.

When Sunny got out, she veered towards the bank of parked cars. Swinging herself confidently into a catering van at the back. Maggie and Nick had already moved on to the brightly lit entrance.

We remained behind, as I fidgeted Reese rubbed small circles with his thumb. "Calm down, we have enter separately. Catherine will be following us in."

I nodded, "I have never been good with waiting. Well while we wait, I need to place protection over us." At his raised eyebrows, I continued, "Well more like a don't notice us but trust us. It will make us unremarkable, not memorable with a little anti-glamour protection." As he raised his eyebrows, "I stepped closer, it might tingle a little." I closed my eyes and placed it.

Reese whistled and held his hand out, looking at it while turning it over. "It feels like something soft around me, protective. When others do something like it, it feels itchy, irritating. But not with you." He smiled at me.

Feeling shy, "I don't really know what I am doing, all self taught."

"I am not complaining, I am impressed." Looking at his watch, he held his arm out for me, "Shall we?"

"Yes, let's do this." I placed my hand on his arm and took a deep breath, as we stepped forward.

Anti-climatically we joined the line of guests, no alarms rang but I kept my eye on the security. There was certainly a lot. I thanked Daisy for the dress, I certainly fit right in as I looked at all the amazing evening dressed around me.

As we reached the end of the line, Reese produced our tickets and IDs. He did it more smoothly than I would have, an air of entitlement surrounded him. I just smiled. We were directed through, there were some gifted in the area, probably scanning for threats. I shivered as their attention went over us. It moved on, success though I did add some extra layers. As we moved on, following the crowd there was a commotion behind us. We turned, as did everyone else. A man had been halted by the gifted, he was protesting loudly. Quickly surrounded by security, so that I could not see him. He got louder, I could hear "Where is my daughter, you bastards. I want her right now." He started to struggle until a woman came and touched him, then he suddenly went quiet. As the man was dragged away, she was clearly visible, the powerful blonde. She was dressed in a pure white sheath with long side slits, showing her athletic figure, the dress almost matched her platinum white blonde hair that was cut into a pixie cut. Cold spread out from her, encouraging people to turn away and move on. Even security moved quickly on. Without me realising, Reese had angled himself between us. "Come on."

I had no interest in confronting her, I had no doubt that she was more powerful than me. Suddenly her head swung around, she looked around intently. Reese kept us moving and I breathed a sigh of relief as I lost sight of her. I hoped that the man was alright but I doubted it. Reese bent his head to whisper, "Never let her touch you." I nodded energetically, in complete agreement.

"Let us get started. Remember you need to just identify them."

He grabbed us a couple of drinks and we moved around trying to fit in. Unbelievably we walked into one of the people we had suspected immediately. A heavy set woman, squeezed into a skin tight dress, that left nothing to the imagination. Almost every guy was staring at her breasts. Reese squeezed my hand as he moved forward to talk to her, appearing mesmerised by her. I pushed down the jealousy that I felt heat my blood. He was doing a job, I reminded myself, as she flirted back.

As I stood a little to the side, I concentrated seeing her aura. It was different, there was an extra red streak that led off her aura. It was almost siphoning something from her. As I moved to look at it more closely, Reese distracted her. Without thinking I put my hand out to touch the red streak and then pulled it. There was resistance, which I overcame pushing my power into it. It reached back, trying to reach me. Gross, I reinforced my shields while pushing more power into removing it. My shields held, it wasn't able to latch on. With its focus on me, it had detached fully from its host. I encased it, drawing all of it inside. It thrashing around, like a snake twisting in on itself. There was something like the echo of a scream but gradually it became duller and duller. With no power it seemed to fade away.

I came back as Reese called out, "Oh my god, are you okay?" I saw what he meant, she had gone deathly pale and collapsed where she stood. Someone managed to catch her, lowering her to the ground. A murmur of voices, asking what had happened. Reese dispersed with the crowd, gone by the time a member of staff had joined.

I saw Catherine and I moved towards her. Facing forward, she asked me "Did you do that?"

"Yes but I am not completely sure about what I just did."

"When are you ever. With no training, no big spell or noise.

You severed the link between her and the demon." She was obviously impressed. "So now there is a new plan, the guardians are to be brought to you. You will sever their links, I will play with the Professor. He will learn of these losses soon enough and then there will be fireworks. I will let the others know."

Before I could say anything she was gone, as a server went past with some champagne I snagged a glass. The change of plan had left me unsettled though I understood the logic. While I was sipping, Reese came up taking my elbow, "Well done. Lets get the next one."

So we started mingling, Reese proved to be charmingly good at small talk. I stood and smiled, as I switched my sight. Despite our mission, I could appreciate that these were interesting people, who I would have enjoyed meeting under other circumstances. I had to remind myself that these were the bad guys, even if by omission. We continued to move through all the rooms, ending up in another room, more richly appointed. I was surprised to see a child standing with his parents, I had not expected to see any children. He appeared to be about ten years old, looking bored. "Hello," kneeling to his level, I switched my sight and saw his red streak. "You are very special aren't you?"

"Yes," he replied seriously, "My parents have always told me that I was made for something and I carry a great power."

Okay, that was a creepy. I looked at Reese, nodding towards the boy. He looked at me and then the child, surprise and disgust crossing his expression.

He also crouched down, "Hi, do you want some pudding? I know where they put them for later." The boy looked torn for a moment, glancing at his parents before shaking his head. "No they wouldn't like that." His colours appeared more intense, I wondered if that meant that the bonding was stronger. That would mean that the bonding must have been more painful, what had his parents been thinking. Looking over at them, I saw that they were intensely proud, basking in his importance.

Forcing myself to, I smiled at them, "What an amazing son you have." We moved on around the corner, I ducked behind some foliage. It wasn't that great a distance and I thought it better to try before taking their son away. Pulling Reese close to me, I thought that it could look like we were doing nothing more than stealing a moment. Trying to ignore the heat of his body, so close to mine. I concentrated in unravelling the red threads. This time they fought more, the boy's own essence fighting me, trying to hold on on to the demon power. Needing more, I kissed Reeses's jaw, feeling him stiffen but taken that boost. Slowly, so slowly with sweat building between my shoulder blades I persevered. Suddenly with relief, I realised that I was making progress, giving me the needed push to finish. Finally they were all separated and it faded as the other had done. I sagged against Reese, his arms supporting me. "Done," I whispered.

"Well done, you did good." He spoke as the crying starting from the boy. I couldn't seen him but he sounded heart broken, confusion reigning. We moved out, looking shocked, no one seemed to be paying us any attention.

Reese moved through the gathered crowd, snagging me some water. "Why was that harder?"

"The boy and the demon were bonded more strongly, I really hope that the others aren't going to be like that. Not sure I have it in me."

Looking concerned, he reassured me as he scanned the next room. "Don't push too hard, if you don't have the energy, then we just identify them and go with the original plan. Remember we think that there are four more." His tone was flat but I recognised concern.

"Okay." He looked shocked that I had agreed and hugged me close. Then his eyes moved to the right and I could tell that he was listening to his ear bud. "They have already identified two, we just have to find two ourselves."

"How come I didn't get one of those."

He grinned, "So the you have to stay close to me."

"Really?" I frowned, though I thought it was cute.

He laughed at my expression, "No, we thought that you would fry them with your gift." Then he paused, looking uncomfortable and unsure. He looked away and then at me from under his eyelashes. "You need energy, you know that I can recharge you."

I blushed, as I realised what he was saying. I felt myself get hot, I was about to refuse but then looked him in the eye. I went blank and could say nothing. He pulled me out of a nearby patio door, leading me into the shadows. He pulled his ear piece out, while pressing me against the cold wall. All I felt was his heat in front of me, he leant slowly in and then paused a hairs breath away from my lips. As he held himself torturously close, I didn't understand why he didn't move. Then I realised that he wanted me to make the final move, I reached up and crushed our lips together. As out lips danced together, his swept his tongue across my lips and I opened on a moan. I could feel my energy building, more than it gad with Grayson. That thought made me pull back regretfully, we rested our foreheads together.

A quick kiss and he leant back putting his ear piece in. Abruptly he pulled me with him, "We have to go they have found two. Are you ready?"

I felt like I could take anything on, my whole body filled with power, I was surprised that I wasn't glowing. Nodding, I rechecked our shields. "Lets go." We reentered the room, and without effort I could see everyones auras. Smiling, I dragged Reese along with me for once. Moving rapidly I was able to scan them quickly. Then I spotted one, a young guy, about my age. There was something familiar about him, I approached him from the side, so that he didn't see me directly. Then I realised where I had seen him before. He had been the guy that had taken Daisy, I recognised his smarmy arse. This would be a pleasure, I had no doubt that he wouldn't recognise me. I looked very different and I had my shield. I left Reese with a look, as I approached him with a smile. He liked to be noticed and responded quickly, not delaying when I asked him outside for some fresh air. I laughed at his joke as we walked outside, Reese following at a distance. I could feel is anger at the risk that I was taking. Someone might remember that I accompanied him out but I wanted revenge for Daisy. Under the stars, he looked up and I hit him with a bolt of energy to the heart. He went over like a rag doll, I quickly took out the demon connection. It was easier than with the child, it seemed relieved to be rid of him. Though that could be me reading too much into something inanimate. I turned to find Reese waiting. He didn't say anything but just held his arm to escort me inside. I looked down at the man and kicked him in his privates, Reese winced in manly sympathy. "Dare I ask what he did to deserve that?"

"He took Daisy." Reese drew back to look at the man again. Then he kicked him harder.

I laughed, he shrugged. "Wish we had time to do more. Your shoes held you back from giving it everything."

He held his arm out and escorted me back in side. I spotted a flash of red in the auras. It seemed that we were approaching the centre of the party and it was crowded, making it difficult to move through. Then the crowds parted and I saw Grayson. Not the Grayson that I first met but an angry, scarred man. He glared at everyone around him, muttering under his breath. He appeared dangerous and unpredictable. The shielding that he had before was gone, his aura was a sickly grey with the red threaded throughout. I ducked when his eyes moved over us but there was no recognition. Strangely I was both disappointing and a relief. Reese had followed me eyes, he gritted his teeth, his jaw tight. "Problem?"

"Just Grayson."

"Of course, it had to be him!" Reese said sarcastically. "He is not going to follow you outside."

"I agree."

Then he swore, "Isn't that his sister?"

I spotted a glowing and slim Cecilia. "Yep, she appears to have had her baby." Most annoyingly she looked amazing, I couldn't believe that she had had a baby only recently, I hoped that Daisy didn't see any pictures of her. She was proudly grasping onto the arm of a tall and distinguished looking man.

"He would follow his sister."

"She has her memories, so she will follow me or raise an alarm." I bit my lip, not sure what to do.

Grayson looked at his watch, "We need to take the risk. We need to move this along. At some point they are going to raise an alarm. I don't like our choices."

I indicated an exit, "Go out there. I will catch her eye and then come out."

He gripped my hand and slipped out. I moved so that I was in her line of sight, breathing deeply to calm myself. I dropped my shielding and felt it when she saw me. Her face dropped and then filled with anger. She felt different, she had something extra. I pretended that I hadn't noticed her and moved to the exit while raising my shielding back up. Sweat gathered again as I moved away, my back towards her. Once through the door I sprinted outside and took refuge behind a tree. I didn't see Reese but I had no doubt that he was nearby. I saw her approach the door, she was gesturing to someone and pointing outside. Oh that wasn't good.

She, Grayson and two other men stepped outside. The men drew guns and it looked like they know what they were doing.

I tried to move quietly, though it seemed as if I was stepping on every twig there was. Every step sounded loud and I could hear my breathing quicken. My dress caught on a branch and ripped. I looked up to the sky and rolled my eyes. As I looked back couldn't see the two men or Grayson, just Cecilia impatiently tapping her foot. I prepared an energy bolt to stun her. Just as I drew back my arm, someone barrelled into me. I gasped for air, pushing frantically at the body on top of me. With some distance I saw that it was Grayson. He stared at me, my shielding had dropped. He looked confused and then understanding, I literally saw when he recognised me. I kicked desperately with my legs, lifting my pelvis up and then twisted to the side.   Grayson roared behind me but I didn't look back. I ran at Cecilia, she screamed and I punched her hard. Turning to Grayson, I pushed power like a punch at him. He stumbled and hit him again. Powered by fear and anger he went flying against a tree and didn't move again. After checking that he was out, I held his head and started unravelling. I was aware that adrenaline was all that was keeping me upright. I uncoiled the red threads, they ran throughout his aura. Finally as I watched the collected coils fade, I heard the roar.

Collapsing back onto the ground, I stared at the stars. I felt something loosen in myself, pulling away. Something had changed but I didn't know what it was but as a shadow fell over me, it could have happened at a better time.

CHAPTER 30

"You are in so much trouble, bitch. You hurt my brother, have done something to the Master and I am owed a favour for giving him a gifted son." With great enjoyment she kicked me in the stomach. "You could have had it all but you are too stupid to have known it." She kicked me again, I rolled over with it. I coughed, it felt like some of my ribs were broken. It had been going so well. As I looked over at Cecilia, I saw her pick up a tree branch. Oh that wasn't good, I braced myself as she hit he across my back. I screamed. Have to distract her, I couldn't see Reese or the others, hopefully they were still on the job.

"How or should I say what is your baby?" I gasped out, spitting out some blood.

"He will be so powerful, I haven given him over to his destiny. I can not have you interfere with that, without the Master, there will be no destiny." She spat at me, "You will suffer and then you are going to fix what ever it is that you have done."

"Can't do that, sorry," I blithely gasped out and then kicked her legs from under her. She went down hard and hit her head on a decorative statue. She stared at me, her eyes opened in an uncomprehending stare. She was not going to be getting up.

I rolled onto my back, hasping at the pain but blow out a breath. "I have to say that you would have been an absolutely terrible mother." With a grunt I continued to struggle to stand up. It took a couple of toys, due to the pain from my back and ribs.

As I hugged a tree, desperately trying not to pass out, I heard fast footsteps from the side. I tensed.

It was Reese, bruises standing out over his face and holding his left arm awkwardly. As he laid eyes on me, relief flooded his face. "Thank god you are alright." He held me with his one arm, "There were four other men." He looked down at the body. "I am sorry that you had to do that but you did the right thing. "Can you walk?"

"Try and stop me."

"That's my girl."

"It will be slowly though," I joked.

Smiling, he helped me move with a careful arm aoround my waist. "I think that we look out of place now," he said woefully bit with a glint in his eye.

I giggled uncontrollably, "I was just starting to like the dress."

"Oh I really liked the dress," he raised his eyebrows meaningfully. He bent and kissed me hard, which then gentled. Pulling back reluctantly he touched his earpiece. "We are okay but there are some casualties." He listened,"Shit," he stiffened. "We are coming."

"What has happened?"

"Catherine met with the Professor but then she has disappeared. There were two teams watching her, I don't know how she has disappeared."

"We need to help," I bravely said but with a wince.

He looked down and wryly said, "No we need to join the backup, neither one of us is up for more right now." Kissing my head, he turned, "Come on." Supporting each other we made a long journey to the others. Passing the doors carefully, I could hear that it was disturbingly quiet.

"Do you think everyone left?" I whispered.

"No, something has happened. Careful!" He caught me as I tripped and he pulled me closer to his side. Every step hurt, making me catch my breath. Reese didn't look like he was doing much better. We were now just staggering along. I focused on making just one step at a time, not the distance. Suddenly Sunny was there, gently pulling me aside and taking my weight as she muttered bad things she going to do to the people who had hurt me. I giggled even though it hurt. "Hey we aren't dead."

She looked exasperated but a small smile lurked at the corner of her mouth. "You are an idiot, come this way, those strange twins can do healing. It's freaky." As I looked back, "Don't worry they will help Reese too."

She helped me to one of the vans , Louise was there with her son. She came forward to help me into a chair. "Sit down Olivia, Harrison will help you. Though I suspect that his power, like yours is somewhat reduced. You did a good job."

Harrison came over, I couldn't read his expression. Flatly he spoke, "Rest and you to relax all your shields. I must warn you this will feel intrusive." Closing my eyes, I allowed myself to feel how exhausted I was. As I was wondering how I was going to end this, Harrison put his hand on my forehead and I passed out.

The next thing, I knew I was floating on a cloud and I stretched contentedly. As I did, I became, I followed them. As I come to, the first thing I noticed with relief was, no pain. Gingerly I took a deep breath, I could do that. Amazing, now this was a power worth having. I sat forward, seeing Louise looking worried. "Whats going on?" She turned around with a start, putting her hand on her chest and then rushed forward to hug me.

"You scared me, is my son good or what?"

"He is an absolute angel. I can hardly remember the pain." I could hear raised voices, "Whats going on?"

"They are arguing about what to do about Catherine, these are her team after all. She isn't the only one, others are to. From one room to the next they vanished." With a more cautious look, "How are your gifts?"

I blow a breath out, "You guessed didn't you?" I got up, holding my arms, "Somehow, they feel reduced."

She stood, lending me support, "Didn't you think about it, where some of your power came from."

"I didn't think about it, I was focused on each step. I guess that they know."

"It's chaos in there now, there is some woman tearing everyone a new one. They will start to move out to the grounds at some point. We are warded here but that is probably reducing as we talk."

"Is Reese, Maggie and Nick okay? They aren't missing are they?"

"No they are here. Reese is being healed. Before you run off, you need to recharge." She held up a hand, "No, eat first." I could tell that she was serious and I was starving. I let her sit me back down, she fed me and then best of all she produced a change of clothes. I took off the sadly ruined dress. I pulled the T-shirt and jeans on with relief, especially the boots. I washed off what make up I could and tied my hair up. Stepping out, I saw that men were getting gear ready. I got to Sunny's van, where I poked my head around the door, she gestured me in and ended a conversation. She came over to hug me, "You look much better, thank god. Come with me." She left the van, "Daisy is fine."

"What happening?"

"They went in to search the place," grabbing my arm, as I turned. "Let them do it."

I shook my head, "No, I know that you want me safe but I can sense more, I can help. You know that."

She sighed heavily, "I know, go." She called after me, "Try not to get beaten up again."

Ha, ha. I made my way straight back to the building. I paused by one of the doors, I couldn't see anyone inside, I closed my eyes and felt out. The breeze, the scent of flowers, smell of food. As I went deeper and deeper, my breathing slowed. I still reassuringly had my core of power, thank goodness. There was more of a steadiness and calmness to it. I opened my eyes and decided to wander around to see if I could sense anything. Touching the walls as I walked, I got some sensations but nothing left out at me. I walked past men searching, what happened to everyone? I could not help but think of the young boy, hoping that he was alright. I realised that I was being drawn to the rear of the building. Why was it always the back or basements.

Suddenly I stopped and stepped back, was that an echo of Catherine? The hair on the back of my neck were standing up. I didn't have my phone or earpiece. Sending out a call to Maggie but all I could feel was her anxiety and fear for her mother.

I pushed on, not wanting to loss this clue. I ended up at a dead end, a wall but I knew that there was something there. I held my palm over it without touching, I could an illusion maybe. Pushing some power towards it, the wall rippled. Excited I pushed more my hands entering the wall itself, it was unpleasant but I winced and pushed through. Stumbling as it disappeared, looking back it appeared as if it had never been. I called out, in case anyone was nearby.

I moved on, the building looked older now, I slowly moved forward. I had the sense that I was in a different buliding, had that been a portal.

I could hear some voices ahead, they sounded angry. I was doing what I said I would try not to do, going off on my own. Pausing, I just could not proceed, especially as then I recognised Catherine's voice. Without another doubt, I kept going. Carefully I peered around a corner, with my heart thumped loudly.

With relief, I could see Catherine. She appeared unharmed, though she was kneeling, her men either side of her in a similar position. They were a little battered and bruised, they had put up a fight. Arrayed against them was that blonde woman, several guards all armed and the infamous Professor May.

I was proud to see that he was incandescent with anger, the suave front that he put on for the world, had been completely dropped and the real him was on view. Spitting with anger, he roared, "How did you do it. You will fix this. Bring my demon back."

Catherine curled her lip dismissively, "No." She gasped with pain, no-one had approached her but she was being tortured. My hands clenched, with the smile that appeared on the woman's face, I knew who was responsible.

Cautiously I felt out to assess the gifts in the room. I was shocked to find that the Professor had none, my own lip curled at his weakness. She had a lot, even now.

Wondering what to do, I was saved the choice as a loud noise came from behind me. Followed by what sounded like an explosion, everyone looked up.

Gesturing wildly, the Professor sent two of the men to investigate. Once they had left the room, I quietly moved forward, using the shadows but also shielding myself. She must have picked up on something as she started to turn towards me. Shit, I ducked down and punched out with as much power as I could. She staggered back but my relief was short-lived.

As she wore at me, I was picked up and thrown to the side. As she advanced on me, Catherine and her men took advantage, rushing the remaining guards.

Catherine charged the shocked Professor, holding her hands out ahead of her. I was distracted from seeing what happened, as blonde came into my view. I rolled away from her next strike, regaining my feet and running. I needed to make sure that this woman didn't touch me, I kept ahead of her as I entered a long corridor. Catherine's best chance was if I kept this the strongest player away from her.

I ducked as something hit behind me, I tried the doors. Finally one opened, a storage room for old furniture shrouded in sheets. Diving under one of the sheets, I crouched down and held my breath.

With suspense the door swung open, crashing with a bang, "Little mouse, where are you? I am going to find you and you are going to feel so much pain." Sheets were swept off, I could hear the swish and thud. "But I won't kill you, not yet. If I had met you before then you would already be dead."

I was scared, very scared. She was saying everything in a flat voice, no emotion. I had no doubt that she meant what she said. I covered my mouth, as her voice sounded so close to me. "I can do this all day, Olivia." At my continued silence, some exasperation sounded, "You care about your friends and that makes you weak and easy to manipulate." There was a snigger, "How else did Grayson end up so easily in your bed? Pathetic."

My face was burning now from anger, chasing away the fear.

"Do you know why you run from me little mouse, why you will always run from me?"

I shrank back from the heels that appeared by my side. I started to pull power, so that I could at least go out fighting. But her next words made me lose my concentration. "Do you know why I hate you. Because I am your big sister Olivia. Daddy's favourite. You were a mistake that was never meant to happen." My heart stopped, frozen with denial. It can't be true, a psychopathic killer sister.

Gun fire erupted outside, she swore turning to the door. "Seems like I will be seeing you Olivia. You can count on it." I heard footsteps to the door and then she was gone, I could feel that she was gone but I remained frozen. My mind not wanting to deal.

Reese's frantic voice called for me, "Olivia, Olivia!"

I carefully looked and felt out, not trusting that it was him. I breathed a sigh of relief as he appeared in the doorway, holding a gun. "Thank god," he pulled me to him and placed a hard kiss on my mouth, leaving it tender and bruised. "After this is over, we are going to be placing a tracker on you. Come on, lets go, we have the Professor."

Those were the words that I had been waiting for but the revelation about my sister had ruined that. She would not be going quietly into the night.

I allowed Reese to escort me to Catherine, who was standing over a restrained Professor May. Looking much less imposing. Maggie stood by, they appeared to be magically restraining him. He hadn't seen me, as I had approached from behind but "Olivia, my daughter. I am impressed by your power but not by your use of it. Very disappointing." Reese and Maggie put themselves between us. They need not have bothered, as I left. There was going to be no big show down, I was not going to indulge his games. I could hear him shouting at me as I walked faster, Reese hurried to catch up.

I stood outside breathing in the fresh night air. Thinking about how the night hid so much, on edge more than before.

Foresight as to what was to come. Reese stood next to me, looking out into the night as well.

"Tonight we won, sent a demon back to hell and captured a monster. The Society will not recover from this. We won."

"Reese we won a battle but there is still a war."

He didn't disagree, "For tonight we won, let us enjoy it, recharge and welcome a baby into the family." He gave me a knowing wink at the word 'recharge'.

Despite everything, I blushed again. "You have to stop that."

"You will have to make me, come on."

I let myself be dragged to Sunny, let us enjoy this night and then we will prepare again but this time I would not be so naive and I was not alone.

"Fuck, Fuck." Olivia's sister threw things around the room, there was the smashing of glass, the ripping of fabric.

The man carefully picked off some non-existent lint from his sharply pressed trousers. He had a bored air that finally registered with the angry woman having a tantrum.

"Why are you not upset, she has ruined everything."

"No, she has delivered us a new opportunity and power." He smiled cruelly, I look forward to meeting this sister of yours.

"What we call the beginning is often the end.
And to make an end is to make a beginning.
The end is where we start from."— T.S. Eliot

ACKNOWLEDGEMENT

Thank you to my supportive and wonderful husband, who let me ignore him while I wrote this.

ABOUT THE AUTHOR

Anusa Nimalan

A busy mother of three lovely girls, a wife and an Emergency Medicine Consultant in A London Hospital.

Printed in Great Britain
by Amazon

86288417R00159